D0446055

Praise for Stacey B___
INAPPROPRI___

"An insightful and hil_____ journey
into the life and mind of Chicagoan Sidney Stein."
—*Today's Chicago Woman*

"Ballis's debut is a witty tale of a thirtysomething
who unexpectedly has to start the search for love
all over again."
—*Booklist*

"Stacey Ballis's debut novel is a funny, smart book about
love, heartbreak and all the experiences in between."
—*Chatelaine.com*

"This is the ultimate read for women everywhere...."
—*Flare.com*

"...chick-lit fans will enjoy this second-chance-at-life tale."
—Harriet Klausner

"*Inappropriate Men* is wickedly funny, fresh, and real."
—*curvynovels.com*

Acknowledgments

*

If you were listed in the acknowledgments of *Inappropriate Men,* please assume that I still love you and am listing you here via asterisk. Unless, of course, you have done something to tick me off, in which case, consider yourself deleted. If you do not know if you were listed in the acknowledgments of *Inappropriate Men,* it means you had better go get yourself a copy, pronto.

If you and I became close after the publication of *Inappropriate Men,* or if you weren't born then, or if we hadn't met yet, but we are fond of each other at the moment, then consider yourself acknowledged.

Mom, Dad, Deborah and Jonnie, who know how much I love them and how inspiring they are to me always.

Scott Mendel, my most favorite agent and friend, and a true mensch in all things.

Margaret Marbury, the best editor a girl could ask for, especially on this project. Whatever clarity of purpose is in this book could not have been revealed without her.

Andra Velis-Simon, PR guru and great friend.

My wonderful colleagues at The Goodman Theatre, for all the support, encouragement and laughter, with special mentions for Bob, Roche, Steve, Kathy, Cindy and my lunch bunch: Julie, Jodi, Rob, Patti, Deb and Jen.

Everyone behind the scenes at RDI/Harlequin Books for all of their hard work and support, especially the gang in the field. There is no better group of sales reps anywhere, and the next round is on me.

Thanks to my fellow writers for being so welcoming of me: Laura Caldwell, Jennifer O'Connell, Sarah Mlynowski, Lynda Curnyn, Laurie Gwen Shapiro, Judy Markey, Cara Lockwood and everyone on the chick-lit loops!

STACEY BALLIS

Sleeping Over

RED
DRESS
INK™

First edition April 2005

SLEEPING OVER

A Red Dress Ink novel

ISBN 0-373-89516-X

To Deborah, for all the years of late-night laughter, whispering in the dark, sleepwalking and sleeptalking and sleepphoning. You are always a joy to wake up to.

February 14, 2003

I look around the apartment to see that everything is in place. I've rearranged my living-room furniture to make plenty of floor room in front of the television. A stack of classic hot-guy flicks sits next to the TV. On the coffee table, an eclectic array of snacks: port-wine cheese spread and Ritz crackers, three kinds of olives, sliced California rolls, pita chips and hummus, mini quiches, pigs in blankets, chicken satay skewers. Thank God for Costco. I don't mind cooking, but I prefer to let someone else do the big work and just heat and eat.

The really good stuff is in the kitchen. I bought large bags of all the members of the "ito" family of foods, Cheetos, Fritos, Doritos and Tostitos. Jars of salsa and nacho-cheese dip. In the fridge is a big bowl of French onion spinach dip next to a bowl of veggies, a huge pitcher of my famous green apple martinis and two rolls of chocolate-chip cookie dough.

One thing is for certain: if the five of us aren't going to

be spending Valentine's Day on romantic dates with gorgeous men, we're going to eat whatever we damn well feel like, drink copiously and watch fabulous Hollywood hunks to our hearts' delight.

I'm reasonably sure that everything is organized, and I'm excited about this slumber party. Who needs a boyfriend when you have amazing girlfriends? Frank can kiss my ass.

Vital Statistics:

Frank Battle

32, doctoral candidate in Slavic languages at the University of Chicago

Commitment-Phobe (read: ASSHOLE)

Likes single-malt scotch and foreign films

Hates cats

Frank and I were together for two years. I thought we were in a really good place, and figured it was only a matter of time before a ring materialized. Until he started looking for teaching jobs. Not in Chicago. I tried to broach the subject of **us,** but he always managed to dodge it, so I got serious. After all, while I love Chicago, I'm not wedded to it, and I would have considered moving. If he had asked me. Which he hadn't. So I made the classic mistake of trying to apply passive pressure. I went to a recruitment meeting for the peace corps. Came home and got all excited telling him about the meeting. At which point he was supposed to grab me and kiss me and tell me I couldn't join the peace corps—he couldn't bear to be apart for that long—and then ask me to marry him instead.

But he didn't bother to propose. He just matched my enthusiasm and told me how proud he was of me, and that he thought it was a great idea. He said that he was probably going to be moving after graduation, anyway, so it would be perfect timing since, and I quote, "It isn't like we were ever going to do the long-term thing." Ouch.

It's funny how we cope sometimes. Inside I was screaming; outside I was calm. I pretended to agree with him, and over the next few months I started the application process, all the time thinking deep down that any minute he would wake up and realize the error of his ways. But he did not. And then I got accepted, with a posting in Kenya, teaching English. He took me to dinner at Le Bouchon to celebrate and I broke up with him over tarte tatin and espresso, claiming that I had so much to do before leaving that I wouldn't have time for him anyway. And he fucking AGREED with me. Just like that. Over. So much for passive pressure—I was halfway to Africa, by God!

I needed to assess. I wanted to take a break from teaching, stateside at least, before tackling a PhD anyway. And a master's degree in English literature with a concentration in the Victorian novel essentially makes one completely unfit for any other type of employment. And since I hate to ever admit that I'm wrong, I decided that the whole thing was part of a master plan the universe has for me, and accepted the offer. So in a couple months I'm heading out for a two-year Peace Corps tour. This, by the way, is not exactly a smart or peace corps–sanctioned reason to join up, and while I'm feeling very satisfied about the decision at the moment, I can't really in good conscience recommend it. I hate to think that I'd be sending hordes of broken-hearted women out into the world to do community service in third world nations, just to avoid having to look at bridal magazines with unrequited longing.

I wander into my bedroom and put on the new flannel

pajamas I bought for tonight's sleepover—light pink strewn with red hearts. Matching fluffy red slippers. I pull my sandy-brown wavy hair back into a loose bun, and catch the reflection in the mirror. I look about sixteen. Not bad for an ancient thirty-one-year-old. The doorbell rings.

Anne and Beth are the first to arrive, with Lilith in tow. Anne and Beth are arguing about which one of them has had the longer day.

"…waiting tables is backbreaking, not to mention mind-numbing, and no one is ruder at lunch than out-of-town businessmen with corporate AmEx gold cards! Hey, Jess." Anne hugs me.

"Jess, will you please tell my darling little sister that stuffy businessmen eating enormous three-martini lunches at Gibson's are nothing compared to the picky tastes of the jaded ladies who will make me run all over Barneys for three hours, try on every damn thing in the store and then buy one shirt!" Beth and Anne totally love each other in that *we aren't just sisters, we're best friends* way, and the teasing has a great deal of humor in it.

I hug Beth next. "Don't ask me to play 'Whose Job is Worse' when I just finished having end-of-the-year conferences with a bunch of parents who've let their nannies and au pairs raise their 'privileged' kids and now blame me for their lazy study habits and lack of concentration."

"Oh, all of you stop it." Lilith hugs me and smacks Beth on the arm. We all go quiet at once, knowing that of all of us, she is the one who has it the hardest, and she isn't complaining.

The buzzer interrupts a round of everyone talking at once, and I go to let Robin in. The greetings begin anew, and I look at my four best girlfriends with a heart at once light with joy and darkened with fear. Two years. Two years is a very long time. It isn't even that I'm scared about getting through two years without them, it's what happens when I come back… It's the fear of knowing that what we share—right now—will never be the same again. Will they—and life—have left me behind?

Everyone gets into their pajamas, and I swear I would have known any of them immediately by their choices. Beth, always the romantic, has donned a flowing white nightgown of soft cotton, with billowy sleeves and a gently gathered tie collar. She looks like a Victorian poetess, with the exception of her curly auburn hair, which she has tamed into two Pippi Longstocking braids. Anne, Miss Practical, is wearing a set of simple gray flannel pajamas with green piping, her chestnut hair in a ponytail. Robin's blue cotton jersey pj's are patterned with whisks and eggs, set off by big plush slippers in the shape of ducks' feet. Artsy Lilith has adorned her generous curves with a vintage set of men's cream linen pajamas edged in blue satin, and a flowing Japanese kimono–style robe in ivory silk with brilliant scarlet dragons and bright magenta cherry blossoms embroidered everywhere.

The apple martinis come out of the fridge, and we decide to watch the movies in chronological order, so *Charade* is up first. We've all seen the film, allowing for much *oohing* and *aahing* over the terribly dapper Cary Grant, and loud moaning by Beth, Lilith and Robin that in a million years they will never be as thin and elegant as Audrey Hepburn. These complaints are deftly punctuated by generous plate refills.

When the movie is over, we take a few minutes to clear the mostly empty snack trays and mix another pitcher of martinis. Back in the living room, Anne sits behind Beth, unbraiding her hair and attempting to French-braid it instead, while Lilith talks about her recent move home.

"It's just so fucking hard, you know? I mean, he's dying. No two ways about it, he gets the tiniest bit worse every day and there isn't a damn thing any of us can do about it. The cancer is everywhere—his liver, his pancreas, his lymph nodes, his brain. And all day long it's just me and the nurse, and his pain." She looks drawn, but resolute as she says it.

"It's an amazing gift you're being given, sweetie," Robin says, an arm around her shoulders. "I know it feels shitty, but when my dad went, it was all of a sudden, a massive coronary. I was here, he was back East, and I hadn't even been home to visit in, like, six months! You're getting to say goodbye and be there for him and with him, and love him right out of the world."

Lilith shakes her head. "I wish I could see it like that. I hate even talking about it, complaining about it, everyone puts this Florence Nightingale spin on things. *Aren't I the best daughter? Giving up my work, moving home, being there for him.* But the truth is, I resent the hell out of him for getting sick, and I'm pissed at my mom and sister for pressuring me into making the sacrifices. Fine for me to be the perpetual temp and starving actor until now, but Mom wasn't going to stop working, Lauren wasn't going to leave the kids at day care to come home. Suddenly I needed to 'get over' my silly little 'acting phase' and take some responsibility."

"Everyone deals in their own way… Ultimately I think Robin is right, you're going to be grateful for this time," I say.

"I totally agree," Anne pipes in.

"Ditto," adds Beth. "You'll come out the other end with the knowledge that after everything he did for you in your life, you were able to do the most important thing for him when he needed you."

"Enough depressing talk. I feel like I've barely seen you guys in the past three months, and Jess is leaving in, like, ten minutes. I want the entire scoop, everything I've missed. Circle up."

Circling up is our private method of getting the important information out in the open for discussion in the most concise way possible. Each of us gets literally one minute to throw out the big events, no embellishment, no defense, no secrets.

Robin goes first. "Got promoted from the line to executive sous-chef after only four months. Apartment still has termites."

Beth is next. "Petey had a raging case of worms, which he picked up at Bark Park, but the medication seems to be working. I'm the fattest employee in all of Barneys with the notable exception of Jamal, the security guard in the loading dock, who is six-seven and must weigh four hundred pounds. Luckily, since Barneys would never dream of carrying anything bigger than a size twelve, I'm thwarted in any effort to actually use my employee discount. And all the skinny little women I wait on think they look so great next to me that they buy all kinds of stuff, which is good for my sales record. On the plus side, I'm loving assisting Mara, the head buyer—it's much more fun than working the sales floor. She says if I keep up the good work, she'll take me on full-time, and I may get to go to New York in the spring."

Anne's turn. "Miss working at Hugo's Frog. Tips are better at Gibson's, but clientele is better at the Frog Bar. Getting ready for a next phase of working life, but can't for the life of me figure out what that should be. Have had exactly zero dates this year. I'm assuming I'm out of luck until spring, as no one ever seems to start dating anyone midwinter—it's too much trouble to leave the house. Wondering if twenty-seven is old enough to be considered a spinster?" Beth takes this opportunity to bash Anne over the head with a handy throw pillow, before gesturing for the circle to continue.

"You guys already know my deal," Lilith says, and passes the floor to me.

"Leaving in two months," I say. "Not freaking out yet, assuming it's the calm before the storm. Got all my shots, paperwork is in order, will be spending my last week up at the cabin with the family, then adventure time. Have decided that if you guys don't write on a semiregular basis, I'll smuggle back some sort of Ebola-type virus and poison your cosmopolitans with it."

Everyone begins assuring me at once that of course they'll keep me in the loop about everything, and miss me like crazy while I'm gone. We spend the remains of the night watching movies, eating, drinking, gabbing and eventually, around 3:00 a.m., we make up little beds on the floor of the living room. In the dark, while I'm sure each of us is having her own private déjà vu of slumber parties from childhood, we whisper and giggle until, one by one, we drift into sleep.

2005

anne

I never thought I'd see him in Lula Café. I mean, he didn't look as if he really belonged, not with those cement-spattered work boots. I had been there all evening, in my favorite corner table, rereading *The Unbearable Lightness of Being,* swilling mocha lattes. Pretentious? Maybe, but everyone's got to be something, and I happen to excel at pretentious.

I actually only go to Lula once a month or so. It's very expensive, and with Beth and me having opened the clothing store such a short time ago and trying to keep ourselves liquid in this sagging economy, my current salary allows for few luxuries. More and more I think I may really want to eventually go back to school for occupational therapy, but I have so many loans from college that I hate to borrow more until I've whittled down the principal a bit. But since the other assistant manager quit, Beth and I have been splitting abundant overtime hours, so I can treat myself a little.

So I'm sitting at Lula, and behind me the door opens. I get hit with a blast of arctic wind. (I love Chicago weather—even in June it can get wintry). Then the door closes, and out of the corner of my eye I catch a glimpse of this guy. He is beautiful. Perfection. I toss half of my latte back in one gulp, burning the almighty hell out of my throat, and watch him cross the room.

The boots make no noise on the concrete, so the only sound I hear, besides my own heartbeat, is the air crashing back together behind him as he walks. He sits in the middle of the empty café, the most conspicuous table. It gives me the perfect angle to watch him from behind my book. And watch him I do.

Like a balloon slowly collapsing, he folds himself into his chair. He glances briefly at the menu, motions for the waitress, brushes the longish hair off his forehead. When he looks up to order, his face is captain-of-the-football-team-handsome. Rugged features, heavy brow, a slightly crooked nose, brutally square jawline. When Joan, the waitress, finishes with his order, he reaches into the pocket of his jacket and pulls out *Manchild in the Promised Land,* one of my favorite books. It shocks me. He looks like a construction worker or something, and you don't expect them to read anything without sports or naked women in it. I don't mean to perpetuate a stereotype, but you just don't think of the average day laborer as possessing a literary mind.

He must have realized he was being watched because he shines his gray-green eyes back over at my table and catches me staring. I'm so dumbfounded, I don't avert my gaze until he winks at me. Then I look down quickly, sure that I'm turning eighteen shades of red and purple. By the time I get up the courage to look back up, he is engrossed in his book.

Okay, now, I'm not man-crazy, in fact, I'm fairly shy. I tend to attract these slight, bookish fellows who want to take me to poetry readings and gallery openings. The last guy I dated took me to this gallery and abandoned me to suck up to some socialite, and I was practically molested by this greasy pervert with a thick Italian accent who turned out to be the artist. I was not amused. Especially when I found out months later that my date had been dating Beth at the time, and knew I was her sister.

It isn't that I'm unattractive; I'm actually pretty satisfied with my looks. I'm very short, and unlike poor Beth, I've never had a problem with my weight, so my figure is about the same as it was in my teens. My hair is straight and light brown, and I keep it long, since I've never been much into girlie stuff and a ponytail is about as much bother as I can manage, hairwise. I just never got the hang of the whole boy-girl thing, and I certainly don't know how to flirt, despite Beth's attempts to tutor me, so I tend to either be part of a large group or by myself. And truthfully, I'm very okay with this. Beth and I have been hanging out a bit since she is also going through an "I'm okay with Me" phase, but tonight she has a date with her bathtub and a book. So here I sit, at Lula Café. Almost alone, except for this amazing guy who is making it impossible to read the sexy parts without thinking about what might be underneath those faded jeans.

We sit for the better part of an hour in that uncomfortable, expectant silence. (At least, uncomfortable and expectant to me). Every time he breathes or turns a page I think he is going to say something. We're still the only people in the place. I'm sure he can hear the blood rushing in my veins. Suddenly, he closes the book and returns it to his jacket pocket. He gets up, tosses a few wrinkled bills on the table, tips an imaginary hat to Joan. He walks by my table, stops, turns around and stands, reading over my shoulder. I feel the flush begin in my toes and make its way north.

"That's a great book."

His voice is deep, honey over gravel, and my mouth is so dry I have to stop breathing altogether. He leans over and picks up a piece of the banana muffin I had abandoned earlier, pops it in his mouth.

"I agree," he says, gesturing at the muffin. "Kundera needs blueberries. Banana doesn't work at all." He winks at me. Then he turns away, and I gape, trying to think of something intelligent, endearing, memorable and sexy to say. I can't find any words, and I hear him open the door and leave.

I scramble my stuff together, toss a twenty on the table (so much for the phone bill), grab my coat and run out the door. He has disappeared without a trace.

I run back inside and accost Joan, who claims she hadn't seen him in the café before.

Just my luck.

Probably wouldn't matter anyway; that type never goes for my type. They always find the tall, willowy blondes or the fiery redheads with the amazing bodies. I figure it's better to leave it alone, and begin to walk home. I tell myself that I shouldn't go back to Lula anytime soon, after all, Joan said he hadn't been there before. And it's too expensive anyway. Nope, I won't go back, certainly not tomorrow.

I pretend that I believe myself.

Lilith

"I think you should do it." I'm saying this very calmly to my friend Bill, who is looking to me for comfort and reassurance with his big, blue semiwatery eyes.

Vital Statistics:

Bill Dillon

38, theater director

Notoriously bad taste in men

Likes campy musicals

Hates auditions

"I've never directed a verse play before," Bill throws back at me. "You know me, I'm all about these witty contemporary pieces that everyone ends up hating, but at least I don't have to deal with the whole 'dialect-period-movement-stage-combat' thing."

Why is it that directors only ever complain? They complain about not getting work, they complain about the work they get, they complain when they don't get the actors they want, and when they do, they complain about them being prima donnas. I adore directors as a group, and Bill in particular, but they do require a lot of attention. And cocktails. No matter, I'm here to convince Bill to take the job he has probably already accepted, and remind him that he is brilliant.

"Well then, it's about time you tackled something profound," I say. "Do they have company members with the chops?" Working small in theater often means that companies require that you cast significantly out of their resident ensemble, which can be a lucky break or a nightmare.

"They're letting me have full auditions, and while I'm required to see company members, I'm not under obligation to cast them if I don't want to."

"As long as you don't ever want to direct for them again."

"Well, there's that." Finally a smile! "Anyway, they have some good people. No one for *Tartuffe,* though. I think I'd want to use that guy I was telling you about if he's available."

"The little dancer?"

"Not him, the other one." Bill motions for another round. This is going to cost me a fortune. "The one in the really bad play I saw two weeks ago."

"Right, right, right."

Bill delicately removes the lemon twist from his fresh cosmopolitan, takes a sip and sighs deeply and dramatically. "I think your new golden highlights are making the blond seep into your usually exceptional brain. Can we focus here for a moment? We're discussing my life and whether I should undertake this enormous French-period verse thing that could guarantee I'll never direct again except in dinner theater in Napanee, Indiana. *'Plain and Fancy, the Amish Musical,'* directed by Bill Dillon, with traditional threshers dinner…"

"You about done, or is there another catty comment you have for my sassy new hair?" I interrupt him before he really gets going. Especially since it took nearly two hundred dollars and three hours at Fringe to get the right shade of golden and caramel highlights that would look remotely natural in my dark brown mop of curls. Thank God for Monique, the genius hair guru.

"About." He smiles at me.

"You want to do it?" I know he does.

"I think so." Meaning he has already said yes.

"You think you can do a job on it?" I know he does.

"I think so." Meaning he thinks it will be brilliant.

"So what's the problem?" Other than the fact that he has ordered a basket of fried zucchini rings that I shouldn't eat, as my butt left the Jennifer Lopez realm a year ago and seems to have landed solidly in the "secretary spread" arena since I started temping for a living. Well, maybe just a couple….

"Fear mostly." Meaning he needs stroking.

"The worst thing that can happen is it sucks."

"Thanks a lot!"

"Do you love me?" I only ever ask this of my gay boyfriends, since the straight boys always seem to feel perfectly within their rights to say no.

"You know I do."

"Do you trust me?" Soothing head tilt.

"Within reason."

"Have I ever steered you wrong before?" Gentle raise of the eyebrows for emphasis.

He raises his eyebrows back at me and smiles. "Blind date with your masseuse?"

He would bring that up.

"Besides that."

He pauses. "Kiwi margaritas." My, that *was* a long night. And, as memory serves, a longer morning.

"Professionally."

"The workshop of the Arthur Miller musical." Damn him, he remembers every little detail, evil thing.

"Okay, once."

"Salesman, exclamation point!" Bill spans the invisible title over our heads with a sweeping gesture. This makes me laugh.

"It wasn't so bad." Actually, it was.

"Lil…" Bill is shaking his head at me.

"So it wasn't Sondheim." By the longest shot imaginable.

"It wasn't Sondheim's cousin's dry cleaner!"

Now we're both really laughing hard.

"The production number with the suitcases?" A whole chorus of dancing salesmen singing a dreadful tune called "Going on a Trip" with a vaguely barbershop-quartet feeling. There are no words for how bad this thing was. "And Willie's…big…ballad…" I may, in fact, pee myself.

Now Bill has tears streaming down his face. "The… dream…ballet."

My God, I had forgotten that part.

"With…the…stockings…and…the…football…" Cirque du Soleil meets Monday Night Football meets Fredericks of Hollywood meets bad peyote trip. All done to lilting strings and oboe solos.

We're convulsed in giggles, and everyone else at T's looks over at us as if we must be high. Finally Bill wipes his round cheeks and looks over at me. "Why would I listen to you?"

"You adore me."

"In spite of yourself."

"So I made a mistake." A really, really big mistake.

"No shit! But you made it with *my* career, because, as I recall, you met the composer and he was yummy."

"He was yummy." So true. "Dumb, grossly untalented, but yummy."

"You and your boys. That man of yours is a saint." Which in many ways he is. Albeit a boring one.

"Today, yes, he is. Ask again tomorrow. Besides, it was a workshop. No one saw it. It isn't like you got reviewed." Bill shakes his head at me.

"It's Molière and you'll be brilliant," I said, going back to support mode.

"All that religious stuff, my Catholic upbringing, it's in fucking verse for Pete's sake!"

"You gonna do it?" Time to cut to the chase. I have somewhere to be.

"Yeah. Will you help?" There's my boy.

"You know I don't act anymore, but if you insist, I suppose I could do Dorine...."

"Oh yeah, just what I need, you *in* the play. I don't want to cast you, darling, I want you to coach." I knew this, but I do love to rattle him about my defunct acting career.

"No dialect, right, just faster, louder, hit your consonants?" I'm a pretty good scene and speech coach, good with casting, excellent with dramaturgy, but the only dialect I can do well is Jewish, which is not much in demand for Molière.

"Exactly. Mostly I need you for work on the verse, some occasional one-on-one scene work if folks need it."

"How much time?" As if my schedule isn't achingly empty.

"One full rehearsal a week, plus a few hours here and there for sessions, and I want you during auditions and tech."

"For you, I can fit that in. Bill?"

"Yeah?"

"It'll be great, I promise." Which I'm pretty sure it will be.

"It had better be." He smiles at me, letting me know he is pretty sure it will be, too.

"And opening night…"

"I know, kiwi margaritas all around."

"Exactly." I check my watch again.

"Okay, I'm convinced. And clearly you have somewhere to be, as you've checked your watch eight thousand times." Busted.

"Sorry, I don't mean to be distracted, but I'm meeting the girls for dinner."

"Ah, the coven is convening."

"Be nice. Jess is coming back soon, so we want to think about what we should plan to welcome her home."

"My God, has it been two years already? Time must fly when you are saving the lepers in Botswana." Bill knows better, but he loves to bait me.

"Or teaching English in Kenya. Lord love the Corps of Peace while they still have funding. Anyway, she gets back pretty soon, and considering how crazy we all are, we want to be sure to get the plan under way."

"Well, give the girls my love, and I'll call you when I get a schedule."

"Thank you, Uncle Bill."

"My pleasure."

We motion for a tab, which Bill actually picks up, to my great surprise and delight, and I drop him at the train and head off to pick up Anne.

I am, frankly, always a little nervous before these events. Even though I've known these women for several years, I do always feel like the country cousin. They all have such deep connections, and all I did was answer an ad for a roommate. And even though Anne and I aren't living together anymore, I'm grateful that they continue to include me in the group activities. It's always nice to be surrounded by smart, fun, strong women who understand me.

Plus, I could really use some advice on what to do about Martin.

Vital Statistics:

Martin Pincus

34, consultant

Can pack for a business trip in 14 minutes

Likes money

Hates going out with my friends

We've been together for almost two years, but as a consultant for Accenture, he spends a lot of his time on the road. We only really see each other a few times a month, and even then we mostly just hang out at his little-used condo, since he's always so exhausted from the traveling that he doesn't want to go out anywhere or do much of anything except watch TV. He keeps talking about how he is going to be able to retire by the time he is forty-two or so, but I think he likes the work too much to stop then. And in the meantime, for someone with a longtime boyfriend, I'm more and more lonely. I want to broach the idea of dating other people, but I'm not sure why, since no one has asked me out in ages. Still, it'd be nice to have the option.

Then again, it is pleasant to have the security of a steady partner, and it takes the pressure off of me to find someone else, the most tedious process imaginable. I'm actually kind of curious to see what the group consensus is on the topic.

In the meantime, there is always the excitement of a new project on the horizon. I didn't mention to Bill that *Tartuffe* is one of my all-time favorite plays; he would have thought I was pressuring him on my own behalf.

Anne told me to pick her up at Lula, which is a little odd, but when I get there she is waiting outside, looking sort of disappointed or maybe just tired. She jumps into my car, and we head off to meet the girls. We've tentatively decided to welcome Jess back with a repeat of the Un–Valentine's Day slumber party. But we also want it to be really special, more like a dinner party, so Robin, who is going to do the food, has invited us over to Ajax for a tasting dinner. Anne and I find miraculous parking in front of the restaurant, and head on in to meet the girls.

robin

After the restaurant closed for the evening, and the gang headed off excited about the plans for Jess's welcome home, Michael asked me if I needed a ride home.

Vital Statistics:

Michael Korman

42, restaurant owner

Makes fabulous vodka gimlets

Likes bedtime stories

Hates nicknames

This is Michael code for "Can I come over, because I don't want to be alone." But since I can deny the man nothing, I agreed. When he saw the state of my living room, he laughed at me.

"This is absolute chaos. How the hell do you live like this?" he said.

"Life is chaos," I said. "The world began in chaos, and the world will end in chaos. We're born in chaos, live in chaos and die in chaos. We should be comfortable in chaos, and yet it disturbs us."

I smile at him, and he smiles back. This is how all our best conversations get started.

"I mean," I continued, "chaos should be the state in which we're the most at home. We should seek it out, not shy away from it."

"Isn't it always the things that we're most familiar with that frighten us the most?" he asks.

"I suppose, but that in itself is a contradiction in terms. I guess it's one of those traits that is commonly human, but unfounded in its conception, and without basis in reason."

Michael grins at me and shakes his head. "We won't make sense of it all tonight."

"Very true. My brain hurts from all of my own bizarre thinking. Possibly it's the Shiraz, but I doubt it."

"I know it couldn't be the wine, not with your tolerance for alcohol," he says with a laugh.

"It's not so bad." Actually, it is.

"For an NFL linebacker, maybe. Give me a break, Robin, do you happen to recall a certain drinking jag in October....?" Oh, crap-a-rama. That was a long night.

"I was depressed, I needed to get drunk."

"But you drank like a candidate for alcohol poisoning. When I got your message on my machine it was nine p.m. and your message said you were calling at eight-thirty. By the time I got to your place at nine-twenty you had already consumed four shots of tequila. Enough to make a normal human being blitzed. You weren't even tipsy. Over the course of the next four hours you quietly and politely drank two more shots of tequila, a kamikaze and four fingers of Johnny Walker Black scotch, neat."

"You forgot the martini." God, I sound like a lush. Luckily I only drink like that maybe once a year.

"Ah, yes, shaken, not stirred."

"Some bartender you are, stirred, not shaken—shaking bruises the gin. Extra olives." I smile in spite of myself.

"That, my dear, is a myth. Whatever. I was sure I was going to have to take you to get your stomach pumped. But by the time one a.m. rolled around, you seemed more tired than drunk. You must have an iron constitution."

"Nope, an iron liver. I have a pickled constitution. There is a difference. You took good care of me, Mikey."

"Don't call me Mikey. All I did was agree that the customer was a shithead, that you deserved to be treated with respect at work, and put you to bed."

"And stayed with me until morning to make sure I was okay."

"If I remember correctly, I fell asleep on the bed trying to keep vigil, and around four-thirty *you* woke up and tucked *me* in, and at ten brought me breakfast in bed. Sneaky minx." I love it when he banters with me like this, it makes me feel very Rosalind Russell, and since he is as close to Cary Grant as I'm ever going to meet, the repartee is delish.

"You deserved it. Putting up with me on your day off."

"Robbie, you will amaze me till the day I die." Sigh.

"Don't call me Robbie. And anyway, amazing you is the general idea."

"Why?" Sometimes I wonder if he is just pretending that he doesn't know.

"If I bored you, Michael, or got predictable, you wouldn't want to hang out with me anymore." Which is actually sort of my biggest fear.

"What makes you think that?"

"Because when we get together you try to make me talk about one of my strange theories on the universe to amuse you."

"Best breakfast I ever ate…." He always changes the subject like that. And I always let him.

"Anytime you are up for the sequel, I finally perfected the baked-apple pancake." Which is true. Hence the size of my ass.

"With brown sugar and sour cream?" As if I would serve it without.

"For you, anything." Really. *Anything*.

"When?"

"Whenever you want." I am getting very good at feigned casualness. As if my heart isn't pounding, praying he will make it soon.

"I haven't been shopping in an age. My fridge has tumbleweeds—how about tomorrow?" He thinks he is being subtle, but I know he is inviting himself to spend the night. Thank God. But I play along.

"Fine with me. With or without slumber party?"

"I didn't bring my jammies." Like that has ever stopped him.

"You can borrow some sweats. Your toothbrush is in the medicine cabinet." I got sick of buying spare toothbrushes in bulk after about the tenth sleepover, and finally bought one with a case that I keep for him.

"I don't get to use yours?" Why this thought doesn't particularly gross me out, I have no idea.

"Whatever works for you." Really. *Whatever.*

"It's a chilly night, I can always go for some cuddling," he says. "You just have to promise not to hog the covers."

"Deal. We can stay up all night and talk about boys."

"What will I have to talk about?"

"You can tell me all the secrets of the male psyche, so I can catch myself a boyfriend." Like, oh, I dunno, you.

"I have a better idea. Will you tell me a bedtime story, Mama?" He grins at me.

"Sure, kiddo."

"Oh boy, oh boy, it's not even my birthday." Michael bounces up and down in his seat like a four-year-old.

"You are such a child. Really, I can't imagine you are as old as they tell you. What is it, like, dog years?"

"It's not nice to make fun of your elders."

"No scolding, Mister Man. I've had a very rough week, after all."

"I know, poor baby. I'm sorry that Gerald was such a bitch this week." Understatement of the year. Gerald is the head chef, and I suspect a little bipolar. In any case, he can be hell on wheels in the kitchen, and it's a very small kitchen.

"He's always fine with me, but, Michael, we can't continue to turn over new sous-chefs every three weeks. I can't run a kitchen by myself. I was in the weeds all frigging week. You have got to talk to him."

"I will, I will. You know he has been nuts since Linda left him." Well, she left him because he is gay; why he just doesn't admit it to himself and the rest of us, I have no idea.

"Then, get him into therapy. It's been seven months, and we're getting a reputation around town."

"First thing Tuesday, I promise." Michael raises his right hand as if he is taking an oath.

"Thank you."

"And I'll give you the money I would have paid the boys who quit, since you covered all their stuff." I smell new shoes in my future.

"You are very good to me."

"Piffle." He winks at me.

"Did you actually just say 'piffle'? Out loud? I think we'd better get you to bed before your mind goes completely."

"Where are the supplies?"

"Sweats are in the bottom drawer. Let's synchronize our watches and meet in the bedroom at twenty-three-hundred hours."

"You're on."

I get into my pajamas while Michael avails himself of my bathroom, and then we switch. I love that he is here. I love that he wants to be here. I'm trying not to think about how much I love it. When I get back into the bedroom, Michael is already in bed. I get in beside him, both of us lying on our backs in the dark.

"In the beginning there was chaos…" I begin.

"Didn't we cover this already?"

"You want a bedtime story or not, Mikey?"

"Sorry. And don't call me Mikey." I know when he is smiling, even in the dark.

"In the beginning there was chaos. And all the world was void and without form. And God created the Heavens and the Earth, and in the darkness the Heavens and the Earth were formed. And God said 'Let there be light.' And there was light. And God saw that it was good."

"Are you going to tackle the whole Old Testament, or just Genesis?" He rolls over to face me.

"Just that first passage. I like the idea of chaos and void and darkness and, suddenly, light. For some reason it makes me feel better to think that God prefers lightness to darkness."

"I never thought of it that way."

"That is what you have me for." He nudges me, and I roll over on my side.

"Indeed I do, lucky me. Good night, Rob," he whispers, and pulls me close to him, two spoons in the silverware drawer. "Sweet dreams."

"We fit well together, don't we?" I whisper back to him.

"Yep."

"Does it ever make you uncomfortable to snuggle with me like this?" Don't ask that, you ninny, what if he says yes?

"No." Sweet tap-dancing Jesus, that was close. "You are the only good friend I've ever had who I can sleep in the same bed with and not feel awkward. Come to think of it, you are the only friend I can sleep with, period. It's nice, though, to be able to be close to somebody just because you want to be close, and not have to worry about all the sexual politics. Truthfully, I wouldn't have thought it possible, but you made me a believer."

I like this; it makes me feel special. Being special to him is more important to me than is likely to be appropriate, but I'm resigned to it, and nestle closer to him, liking the feel of his breath on the back of my neck. He chuckles quietly.

"It's a good thing you are such a coward or we might not have ever found out how nice this is."

I blush in the dark, remembering.

"Michael, it's Robin. Can you come over?"

"Sure, kiddo. What's wrong? You sound awful."

"I'll tell you when you get here."

"On my way."

It takes less than fifteen minutes for him to appear at my door.

"You are absolutely green. And those are the biggest, deepest, darkest circles I've ever seen under your eyes. When was the last time you slept?" He looks very concerned, bless him.

"Two, three days ago." Sad but true.

"Good Lord, why?"

"Night terrors."

"Excuse me?"

"Night terrors—nighttime panic attacks. I think I hear people coming into my apartment." I'm not faking damsel-in-distress, it really is my only mental defect.

"Honey, it's an old building, it makes noise."

"I know that. I know that it would be nearly impossible for anyone to get in, I know that the chances are one in a million, I know, okay? I know it for certain all day long, and then I get into bed and I hear noises, and I can't fall asleep for ages, and when I do drift off I either have terrible dreams, or I wake up every fifteen minutes and think I see some big scary guy standing in the doorway looking at me. It usually only happens once in a while, but it's been three days in a row, and I think I'm going out of my mind." My pulse races, and I'm nearly hyperventilating.

"Hush, hush, it's okay. You're just stressed and your mind is playing up a rational fear. Think it has anything to do with that attack in the library last week?"

"I don't know, all I know is I can't spend another night suffocating."

"You have trouble breathing when this happens?" He looks worried.

"Just when I have to pretend to be the bed."

"What?"

"Here, come look at my bed." I take him by the hand, lead him into my bedroom and point at the bed.

"Looks poofy, but otherwise, it's a bed."

"It is poofy. I have a huge feather bed on there, and a thick down quilt."

"Feather bed?"

"Yeah, you know, like an enormous down pillow you put over the mattress."

"Sounds comfortable." He still seems puzzled.

"It is. Now look." I pull back the comforter to reveal a perfect outline of a body, legs wide, like a kid began to make a snow angel there. It begins to dawn on him what I meant.

"You fluff that feather thing up, then lie down so that most of it is still the normal height, and then…"

"And then I pull the blanket totally over my head, and put the pillows on top so if the scary guy looks in my room he will think no one is home, and I try to sleep without moving, sweating like a pig, and I can't breathe very well under there, as you can well imagine."

Michael can't help himself, he has to laugh. If I weren't so fucking exhausted I would join him in merriment. Instead, it just sort of pisses me off.

"Look, never mind, okay? It was stupid. I shouldn't have bugged you on your night off. I'm sorry."

"Aw, come on, just because I'm laughing doesn't mean I don't want to help, sweetheart, it just tickled me, the idea of you pretending to be a bed so the boogeyman won't get you." I have to smile in spite of myself.

"I told you already, I know I'm completely ridiculous. Why do you think I waited three nights to call you? It seems the most illogical thing in the world, until I try to go to bed, and then logic takes a holiday."

"Look, I'll be back in an hour. Will you be okay till then?"

"Sure. Where are you going?"

"Don't worry, I'll be back."

Fifty-five minutes later, he was. With a bag.

"What's in there?"

"My pajamas, toothbrush, basic necessities. You are going to make yourself sick if you don't get some sleep, so I'm not going anywhere until you kick this thing."

"Michael, I didn't mean you had to move in, I just—"

"Quiet. You asked for my help, you have to take it, no questions asked. Is that what you sleep in?"

"Yep."

"I'm going to change, go get into bed."

"Yes, Doctor."

He joined me a few minutes later, dressed in baggy pajamas, carrying a book.

"What's that?" I gesture at the book.

"Bedtime story."

"Really?"

"The Hunting of the Snark, you know it?"

"An old favorite."

"Good. It was all I could find. Well, scoot over." I moved to the left side of the bed, and he sat beside me, leaning his broad shoulders against the headboard.

"God, this is really comfortable. Come here." He pulls me close, so that my head rests lightly on his stomach. Then he begins to read. I don't remember anything after the first few lines.

He stayed for four nights, holding me close in the big soft bed, until I was pretty sure I would be able to go it alone, only leaving after eliciting a promise that I'll call him at any hour if the terrors come back. They don't, but it becomes typical for him to crash at my place when we go out after work, sometimes falling asleep on the couch, more often sharing the bed, always at ease together. The girls all think I'm crazy for letting him stay over like this; they think I'm just setting myself up for heartbreak, but I can't help it. Sleeping safe in his arms, waking with him beside me, these are nights of pure joy and sublime security, and I can't deny myself that pleasure, even if it's detrimental to my emotional health.

I rouse myself from my memories. "No, I don't think I could do this with anyone else." Nor do I want to.

"I'm honored. Good night, darlin', sleep well."

"Good night to you, too."

And then, in a very bad Jimmy Durante imitation, Michael says, "Good night, Mrs. Calabash, wherever you are."

beth

I've been so exhausted lately when I get back from the store, that it's all I can do to walk Petey before collapsing onto the couch in front of the television. I know it's just a temporary thing; we lost an assistant manager a couple weeks ago, and I want to be very careful about her replacement, so in the meantime, the workload has doubled. But I love being in charge, and I love working with Anne, and luckily for us, we're staying in the black, which is something to say in light of the current economy.

I've essentially given up all hopes of a social life until the store is really settled. "Life is the age-old progression toward death. The only thing man can do is attempt to make his own time satisfactory to himself." That is what Sasha always said.

Vital Statistics:

Sasha Brunowsky

37, philosopher

Pretentious as hell

Likes coffee and cigarettes

Hates all non-intellectuals

Being a philosopher, he expounds pompously on any subject that presents itself, to anyone without the foresight to flee. I didn't take to my heels, but instead moved in with him one week after we met.

Sasha and I found each other at a gallery opening in the River North area of downtown Chicago. I was sleeping with the artist, Antonio, and Sasha was sleeping with the artist's wife, Sarah. Antonio and Sarah were being very cozy, and Sasha and I, feeling depressed and unloved, were standing by the refreshment table trying to get drunk off the cheap California white. Sasha introduced himself by telling me that my hair reminded him of a brushfire he witnessed as a child.

Being incredibly self-conscious of my unruly red mop, I, naturally, got drunkenly defensive.

"Excuse me, I don't believe I know you well enough for you to act like an asshole in my presence." I can be an icicle when I want to be.

He got really flustered. He thought he was being poetic, and I thought he was being rude.

"I'm sorry, I didn't mean to offend. That brushfire was one of the most beautiful things I ever witnessed in my entire life."

I warmed to him slightly, and decided to give him the usual five minutes to redeem himself.

"Really. How is that?"

"Well, I was seven, and the only fires I had ever seen were in fireplaces and had always struck me as artificial and contrived…."

"At seven you thought they were artificial and *contrived?*"

My God, he was pompous. Cute, but pompous.

"Well, I'm sure had one asked me, those would not have been my exact words, but that was my general Feeling about them," he says, emphasis on the *"f."*

Great, the man speaks in capital letters. How positively Self-Absorbed of him. Well, he has four and a half minutes left.

"We were driving to Kansas City to visit my grandparents, and in the middle of Iowa we drove by this brushfire. It went on for what seemed like miles, right along the side of the highway, and I could feel the tremendous heat from it even inside the car. It was probably three in the morning, but bright as daylight and the roar was deafening. It was the first time I had ever seen fire as it should be, Wild and Untamed and Dangerous. It was incredible. I've never seen anything quite like it."

Okay, he got me, the story was a good one. And with two and a quarter minutes to spare.

"Want to get out of here?" he asked. "Go have a cup of coffee or something?"

He was very sincere, and I felt bad for being bitchy. Besides, Antonio wasn't paying any attention to me anyway.

"Sure, why not."

Well, Sasha fetched our coats, I bid farewell to Antonio and told him I would be in touch, maybe, and we set off for Tempo, a great twenty-four-hour diner on State Street. We got a corner table, ordered coffee and fries and talked for hours. I told him about my ten-month relationship with

Antonio, and he told me about his two-year relationship with Sarah. When we had exhausted our childhood, siblings, parents, relationships and other sundry information, it was almost 2:30 a.m., and we were both getting glassy eyed. He invited me over for a nightcap, and I agreed.

His studio was small, but neat, and very cozy. We sat on a huge futon in the middle of the room and sipped Cointreau, and I fell in love. It was so like me, quietly falling in love with some bastard on the night we meet. He was trying to tell me some of his philosophies on life, none of which I understood, all of which sounded brilliant.

"All women have a part of their soul that is tormented. And it's the direct relationship of this tormented part that determines each woman's tolerance for biological changes in her body." This is his explanation for PMS and why pregnant and menopausal women get goofy. Pretty interesting stuff. Especially with his hand up my skirt. He turned out to be an accomplished lover—which, in my current emotional state, felt a lot like tenderness—and a cuddly sleeper, if a little bony.

When I awoke to fresh bagels and lox in bed, it was all over. Once again, Elizabeth, the worldly and independent thinker, steps aside for Beth, the insecure and love-starved. I mean, who wouldn't melt when a guy wakes you up for breakfast in bed, looks deep into your eyes and says softly, "I've found my Muse, and she sleeps like a child curled up in my arms. My life is devoted to the discovery of her, so that I can reevaluate my own beliefs as they relate both directly and indirectly with hers." Powerful stuff at 9:00 a.m., especially for a twenty-six-year-old, y'know?

One week later, I moved in. In the month after that we found a bigger apartment. In the next three weeks we bought a puppy and an aquarium full of exotic fish. Life was fabulous. We cooked gourmet meals for each other, gave each other backrubs and foot massages. I made chicken soup from my grandmother's recipe, and he made matzo balls from his. Things were terrific. The dog was house broken, the fish were still alive, I could leave the door open when I went to the bathroom. It was a *serious* relationship. I was even thinking about marriage, in a vague sometime-in-the-future way. We had our tiffs, but more for the sake of making up than for principles.

But after the first three years the fights were more frequent, and the making up was not as much fun. And sometimes he would give me the silent treatment. He didn't speak to me for almost two days once because I "insulted the intelligence of an Incredible Thinker, and acted like a Socially Maladjusted Child in the presence of minds I could not even begin to understand." I had told one of his philosopher friends that I didn't think vegetables had souls, but if they did, it certainly would not be the determining factor in how they tasted.

It began to seem as if he hated me, but when I threatened to leave he would analyze my life and tell me that it wasn't him, but rather "Extreme Disappointment in a job and lifestyle which you feel is not quite good enough for you, but which you are powerless to change because you Fear Failure and Loneliness." Then he would tell me I was the only woman he could ever love, and that if I left I would not only ruin my own life, but that I would take with me "the true factor of great thoughts," which I inspire in him. I was in turmoil. I could never put my finger on it; it was just something lurking beneath the surface of the relationship. It was just bad enough to make me miserable most of the time, but not bad enough to make me leave. It continued like that for nearly three more years.

It is not that I didn't still love Sasha, I did, I just didn't seem to like him very much anymore. His philosophies had ceased to be enlightening or innovative; in fact, they had become as trite as any repeated cliché. And his looks, which had always intrigued me, had become less and less appealing. Sasha is very tall and thin, with pale, fish-belly white skin and dark hair, and huge gray eyes behind the most enviable eyelashes that ever existed. But after a while, Sasha just looked sickly and malnourished to me. Skinny instead of lanky. In need of some poundage and a little sun.

Then one day, on my day off, I decided to sneak into one of Sasha's morning lectures. I figured it might give me some insight. I did the whole incognito bit: big hat, dark glasses, trench coat, sat way in the back of the hall, low in my chair. And for some reason it really got to me. There I was, upset with the monotony of the relationship, and suddenly I find this side of him that he never showed me. I couldn't figure out what the hell he was talking about, but whatever it was, he was doing it so animatedly, with such fire and passion that, being the emotional faucet I am, I just sat in the dark and cried. It was remarkable. I had never seen any of that passion in him. He was in love with the words pouring from his mouth. If he would just show me once in a while that he loved me as much as his philosophies, maybe I wouldn't be so miserable. The only time I caught even the barest glimpse of that fire was when we fought.

I left before the class ended, then walked home in the pouring rain, getting drenched and feeling like a character out of a midnight movie on AMC. I found my DVD of *Casablanca* and a pint of Ben & Jerry's Chunky Monkey, then settled in for a good loud cry. I was just starting to get into the movie when the phone rang.

"Hello?" I hoped I didn't sound as if I'd been crying.

"Beth? What is up with you?"

It was Kate, my oldest friend in the whole world, who seems to instinctively know when I need her. Unfortunately, she lives in New York, so we don't get to see each other too often.

"Oh, Kitten, I—" I lost it.

"Honey, what's wrong?"

"I hate him. I really hate him."

"Mr. Wonderful?"

"Uh-huh, hic—" Super. Hiccups. My favorite.

"Shh, calm down, I'm on my way."

"Katie, you are in New York!"

"Well, jumpin' Jehoshaphat, so I am. Hang tight, it's going to take me about five hours to get there, but I could use a long weekend in a real city for a change. On my way. Ciao." *Click.*

Kate is the most impulsive person I know. She also has the largest trust fund in the western world, so she can afford to be spontaneous, and flying to Chicago for a weekend because I'm upset does not surprise me in the least. Plus, if I'm to be honest, I could not rely on the gang anymore where Sasha was concerned. Jess never liked him to begin with, so her letters just told me point-blank to dump him. Robin, ever the romantic, thought we should go to therapy. Anne had put a complete moratorium on the topic. And Lilith had just lost her dad, so complaining to her about anything seemed terribly selfish and inappropriate. Kate was exactly what I needed.

Five hours later, on the nose, the phone rang again.

"Okay, hon, I'm in the most expensive suite in the Inter-Continental, and I just sent down for an entire chocolate cake and two bottles of my uncle Dom. Get over here, and bring a nightie and a toothbrush."

I figured I needed a couple days of girl stuff.

"I'm on my way."

"Great. Suite P3. Penthouse."

I threw my stuff in a knapsack, fed Petey and the Fishes, scribbled a note to Sasha and caught a cab to the hotel.

Kate looked super, as always. She's nearly six-feet tall, with perfect skin, high cheekbones, thick golden hair and the hugest, bluest eyes I ever saw. Not to mention the body of a Greek goddess. If I had known at seven that the goofy-looking buck-toothed kid with the knobby knees would turn out so gorgeous, I would have thought twice about becoming her friend.

The suite was a duplex affair, with two bedrooms, an enormous living room, a conference room and a bathroom the size of my whole apartment, complete with sunken Jacuzzi built for two. The living room had heavenly goose-down couches. We perched ourselves on them with the cake and the champagne and two boxes of Kleenex, and I began telling my saga.

Kate's way of listening is great: if you cry, so does she; if you laugh, she rolls with merriment; if you tell her someone did something mean, she will call them every name in the book. She is the ultimate ally. She somehow knows how to ask the questions that, if you answer honestly, will contain the best solution to your problems, whether or not it's the solution you want to find. When I got to the part about sneaking into Sasha's lecture that morning, she started asking questions.

"Whoa, you may not see that passion in him when he talks to you, but how about in bed?"

"He's got it down to a science. Ten minutes foreplay, four and a half minutes intercourse, two hugs, then snoresville. You could set a timer to it. It's very sweet, very quiet and very dull. In the beginning I was relieved—you know how kinky Antonio was—but, to quote Lilith, at this point, it 'works on my nerves.'"

"Keep talking."

"Hey, I like to be able to do two things at once. Like make love and mentally do the grocery list, or make love and decide what to wear tomorrow. By April I should be able to make love and file my tax returns at the same time. Who knows, a couple more months and I might not have to be in the room anymore!"

My vehemence surprised me, and I began to think that everything has been worse than I let myself believe, that I convinced myself it was merely annoying so that I wouldn't have to face the prospect of actually leaving him. And of course, Kate sensed this in me.

"If you are so unhappy, why are you sticking around?"

"I don't know what else to do. Antonio made me miserable, too, but when I left him I had found Sasha." I admit it, I'm basically weak, and nothing scares me more than not having a boyfriend. And I'd rather be miserable and have someone to wake up with than miserable alone.

As if hearing my thoughts, Kate says, "You can't live your whole life focused on simply not being alone. I think if you can convince yourself that you can be happy without a man, you will be able to wait for one who will make you happy, and you won't be so afraid of being alone anymore."

"You think I should leave him, don't you?"

"Well, don't you? Haven't you had enough? Look, only you can make the final decision, but I'm here for two more days, and I'm an expert packer if you want help."

"Where am I going to live?"

"How about the warehouse? It's heated, has a phone jack—we could call the phone and electric companies today."

Kate had inherited an empty warehouse on Cortland Street from a great-uncle she'd never met. We had talked about converting it into a loft and moving in, but then Kate had moved to New York, so we never got around to it. It's humongous: 5,000 square feet with a loading dock at one end, a bathroom at the other and not a wall in between. Great space if you have a zillion dollars to fill it.

"I don't know, Kitten, it's so big. And I can't just take it from you."

"I'll rent it to you, four hundred and fifty dollars a month. You pay your own utilities, and any repairs you deduct from the rent."

"I don't know. Can I sleep on it?"

"Of course. Tomorrow we'll go shopping."

"I can't afford much more than a bed, maybe a lamp…."

"So what else do you need in life? We'll go to all the thrift stores, and I'll help some, 'kay?"

I knew I really didn't need to think; my mind was already made up. Kate just took away the last of my excuses.

"You are saving my life! How can I ever thank you?"

"Just love me unconditionally and do something to make yourself happy."

"Deal."

So Kate and I called the girls and everyone got into the

community spirit. Anne and Lilith showed up with a rented van chock-full of stuff. Lilith's mom had sold the house and moved into a smaller place after her husband's death, and Lilith and her sister hadn't needed the overflow, but no one wanted to get rid of anything, so they'd put it into a storage unit. We unloaded a great dining-room set, a king-size bed, a dresser, a bunch of tables, chairs and lamps, as well as some dishes and kitchen accoutrements, with Lilith's mom's blessing. Then off to the Ark thrift store on Lincoln to fill up the space with some mismatched couches. After a quick pizza lunch at my new table, the four of us returned the van and headed to the clearance rack at Bed, Bath and Beyond, where we bought a pile of irregular bedsheets. Back at the warehouse, with the help of a staple gun and years of vicarious DIY-television expertise, we reupholstered my new furniture and improvised curtains. Home Depot had a surprisingly decent selection of inoffensive colors in the "oops" rack, allowing me to buy $24-a-gallon paint for $9, and we sectioned off areas of the expansive walls to help visually define some "rooms."

Robin showed up having cut out early from work, with a picnic hamper full of goodies and a plastic jug of Michael's secret-recipe vodka gimlets. By midnight, the place was in surprisingly good shape, and we wrote a tipsy group letter to Jess on the back of a series of paint-chip strips, explaining our adventure. The girls went home, promising to check in the next day, and Kate and I returned, exhausted, to the Inter-Continental, where we made great use of both the Jacuzzi and the last of the gimlets. In the morning Kate offered to come home and help me pack, but I thought I had better do it myself, so she headed off to the airport, promising to come visit again soon.

My whole life I had been an independent thinker, but emotionally dependent on men. From the time I left Daddy's "nest," I had drifted from relationship to relationship, man to man. It was finally time for me to be the woman I know I really want to be. I only wished I was guaranteed that I'll like the new-and-improved me. And that other people will like her, too.

I went back to the apartment, packed my clothes and realized for the first time that I wasn't sad. A little worried, but excited, and more than vaguely proud of myself. All that was left was to say goodbye, which I supposed would be the hardest part. But I knew if I could look him in the eye and tell him "I'm leaving you" then I really would be able to walk out the door and not look back. I made two trips back to the warehouse with milk crates full of books, CDs, Petey's bowls and food and other detritus, leaving only my clothes to arrange. When Sasha got home I was sitting in the living room on top of my biggest suitcase.

"Elizabeth?"

"Sasha."

"What's going on?"

"I'm leaving."

He looked around the half-empty apartment, then glanced at me in disbelief.

"Why? What have I done?"

"I don't know, Sasha, I'm just unhappy. I have been for a while."

"I don't understand. Are you having your period?"

"No, goddammit, I'm not on the rag, I'm out the fucking door, okay?"

"You obviously don't want to leave or you wouldn't be

so angry and defensive. Put down that suitcase and tell me what's going on."

"You must get it through your thick skull that I'm not playing around, Sasha, I'm really leaving you. I don't want to hurt you, but I've been miserable for a long time and this is the best thing for me."

"Did Kate put you up to this?" he quipped patronizingly.

"Sasha, no one put me up to this but me. Look, I don't know, I just can't do this anymore."

"Beth, you know in your heart that this is not the right decision. I understand that you feel something is lacking in our relationship, but running away is not the answer. You must dig deep into your subconscious and determine the true cause of your depression. You'll probably find that it's not me, but rather your own feelings of inadequacy."

He looked so smug, and sounded so stupid, that I really wanted to laugh. And suddenly, I knew I would be okay, after all.

"Sasha, I'm sorry. But I'm leaving you, and nothing can change my mind now. Please don't make this difficult for me."

"I won't make it difficult. Your own mind will make it impossible for you to walk out the door. You will try to go, but your very limbs won't respond to your wishes."

"Goodbye, Sasha."

"You're going to be miserable."

"Sasha, I'm taking Petey. You'll just forget to feed him."

"See? You are wanting me to fight for custody of the dog, our symbolic child, in order to stall you and keep you from leaving."

I attached Petey's leash, picked up my last suitcase and my purse and opened the door.

"My new phone number is on the counter. If anyone calls for me, please give it to them."

"You'll be back—once you're done Finding Yourself."

"Don't wait around for something that isn't going to happen, Sasha. It will make your life awfully boring."

One, two, three steps and I'm in the hallway. *Click,* the door catches behind me, deep cleansing breath, and off we go down the stairs.

That was it. I got settled in the warehouse, fell into a routine, and hung out at Barneys learning everything I could about the business. Then Gram died and left Anne and me a small inheritance. I wanted to open my own shop, and Anne wanted to get out of the waitressing biz, so we became business partners. Our store, Girl Stuff, has been open a little over a year, and so far, even with my current state of exhaustion, it's been the best thing I could've done.

It's so much fun to work with Anne. She has turned out to be a natural at retail sales, always able to make a customer feel at ease, and especially good at helping people pick out gifts. She makes me very proud, and I have fantasies about the two of us as moguls, heading up a chain of Girl Stuff stores in every city and getting front-row seats at the best designer shows in Paris and Milan and New York. Anne just shakes her head at me when I tell her about how much fun it will be, sitting between Madonna and Gwyneth and acting bored. I can't seem to get her to imagine it the way I can, but I know she'll come around.

"Life is the age-old progression toward death. The only thing man can do is attempt to make his own time satisfactory to himself." I wonder if Sasha will ever realize that he finally came up with a philosophy that actually applies to real life?

Lilith

I'm sitting with Bill at auditions. Jeanne comes in with our take-out lunches, and not a minute too soon, because I'm fainting with hunger.

"That was the last one for Elmire. You have twenty minutes for lunch and then we have two guys to see for Tartuffe, three for Valere, four for Damis, three for Cleante and two for Orgon." Jeanne is all perky blond efficiency, like so many interns.

"Thank you, Jeanne," Bill says to her. "Let us know when the first one gets here." He pops open a can of Coke and lights a cigarette.

"The first two are here already. I sent them across the street for coffee. They know they are way early. Eat your lunch."

"So eager these actors, one would think they were anticipating being paid."

I can't stand it when Bill gets smug in front of the next

generation, so I figure I had better help her find her exit cue. "Thanks, Jeanne."

"My pleasure."

I open the sack and hand Bill a sandwich, a bunch of grapes and a large cookie, taking out my own salad and pear, and a bottle of water. Then I bum one of Bill's smokes. He is looking serious.

"What do you think?"

"I think Eva is perfect for Dorine, either Jen or that first girl for Elmire, Tanya for Mariane and whatshername for the mother."

"Whatshername?"

I flip through the stack of head shots in front of me. "This one. Sherry Healy."

"I mostly agree, but I think I want to do callbacks for Elmire."

"Good idea." I put out my cigarette and open my salad.

"I hate my set designer." Bill sighs deeply.

"Be good."

"Stairs, for chrissakes. He put a frigging staircase in the middle of the damn set. I said, 'Aldo, where do you hear reference to a staircase in this play?' He said, 'Bill, the metaphor here is so obvious I can't believe you are questioning it.' I said, 'Aldo, when I want literal translations of obvious metaphors in my set I'll let you know. In the meantime lose the stairs and find me my armoire.' So he says, 'Why do you keep insisting on that armoire? It's so unnecessary.' So I said, 'Aldo. Please go home and read the play. *Tartuffe.* By Molière. The French guy. Then call me and we'll have another discussion.'"

I'm trying not to laugh. "So what did he say?"

"He told me I was a small-minded idiot without a single artistic cell in my body."

"You're sleeping with him." Bill always does this.

"Of course."

"I hate auditions." Which I do. Hate watching them almost as much as I used to hate having to do them.

"I know."

"Why do you make me come to auditions?"

"Company. Plus, if anyone turns out to be miscast I can blame you." He is only half kidding, the prick.

"Great. My fault again."

Jeanne comes back in with a new stack of head shots just as we're finishing up our little luncheon.

"Here are the afternoon guys, Tartuffe's on top. I'll send in the first one in about three minutes."

Bill smiles at her. "Thanks, Jeanne."

I light another cigarette and pick up the picture on the top of the pile; a quirkily handsome gentleman with a twinkle in his eye. "Who's the snack?"

"Down, girl, he's my first choice unless he does something really stupid like audition with some Mamet thing. You know, the one who isn't the little dancer."

"Very funny. He's sort of dishy. Info?"

"Enigma. Rumored straight and married. Wife not in the business. He works out of town a lot, but sort of an underground local favorite. Everyone loves him but no one seems to really know him. Dry wit, smart, good actor."

"I like him already."

"I'm in hell." Bill shakes his head and laughs.

"I thought you wanted to hire him?"

"And now you want to sleep with him."

"Give me a break. I think his head shot is cute. I don't want to sleep with him—I haven't even met him yet." But he is very cute....

"Trust me, you want to sleep with him."

Intriguing. "What have you heard?"

"Hazel eyes."

"How hazel?"

Bill holds his hands apart a very respectable distance, implying a quality that has nothing to do with eye color. "This hazel!"

I laugh. "Oh, my. Is it warm in here? How do you know?"

"Tommy shared a dressing room with him in Connecticut."

"Really!" Even more intriguing.

"I shouldn't encourage you."

"Reverse psychology. Just think what would happen if you discouraged me!"

"Good point."

"I wish you hadn't told me." I lie so prettily.

"Why not?"

"How am I going to look at him when he comes in here?"

"Like a person. My God, he is a human being, not a piece of meat, and you may be working closely with him if he takes this part, so *behave.*"

"Yes sir, Mr. Director."

"That's better."

Noah is escorted into the room by Jeanne, jaunty in linen slacks and a tweedy cap.

Vital Statistics:

Noah Rogel

36, actor

[Rumored to be] both amply endowed and married

Likes verse plays

Hates giving a straight answer

He is even better-looking than his picture, and smiling broadly. Bill moves forward to greet him, but I hang back, suddenly a little shy, and notice that little flutter in my stomach, which has never been a good omen.

"Noah, great to see you again." Bill's voice always seems to drop a half octave or so when talking to straight boys. Very butch.

"I really appreciate the call, especially after that last thing you saw me in."

Bill laughs, and then puts on his reassuring voice. "That show is why you are here. Very few actors can rise above a bad play and give compelling performances. I was impressed."

"Thank you. That is very gracious. Nice people to work with, but I'm mostly glad it's over."

Bill gestures for me to come out from around the table. "Noah, I want you to meet Lilith. She will be helping with speech and verse, and maybe working some scenes with you."

Noah takes a step toward me and smiles warmly.

"It's a pleasure to meet you." His grasp is firm and cool, I'm afraid mine is clammy.

"Likewise." It's all I can manage at the moment. Luckily Bill saves me.

"Noah, you ready for us?"

"Sure, I have two monologues. One is Molière, the other is Shakespeare."

"That's fine. Let's hear the Molière first, we may not need to hear the other." Bill and I walk back around to sit behind the table.

"Okay by me."

Suddenly there is a loud, shrill beeping coming from Bill's pants. He peers down at his waistband.

"Goddammit! I'm sorry, Noah, I have to call this person back. Can you sit tight five minutes?"

"Take six."

"You're an angel. Lilith, play nice." Great.

"Okay." Bill zips out the door and leaves me alone with Noah. Time for small talk. I figure it is my responsibility to put him at ease. "You look really familiar to me. What have I seen you in?"

"Probably nothing. I work a lot out of town, and the stuff I do here is mostly terrible." Self-deprecating is sweet, but from Bill's reports, the guy has serious chops. Still, can't hurt to play along.

"You're better away from home?" I quip at him.

"Not really, but you wouldn't have seen it."

"Where do you hang out?"

"I try to avoid it."

"Antisocial?"

"Anti-hanging. Vertigo." Okay, a sassy one. I can do that.

"I see. So no actor bars for you?"

"Well, *bars,* sure, gotta go there." I want to laugh, but he is playing this so serious.

"Now we're getting somewhere. T's?" One of my favorite hangouts.

"Sometimes… I have a friend who likes it there."

This is my territory. "I know everybody. Who's your friend?"

"Well, more of an acquaintance, really."

"Okay, and he is…"

"Well, not really an acquaintance, more of a guy I met a couple times."

"Does he have a name?"

"Actually, I don't know him at all, but he looks like someone I know."

This finally breaks me. I start to giggle. "I give up."

Noah smiles. "Do you go there a lot? T's, I mean?"

"I'm something of a regular. It's near my house. I know the owner."

"Where do you live?"

"Andersonville. You?"

"Michigan." He can't be serious.

"Really? Michiana?" The short stretch on the border of Michigan and Indiana is a long commute, but doable. If one is insane.

"Upper Peninsula." I knew it. What an odd little duckling we have here. I'm starting to be awfully interested. But I'm playing along.

"That's something of a schlep."

"By the time I get home I have to leave again." The king of deadpan, this one.

"Must be rough on your car."

"I walk usually."

"Very Zen."

"Exactly. What makes someone a regular?"

"Excuse me?" He broke the rhythm, and now I am not exactly sure what we are talking about.

"At T's. What makes you a regular?"

"Well, I'm there every Thursday without fail, and sometimes one or two other nights during the week."

"That is pretty regular."

"If you're going to be a barfly, it's important to have a home base." I'm wishing this didn't make me sound so much like an alcoholic. Well, too late now.

"So are you going there tonight?"

"It's Thursday, so I'll be there. Have to go to a show first."

"What show?" He really has the loveliest crinkles around his eyes.

"Irish thing at the Theater Building."

"It's supposed to be good."

"Want to go? It's an industry night." What the hell am I *doing?*

"Maybe. What time?"

"Seven-thirty. Bill is coming with me. You could meet us there if you want. Suck up to us at intermission. Bill loves an ass kisser." Must let him know I wasn't asking him on a date.

Noah laughs a little embarrassedly, and I realize what I've said. Note to self: don't tell people that a blatantly gay man loves ass kissers.

"Oops. Guess that came out wrong." Good Lord, I'm tongue-tied! And now, blushing. Noah laughs harder.

"Now cut that out. I'm all ferputzed. What I meant was, well, I suppose brownnosing also gets tainted under the circumstances...." Might as well go with it. We both crack up.

I regain some of my composure. "Anyway, the invitation is open."

"Maybe I will."

"Excellent." At this point Bill comes back into the room, looking slightly put out.

"I'm so sorry, Noah."

"No problem at all."

Bill's look worries me a bit. "Issue?" I ask him.

He smiles wanly. "Later."

"Okay."

Bill and I get resettled at the table, and Bill looks up from his notepad.

"Noah, whenever you're ready."

Noah takes a moment, and then delivers a monologue from *School for Wives* that literally gives me gooseflesh. In the good way. He is sort of extraordinary—genuine, honest and pretty damn good with the verse. I'm impressed, and I can feel Bill relaxing beside me, knowing that he is going to have the right lead for this show. When Noah finishes, Bill gets up to shake his hand.

"Lovely work, Noah, really."

"Thank you."

"I don't think we need to hear the other verse. We will know by the end of today what the deal is. I'll call you tonight if that's okay."

Tonight? "From the Theater Building?" I ask.

"Sorry, pumpkin, can't go."

"Phone call?"

"Later."

Sigh. "Dumped again."

Bill turns to Noah. "Noah, you busy tonight? Squire our Lilith to the show in my stead? The ticket is wasted, else."

I'm mortified. Noah appears calm.

"Well, we can't have you out in the world squireless, if the offer still stands…."

I'm in hell. "That would be great." In bizarro world.

"Seven-fifteen?"

"I'll meet you in the lobby." *I'll be the one looking totally appalled.*

"See you there. Bill, thank you again."

"I'll leave you a message tonight, or call first thing in the morning."

"Terrific."

Noah goes out, and Bill turns to look at me, grinning ear to ear.

"What did you do?" I love him, but I may have to kill him.

"I was dipping a little."

"Eavesdropping? For how long?"

"Long enough to hear you invite the snack to the show."

"Bill! You don't have other plans, do you?"

"Nonsense, Lili, I have a design meeting."

"Glutton for punishment?"

"Glutton for angry little set designers."

"Oh, Lord."

"You clearly wanted him to come. I gave him an extra push, you can thank me later." Bill looks very pleased with himself.

"Should Martin thank you as well?"

"Hey, you know I stay out of that relationship. Martin is your deal. Besides, Noah's married, supposedly. Two attached people can go out and have a lovely time. Anyway, I know you. You always work better if you have a crush on someone. You'll start showing up for extra rehearsals and things and I'll get double the work out of you for the same pay." Sadly, he is right.

"You insidious, nefarious—"

"Attractive, lovable—"

"That's it. We have eight thousand people to see, and I'm leaving at five, because now I have a date, and I'm not nearly cute enough for a first date."

"Fine." He looks like the canary that swallowed the cat, damn his eyes.

"Fine."

Bill yells to the general direction of the door. "Jeanne? We're ready." Then he turns to face me. "Brownnosing, indeed."

Argh.

jess

The thing is, I always believed that we would end up in this place, together. Not really, you know, not consciously, but somewhere I must have believed it, because once it was in my head, even the littlest bit, as illogical as it was, it still made sense somehow. I mean, it seemed such a bizarre version of reality that the only way it could be resolved was to, somehow, become.

Maybe that's too strange. What am I really saying? Okay, I'll try it a different way. You know how you fantasize about something, not even something you necessarily want or need, but it sticks in your head for some reason, unknown even to you, and it seems like you could never in a million years actually live out that fantasy, but then one day some little piece—a minor piece, really, but a piece nonetheless—actually happens, and then you feel like, wow. Like that little piece is just the first domino, and now the chain reaction is inevitable. That's how we were. Inevitable. I'm beginning in the middle, really, but I don't know where the hell else to begin.

It was an accident.

I was in the Peace Corps. No, that's still in the middle.

Okay, back it up. When I was eight years old, we went to Hama's cabin for the summer. Just me and Amy, and Mom. Dad had left, and things were very weird, and so Hama, that's my dad's mom, invited us to come up to the cabin for the summer. My aunt Georgia was going to be there with my cousins Mark and Teddy, and it would be good for all of us to be away from the city for a while. What I figured out later was that the money Dad was supposed to send to overnight camp for Amy and me was the traveling money he used when he left. It didn't matter. We loved Hama, and Mark and Teddy were okay for boys, and I think it was good for Mom to be away from the house. She could kind of tune out and pretend that Dad was just on a trip or something, just away temporarily.

Plus, I think it was good for her to have access to her sister-in-law for support and encouragement. After all, the two had been college roommates, and the best of friends, which is how my parents met. Aunt Georgia was fun and vivacious and scandalous, and we worshiped her. She was a free spirit, much the antithesis of our conservative mother. She wore colorful floaty muumuulike dresses and peasant blouses and love beads, and her sandy hair was always tied in ribbons or scarves with beads, or plaited in two thick braids like an Indian princess. It was impossible to imagine her growing up with my father, who, until he took off, was the epitome of stability and predictable living.

Aunt Georgia had a degree in Middle Eastern philosophy and library science, and worked at the university library where she gave expert research assistance, and less expert love advice to the students who buzzed around her like lazy bees. She was raising her two boys alone, mostly because she had no clue who their fathers were. Teddy is half African-American, and apparently even that did not narrow down the field much. Georgia claims it could be any one of a four-man delegation from Jamaica who spent one semester team teaching Afro-Caribbean literature and oral tradition.

Teddy, the younger of the brothers, is the handsomest devil you ever met. His complexion is fairly medium, like a good-quality milk chocolate, and he has very African features, full lips and a broad well-defined nose. He has green eyes that go hazel when he's angry, and tight light brown curls. He gets away with murder. Mark, the elder, was the product of either a fling with a Royal Naval officer en route to a posting in Scapa Flow, or a short-lived romance with the dean of admissions. It's impossible to tell, as Mark looks just like Aunt Georgia. Lithe, willowy frame, nondescript brown hair, muddy eyes. He has grown into his looks, or at least learned how to play up his best features, but as a kid, well, that summer I remember a gangly boy of eleven, with a sensitive nature and a physique reminiscent of a praying mantis—big hands, big feet, long legs and a tiny little head.

I loved my cousin Mark the way all young girls love broken things. The doll with the missing arm, the three-legged dog, the stray cat with the missing ear and cloudy eye. Mark needed taking care of; he was no match for Teddy's charm, looks and athletic ability. Being the smart one is no help at eleven, and Mark's self-esteem was at an all-time low. The girl Mark had a crush on liked Teddy, and though Mark had too much pride to admit it, he was sad for himself and jealous of his brother, and so, naturally, I wanted to help him. Secretly, of course. I devised elaborate plans to give him the boost I felt he needed, only in such subtle ways that he never would suspect. Pretending to break the chain on my bike, wanting to build a tree fort in the woods, letting him win all the tennis games and swimming races and diving contests... Later, of course, he claimed that it was, in fact, me who needed the attention, and that he only hung out with me so much because he wanted to keep my mind off my parents but he's a man, and we all know they will say anything to avoid admitting that a girl helped them.

That was the summer we started the diary letters. I kept a diary, which I wrote in faithfully. Mark liked the idea of a journal, but felt stupid "just writin' to nobody but me— I know what I did today." So I came up with the diary letters. Once a week, we would write a letter to each other, telling all of our innermost secrets, and adventures, and even boring day-to-day stuff. The other person was in charge of keeping the letters safe and organized. We've done this faithfully for the past nineteen years. In high school we wrote sometimes twice a week (there are so many more melodramas at that time). In college, we went to once a month. We finally settled on every other week when Mark was in medical school. He had exams every other Friday, so he knew he could write the weekend after the exam without jeopardizing his study schedule. But, ultimately, it was the letters that were the problem.

When I started high school, I fell in love with this incredibly artistic senior. His name was Rush, if you can imagine, and he was *to die for.* He had the locker next to mine, and he smiled at me between classes, and he smelled like a mixture of bay rum cologne and pot. All of his notebooks were covered with intricate doodles, and the inside of his locker was an ever-changing collage of pictures and matchbooks and bits and pieces. He wore a long, tattered tweed overcoat with a cream silk scarf, and kept his brown hair tousled and falling in his eyes so he could flick it back with meaning when he talked.

I loved him.

I started doodling with a vengeance. I began collecting meaningful bits of garbage to paste up in my locker. And my diary letters to Mark began to contain photos and magazine articles, mix tapes (with hand-drawn covers), movie-ticket stubs and long, mournful poems about the godlike Rush and my unrequited love for him. Mark often wrote that he would run out of room in his attic if I kept sending him every damn piece of crap I ever laid my hands on, but he conceded that the photos were useful. They put faces to names, and when we visited each other for weekends or school holidays we could exchange meaningful eye contact at parties without having to whisper snippets of anecdotes at each other. So maybe it wasn't really the letters that were the problem, it was the pictures.

Shit.

I'm still all over the place here.

Okay, fast-forward to two years ago. I'm thirty-one, Mark is thirty-three. I've completed an M.A. in the humanities, and have been teaching in a fancy private school, and Mark has completed his residency, and is a pediatrician. I join the peace corps for a two-year stint in East Africa. Four months before I leave, I get a relatively long diary letter from Mark, discussing primarily his good friend Harrison. This is not uncommon; they went through medical school and internship and residency together, and both landed attending jobs at Children's Memorial. I know it sounds weird that we kept up the letters even though we live in the same city, but it's a force of habit now, and the whole point was and is to keep a record for the future, so the letters continue faithfully. Sometimes we try to get together for dinner and deliver them in person. I can't help that we're strange.

All of that is beside the point. The point is that Mark keeps writing the letters, and that a major theme of these letters is Harrison.

Vital Statistics:

Harrison Mannerly

33, pediatrician

Bad boy

Likes broads and booze

Hates answering to anyone but himself

Mark says it's damn lucky he is a brilliant surgeon; otherwise he never would have finished his residency. The current letter is full of touching and heartfelt concern that his buddy is going to sabotage his career, that Harrison made a pass at the chief cardiac guy's trophy wife, blah blah blah. There are three photos enclosed, all of Harrison. One shows him asleep in the on-call room, in green scrubs, one arm thrown over his head. In the second, he's kneeling to talk to a very dirty and frightened-looking little boy. In the third, he's sitting alone in what looks to be a waiting room or lounge, with a very faraway look on his face and a tiny smile playing around the corners of his mouth.

Here's the beginning of the trouble.

My friend Brian, an art director for a local advertising

agency, came over one afternoon, swiped the three pictures off my desk and framed them together in one small simple wooden frame, beautifully matted in ivory and blue, looking for all the world like some professional photo essay— "A Day in the Life of Dr. Mannerly" (yes, that is really his last name). I end up hanging it over my desk, and every day I look at it, I like it more and more. So I decide to take it with me to Kenya, since it's not very big, to hang on my wall and remind me of home. No ulterior motive, just something from home to look at.

Did I mention he is very handsome?

Perhaps it's relevant now. Harrison is handsome in that casual athletic way that few women can resist. He's at least a couple inches over six feet, with a trim athletic build. Wide shoulders, thick, dark brown hair with a hint of wave, hazel-green eyes, pouty bottom lip, great cheekbones, strong chin. I'm gushing, I know, but he really is a kind of natural Adonis. You know he knows he's amazing looking, but he shrugs it off.

I think that's why the photos looked so, I don't know, like real art, I guess. And I suppose if I'm honest, the prospect of two years looking at one item on my wall, well, why not a hottie?

At a Peace Corps informational meeting, I meet this woman who is just back from her P.C. tour in Tanzania, and when she hears my plans, she gives me this plain gold band she is carrying in her change purse. She says it saved her from numerous problems in her village. She just wore it on her left hand, and people assumed she was married. They were too polite or scared to ask for details, and she swore it made her life easier, being all alone in a polygamous society. They respect the sanctity of marriage, odd but true. Anyway, it has been strongly suggested to all of us that we remember that one of our functions in the villages will be to implement AIDS awareness and family planning groups, and to refrain from romantic fraternization. A little Victorian, I know, but in a country where over ninety percent of the bar girls and prostitutes (often the same thing) are HIV positive, it's better to live like a nun. The idea of eliminating romance as an issue was very appealing to me, so, in the airport, I put the ring on.

When I got to my village, in the westerly part of Kenya, not far from the Ugandan border, I hung up my picture, and wrote to Mark and the girls, detailing my whirlwind week of travel, briefings, settling into my little mud hut. Mark promised, in his first letter, to try to write more often, since, in addition to keeping up with his diary, he was going to be a major source of "First World" news. And, bless him, he did. Letters arrived about every five or six days, with clips from the *Reader,* and detailed descriptions of work, and his new romance with (gasp!) an older woman he met in his building. After the first couple months, the "wedding" ring didn't seem so strange on my hand.

I fell into a routine, teaching English in the local secondary school, working at the clinic, and I began to make friends. A fellow teacher was over for tea one day, and she commented that my husband was handsome. I didn't know what to say, so I just smiled, quietly. Soon, it was natural for me, and no one else thought twice about it; I mean, I wore the ring, I got letters frequently from a doctor with the same last name as me and I had pictures of a doctor on my wall in my hut. Sherlock Holmes himself would have been hard pressed not to draw a conclusion there.

Okay, fast-forward again. I'm now thirty-three, and Mark

is thirty-five. I'm six weeks from finishing my tour, and just in time, because Mark is going to marry Gemma (the older woman) this summer. Mark writes that Aunt Georgia is only tentatively optimistic about this union, and claims that it's not because she gets more and more conservative the further away she gets from the Seventies, it's just her fear that Gemma, thirty-eight, won't have time to produce grandchildren for her. I've been accepted into the PhD program at University of Chicago, where I'll be teaching freshman comp classes to pay the bills. I get a letter from Mark saying that due to prewedding chaos he won't be able to put me up, but that Harrison has a two-bedroom condo in Wrigleyville, and is never there (the life of a surgeon), and I can crash there until I can find a place to live. No biggie. It doesn't even occur to me to be weirded out about moving in with my "hubby" for a few weeks. In fact, I'm kind of looking forward to it—after all, it will be the perfect chance to see if reality matches Mark's letters. I've only met Harrison in person once, their first year of med school, and he was so smashed he said, "How do I do?" instead of "How do you do?"

I decide to tell the girls that I'm arriving home a week after I actually am, so that I have a few days on my own to ease back into the world. Staying with Harrison is one of the ways I'm going to be able to pull this off, since I can keep a low profile. And as much as I love them, I'm not up for the kind of intense togetherness that would result from staying with any of them. Plus, I'm a little afraid of not being able to go right back to the person I was before I left.

I finish up in the village, have one last bout of mild dysentery, buy six Valium in Nairobi where it is an over-the-counter drug and trek thirty-four hazy hours to O'Hare, via Frankfurt and New York. I take a cab to the address Mark gave me, find the key inside the concrete turtle on the front lawn and let myself into Harrison's casually elegant, if sparse, condo on the second floor. After calling my mom and Mark and my sister, Amy, to assure them of my safe arrival, I wander in search of a correct timepiece. The clock in the kitchen says seven-fifteen, the rainy grayness outside giving no clue as to a.m. or p.m., and I'm so wiped I could care less.

This is really where the problem began. Really.

I explore the apartment just long enough to find the bathroom and the two bedrooms. I take a long, hot shower, and wash my hair three times, just because it feels so good. Then I spot it, half hidden on the side of the sink, just within reach. The razor.

Let me tell you something about living in a rural area of a third world nation. To say that they've some serious health risks is a huge understatement. Parasites, bizarre diseases—you name it. I had to get twelve different inoculations before I left, and they only cover the stuff we know about for sure. When I got to Kenya I made two major changes in my personal habits. First, I quit biting my nails. Sheer terror of putting my hands in my mouth. Second, I stopped shaving my legs and armpits. The danger of possible deadly infection entering my body through a nick was not worth smooth legs. Besides, I had to keep my legs covered to midcalf anyway, so the offending hair was little seen. But the sight of that gleaming triple-bladed wonder on the side of the sink was too much to resist. By the time I've finished in the shower I'm as clean and hairless as it is humanly possible to be, and in spite of the couple little cuts on my shins and the rash I've raised in my armpits, I'm gloriously happy with my new self.

I raid the freezer, and nuke (my God, microwave cooking!) a frozen dinner, which I eat with surprising relish. Two years of maizemeal paste and fried greens and Lean Cuisine becomes a delicacy. When I get to the bedrooms, I'm entirely perplexed. There is no indication that anyone uses either of them regularly. No telltale signs, no stuff on the dressers, no pictures at bedside, no dirty clothes in the hampers, nada. Both closets are full of clothes. The only clue is the treadmill. One room has one, the other doesn't. So is Harrison the type to keep it in his bedroom to remind him to get on it occasionally, or is he conscientious enough to keep it out of sight in a little-used guest room? Remembering his handball rivalry with Mark, and the lean lines of his physique in the photos, I decide he must keep it in the guest room, and throw my wet towel over the handle bars to dry. I never bought that "asleep before her head hit the pillow" crap until now. I don't even remember getting into the bed. I just remember the intense drive-in-movie dreams that come with extended use of antimalarials, and waking up kissing Harrison.

Now I've jumped too far ahead.

There are three things you should know about me. I hate sleeping alone. I do it often. In bed, I automatically move toward the warmest spot. When I returned from Kenya it had been twenty-nine months and fifteen days since I shared a bed with anyone for any reason.

All I really remember was the cave dream, where I've been running from something awful, but I find the cave just in time, and when I get inside it's warm and safe and cozy and I know nothing bad can happen. Now, usually, this dream leaves me very empty, like I'm watching a movie with emotions that have no connection to my own existence, but this time I really felt, you know, safe. Tremendously safe. And warm. And in those few minutes of semiconsciousness before I woke up, when you hear and feel and think but can't quite open your eyes or interact with the world yet, I felt the sweetest thing I ever felt in my whole life. Someone was holding me tightly, and kissing me deeply, and whoever it was tasted of scotch and smelled like cigarettes and some spicy aftershave, and I think I knew it was real, but I never wanted it to end.

Then my mother sent a FedEx to my cerebral cortex, which sounded vaguely like a baby crow.

"Who is that, and why are you all tangled around him like some cat in a ball of twine? He could be an intruder or killer or rapist, God forbid, or some loser with herpes and no job, so why are you, Jessica Xavier, making out with Mr. X like a teenager in heat? Caw caw caw…"

My mother, even in telepathic messages, is very convincing. I opened my eyes. And there, in the pale-green light of the digital alarm clock, was Harrison, eyes closed, kissing me with such quiet tenderness that when I pulled myself away from him my throat was uncomfortably tight. He snuggled into my hair, which I was suddenly glad was so clean, and murmured, "Hey, beautiful."

God help me, for ten seconds, I imagined that he had somehow, well, had maybe gotten a small crush on me, you know, through Mark's glowing descriptions, and had only offered the use of his apartment in order to fulfill some seduction fantasy… Then I snapped out of it. The smoke really cleared when he whispered, "Do you want me to drive you home, or can you spend the night?"

He thought I was a fucking one-night stand, some sleazy heifer he picked up in a bar for the price of a couple drinks and some meaningless compliments. I don't know why I was so mad, and disappointed, or why I wanted to hurt him. All I knew was that he had obviously been so drunk when he got home that he didn't realize there was someone in his bed, and when he did connect to this information, he didn't remember not bringing her there.

It was then that I was made painfully aware of something Harrison and I had in common. We both sleep in the buff. And his insistent erection pressing the side of my hip was more than I could bear.

I rolled over, away from his unwanted embrace, and felt around on the floor until I located something made of fabric. Under the covers I struggled into what turned out to be Harrison's shirt, and he must have really woken up, because he said, "Well, if you must leave, at least let me take you home. I'll get dressed in a flash." Ooh la la, chivalry is not dead. It was then that I did something minorly evil.

"Sweetheart, why would I leave if I'm moving in with you?"

"What? Come again?" Harrison propped himself up on one elbow, getting more and more awake by the moment.

"You said we should move in together to save money before the wedding. You said this was my home now, at least until we can find a bigger place in the suburbs—can't raise our babies in the city, darling. You did mean it, didn't you? I told you I would never, you know, except with the man I was going to marry, and you said—"

"Whoa, baby, slow down, I just gotta clear my head and remember…."

He must have seen the look on my face, and suddenly I

felt bad. I mean, he probably fell into his bed drunk and woke up with a naked woman pressed against him. As I said before, I gravitate with a vengeance, and I decided to forgive him. I smiled broadly in the clock light.

"You're joking with me?"

I laughed.

"You're fucking joking with me?"

I laughed harder.

"I don't believe, of all the cruel… Hey, wait a minute."

I swear I could actually see a huge cartoon lightbulb click on over his disheveled head.

"You're Jess."

"Nice to meet you."

"Mark's cousin Jess. You're staying here."

"Exactly."

"Why aren't you in the guest room?"

"I didn't know which room was the guest room so I guessed."

"You guessed wrong."

"Sorry, I was really tired. I'm still really tired."

"I have a feeling this needs more awareness than I can muster right now, heart attack notwithstanding, I'm not fully awake yet. I did two emergency surgeries tonight, and caught the last hour of a birthday party, and I'm beat, so can we table this till morning? I'll buy you breakfast and you can tell me all about this three a.m. practical-joke fetish you seem to have." Then he noticed he was naked, and pulled the sheets up to his neck like a timid bride. I raised one eyebrow at him, and he tried to imitate me, but his face screwed up with the effort and he only managed to look as if he had something in his eye. I lost it. He joined me.

We laughed so hard that soon the tears were rolling, and

finally, we fell back on the bed, trying to catch our breath. When the last giggles subsided, I said I would see him in the morning, and got up. Had I taken more time to investigate, I would have realized that the guest room was easily discernible from Harrison's room. There were no sheets on the bed, no pillowcases under the shams, no blanket under the coverlet. Quiet searches of all available closets revealed no spare linens of any kind. I returned to the scene of the original crime and gently nudged Harrison's shoulder.

"Where might you keep the linens for the guest room?" I whispered.

"Shit."

"Could you be more specific? Are they dirty?"

"No, they're pristine. In fact, they've never been used."

"Great, do I need a map? Secret password?"

"Nope. Bed, Bath and Beyond, corner of Clybourn and Willow. I knew I forgot to do something this week."

"Sleeping bag?"

"Un-unh."

"Okay, well, I've had worse accommodations, but you lose a Michelin star for this." I turned to go.

"Jess."

"Yeah?"

"At the risk of sounding improper, I swear I'll be a perfect gentleman if you want to crash here."

"You know what, Doctor? I'm too tired to think about propriety, push over."

"Want to hand me something to sleep in first?"

"Excellent idea," I replied.

He directed me to the right drawer in his dresser and I tossed him a pair of running shorts and a T-shirt, and went to the bathroom while he made himself presentable. When

I got back to the bedroom he had straightened the covers and pillows, and arranged himself very respectably on the far side of the bed, facing the door. He was already asleep again, which didn't surprise me. Mark had told me that residency, with its grueling hours, trains you to fall asleep instantly. I walked around the other side and got in as gently as possible, facing the window, and back to back, with a two-foot-wide chasm between us, I, too, fell back to sleep.

Harrison was true to his word: he never laid a finger on me. And the next morning he took me to breakfast at Nookie's and we ate huge omelettes and puzzled out the previous night. We talked about Mark and my tour in Africa, and generally got to know one another under relatively sane circumstances. Then we bought new bedding for the guest room. And pajamas, just for the sake of etiquette. Normalcy returns. Almost.

We spent the early part of the afternoon running errands, debating what to get Mark and Gemma for their wedding gifts. Then, around four, Harrison was called in to the hospital, and didn't get home until ten-thirty. I kept him company while he ate the leftover pasta I had cooked for dinner, and we both went to bed (in separate rooms) at around eleven-thirty, falling asleep to the distant rumble of thunder. I dreamt about riding on the bow of a sailboat, the spray of the water in my face, and falling off, and no one knew I was gone. When I woke up, I was drenched, the bed was soaked and a steady stream of water dropped onto my head. I turned the light on, identified a steady leak in the ceiling and headed for Harrison's room.

"Harrison. Wake up. We have a problem." I flipped the light on. Blinking furiously, and rubbing his 2:00 a.m. stubble, he finally looked at me, puzzled.

"What's the matter?"

"Have you ever had a waterbed?"

"No, I...what?"

"You do now."

Then he sat up and looked over to find me dripping on his rug.

"What the hell happened to you?"

"You seem to have a leak."

"Wait a minute, dammit...oh shit."

Harrison jumped out of bed, and while I tried not to notice how good he looked in his new pajama bottoms, he ran to the front closet and grabbed a large bucket, which he placed at the head of the guest-room bed.

"Fucking contractor swore this was fixed."

"You've had this problem before?" I asked.

"That's how it became a guest room. The bed was the only piece of furniture large enough to cover the water damage from last time, cheaper than new flooring."

"Lovely."

"Well, looks like you're bunking with me again. Sorry."

"Tomorrow I'll find a hotel or something."

"No, don't do that, you'll go broke staying in the decent places, and I won't let you stay in the indecent ones."

"Your concern is touching for someone who, in the span of twenty-four hours, has molested me in my sleep and sent me off to drown in his guest room."

"First of all, you could've molested me first, and second of all, oh hell, I can't think of a second of all. Come on, this is why we bought pajamas."

"A brilliant suggestion on my part, I might add."

"Yeah, yeah, yeah, you're fucking Einstein. Can we go to bed now? I'm still on call tonight, and I'd like at least a couple hours of sleep before they wake me up to bug me about upping somebody's pain meds."

"After you, Dr. Cousteau."

"Does Mark know you're such a smart-ass?"

"Yep."

"Just checking."

I remember waking up from a vivid dream, with my heart racing, and Harrison rubbing my back, shushing me, then pulling me close to him and whispering calming words into my hair. When I woke up for real, the next morning, he was already gone.

slumber party: the sequel, as told by jess

I steel myself outside Beth's door. I'm excited and trepidatious, and frightened that things won't be what they were. The buzzer echoes behind the steel door of the warehouse, and I'm startled by the vastness it implies. The door makes a loud metallic creak when it opens, and on the other side I find Beth grinning at me widely. All my fears melt away as I allow myself to be pulled into Beth's expansive embrace while the shrieks of my other friends cut through the air. Soon the five of us are trapped in a strange and delicious group hug, and everyone is weeping and laughing and talking all at once.

Finally we settle down. Beth gives me the tour of the warehouse, Robin returns to the kitchen where she is putting final touches on a plate of nibbles, and Anne and Lilith begin mixing up a pitcher of margaritas. Lil hands one to me— I pronounce it delicious—and soon we're settled in Beth's designated living-room area. I'm on the couch, flanked by Beth and Robin, and Anne and Lilith are sitting on large floor pillows on the other side of the coffee table. Petey decides to get in on the action, and dislodges himself from his dog bed in the corner to flop down next to Anne with his big head in her lap to be petted.

Robin has made a large plate of hors d'oeuvres, endive spears stuffed with Israeli couscous and marinated vegetables, walnut halves topped with herbed goat cheese, prosciutto-wrapped figs and parmesan crisps with artichoke puree and pomegranate seeds. Since they were all true to their promise to keep in touch while I was away, I only have the events of the past few weeks to catch up on.

"I think I'm falling in love with Noah," Lilith begins.

"The guy you wrote me about from Bill's show?" I ask.

"The very same," Lil continues. "We hang out all the time, go see shows, have drinks, picnics in the park. It's all so romantic and yet not, you know? I mean, anyone who saw us together would think we were involved, but he never lays a finger on me. I feel like I'm in one of those stupid movies we all hate."

"What about Martin, how are things there?" Beth asks.

"We're officially 'seeing other people.' When he is in town I make time for him, but when I told him I needed more from him he said he just couldn't right now, his work is too busy and important. He doesn't like that I wanted the option of dating other men, but he also wasn't prepared to let me go altogether. It's good enough when we're together, but when he's gone I mostly think about Noah. And I know he is married, and I know that he probably doesn't want me, but then we see each other and there is such spark, and ease and comfort. It's making me crazy."

"I know the feeling," says Robin.

"Ah, yes, how is Michael?" Anne asks.

"The same. Adorable. Unavailable." Robin pops another walnut into her mouth and sighs.

"You guys still having your weird sleepovers?" I ask.

"Of course. And the weird thing about them is how not weird they are. We just hang out and talk, and then he doesn't want to go home, so we get in our pajamas and curl up in bed and sleep. In the morning I make him breakfast and send him on his way."

"Why don't you just jump him already?" asks Anne.

"Have you tried getting him drunk?" Beth inquires.

"Great ideas, guys. He's my boss and my good friend— I should really attempt to rape him in his sleep, or worse, have some drunken fling he'll regret in the morning, and make everything creepy. It's so hard, though. Sometimes, in the middle of the night, when he's spooning me, I can feel him twitch against my lower back. You know how guys are, all those middle-of-the-night half erections. I know it's just his body being normal, but when I feel it I want to just reach behind me and grab his cock—"

"Robin!" Anne is blushing and looking horrified.

We all crack up, since Robin even saying the word *cock* is awfully incongruous.

"I'm sorry, I don't mean to be graphic, but I haven't had sex in ages, and he is so damn fine...."

"Don't apologize, we've all been there. I almost got into trouble with my gracious host my first night back," I confess.

"The good doctor? Really? Dish, please." Beth is eager to hear the story.

"Okay, look, don't be mad, but I didn't get back this Wednesday, I got back last Wednesday. I know that I should've told you, but I can't really explain, I just needed some time to acclimate."

"That makes sense, sweetie, no big deal." Anne is always the empathetic one.

"Anyway, he was at the hospital when I got in, so I was on my own in his apartment…." I tell them about my first night with Harrison, and about the fact that we've continued to share his bed. The girls crack up about the leaky ceiling, and are very curious about the handsome doctor, especially since they've seen photos of him.

Beth interrupts my tale.

"Let me get this straight. Are Anne and I the only ones without some odd nonrelationship? Robin is having slumber parties with Michael, Jess is bunking in with Dr. Shaggable, Lil is having some bizarre Arthurian courtly romance…" Beth stops her diatribe midsentence, looking over at her sister, who is blushing deeply and avoiding eye contact. "Anne?"

Anne looks back at her sister.

"Anne!" Beth is flabbergasted.

"It isn't what you think. I'm not seeing anyone, or sleeping with anyone or anything like that."

"But…" prods Lilith.

"But I sort of had this strange experience with this guy and I can't stop thinking about him…." Anne tells them about the man at Lula, and admits that she has been hanging out there, hoping he will come back.

"I wondered why you've been going there a lot lately—you used to complain about how overpriced it is!" Lilith is hugging Anne and laughing.

"You sneaky bitch, why didn't you tell me?" Beth throws a balled-up cocktail napkin at her sister.

"Because I'm embarrassed! I mean, he could be married, he could be gay, he could be a serial killer, he might not even live in Chicago!" Anne is laughing at herself now, relieved that no one appears to think she has taken total leave of her senses. "Besides, I don't have to tell you *everything!*"

"You most certainly do, missy. I'm your older sister and your business partner, that means no secrets, *ever!*" Beth shakes her finger at Anne in fake scolding.

"Hey, none of us can point a finger, we're all fucked up when it comes to men!" Robin reaches over and grabs the finger Beth is still pointing at Anne.

"Speak for yourselves, I'm very normal, all things considered," Beth says, retrieving her finger from Robin's grasp.

"Oh yeah!" I say. "How many dates have you been on since Sasha?"

"One."

"Elizabeth…." cautions Robin.

"What? I've been on *a* date," Beth replies.

"Beth, being Bill's beard in my stead at his cousin's wedding doesn't count as a date." Lilith is shaking her head.

"What, I got dressed up, went out with a man, ate, drank, danced…" Beth is giggling at herself.

"Oh yeah, great, one date with a gay man does not a healthy social life make!" Anne pronounces.

"Well, it isn't like the online dating thing worked, all those e-mails and not one date," Beth says. "I've been too busy with the store to meet anyone, and straight men don't shop at a place called Girl Stuff unless they're with their girlfriends or wives!" We all laugh. "Okay, okay, I give! I'm just as screwed up about guys as the rest of you!" Beth throws her hands in the air.

"Well, I'm glad that's finally settled. Now we can eat dinner!" Robin gets off the couch, goes to the kitchen and begins to arrange serving platters and bowls. The rest of us tidy up the snacks, refill drink glasses and help Robin with the food. There is a big salad of romaine hearts, hearts of palm, artichoke bottoms and grape tomatoes in a spicy lime vinaigrette, a roasted leg of lamb with an herbed yogurt sauce, wild rice with currants, pistachios and fresh mint and crisply roasted brussels sprouts. We take the platters to the table and dig in, praising Robin's fair hand in the kitchen and toasting my return to civilization.

After the dishes are done, and we've gotten into our pajamas, we sit in a circle on the floor, sipping Robin's decadent homemade hot chocolate and eating shortbread cookies Anne brought over from Bittersweet Bakery, and chocolate-covered dried cherries and blueberries that Lilith picked up at Long Grove Confectionery. I take the opportunity to give them all the gifts I brought them back from Kenya, beautifully woven wrap skirts called kangas, small soapstone carvings from Kisii, elephant-hair bracelets, and necklaces of handmade silver beads. In addition I have a traditional bean pot for Robin, a pair of garnet earrings for Beth, a signed copy of Chinua Achebe's *Things Fall Apart* for Anne and an antique wooden mask for Lilith. I teach them all how to wear the skirts, and Beth puts on a compilation CD of world music that one of her vendors had given her, and soon the five of us are dancing energetically, wearing our kangas over our pajamas, adorned with Kenyan jewelry. Petey's whine eventually puts an end to the dancing, and Beth throws a coat over her getup and goes to get his leash. I offer to keep her company on the walk, and the rest of the girls decide to get the beds made up. As the guest of honor I will get the couch, Anne will bunk in with Beth, and Lil and Robin will be sharing the inflatable Aerobed.

Waiting for Petey to do his business, Beth slips an arm around my waist.

"I'm so glad you are finally home."

"Me, too. I really loved it there, but I was ready to leave. Thank you so much for doing this for me tonight. I feel like I'm having two years' worth of joy in one evening."

"I'm glad. We're all so proud of you for what you did, and I for one am so relieved that you didn't come back all granola crunchy and Greenpeace-y!"

"You know me better than that, I hope!"

"Well, one never knows—you kept writing how much it was changing you. But as far as I can tell, you seem mostly the same. A little more worldly, maybe, calmer, more centered or grounded or something. And happy. You seem like you're really happy. Not 'something good is happening right now' happy, but deeper. Content."

"You nailed it, it's so hard to explain, it's just an internal shift. I am happy. Glad to be me. Glad to be here. Feeling lucky and blessed to be in the world and of the world."

Beth gives me a hug, and then goes to clean up after Petey. We walk once more around the block, enjoying the crisp night air and the comfort of each other's company, and then return to the warmth of the warehouse and our friends.

robin

"What's that look, kiddo?" Michael breaks into my mini daydream of how good my grandmother's armoire would look in this living room. We're sitting in Michael's new condo, surrounded by stacks of boxes. I'm trying desperately not to imagine myself living here.

"What look?"

"You have a look." Michael's head tilts sideways as he looks at me.

"I do not. I'm lookless."

"You are thinking about something far away."

"Nope. Just admiring your new digs."

"You really like it? It was very impulsive of me." Michael bought this place from a guy his brother plays poker with. In about three days. He hadn't even been in the market for a place.

"I like it very much." Which is true. "I think you and Andrea will be very happy here." Which is a lie. "Speaking of which, how is the light of your life?" Might as well hear it from him.

"Too far away, love, too damn far away." The sadness in his voice is tangible. It fills the room like smoke. And my heart breaks a little, both for his sadness and my own. Well, must try to be supportive.

"I'm sure she misses you, too. Just hang in there, it will all be a happy ending in the long run."

"I hope you're right. She claims that this transfer is just for a year, to get the L.A. office up and running, and then she'll be back, but I'm not so sure that she means it. How about you? Any new men in your life?"

"Just the old ones, with different faces."

"Someone will come along."

"I thought that, too, ten months ago. Nope, I'm incapable of generating physical attraction in men of my own species."

"Robin, stop that. How many times do I have to tell you not to keep putting yourself down like that?"

"None. I'm through. I'm joining SDA."

"I'm afraid to ask."

"Self-Deprecators Anonymous. Hello, my name is unimportant and I'm an addict. I started with a little joke every once in a while, just to liven a mood without making anyone else the butt of the humor. Pretty soon, I couldn't stop. I had no sense of what was funny unless I cut myself down. I've been straight for two weeks, and yesterday I told my first normal joke. It was a knock-knock joke, and got no laughs, but I felt a weight lift from my shoulders. Today, I'm ready to tackle the world. I might even try to accept a compliment gracefully."

"You are really crazy, you know that, Robbie?" He refills my glass.

"But I made you smile—that is worth being crazy. And don't call me Robbie."

"Why?" he asks.

"Why what?"

"Why is it worth being crazy?"

"Because you're one of my best friends. You're always here when I need you, you make me feel good about myself. And because you have a piece of something green stuck between your front teeth, and every time you smile you look really silly."

Michael uses his finger to retrieve the offending morsel, and then pinches my leg. "Thanks for telling me three hours after dinner."

"It's just us. Besides, Mikey, this gets you back for the time you let me walk around for two hours with half of my skirt tucked into the back of my underwear."

"I thought you wanted it that way. And don't call me Mikey."

"Right."

"Anyway, it's just a matter of time until you find some great guy who will see what I see." Intriguing.

"When you see me, what do you see?"

"Eyes. Luminous eyes that change from blue to green to gray so fast it's almost bewitching. Chameleon eyes." Wow. I keep forgetting he has that poetic side.

"Chameleon eyes. I like that. It makes me feel like a sorceress of some sort."

"Well, aren't you?"

"Not consciously. I don't have any specific magic that I'm aware of. Every morning I'm still the woman I was when I went to sleep, just better rested."

"What about nonspecific magic?"

Hmm. "I'm not sure. I think we can all do some kind of nonspecific magic, but that we're unaware of what form that magic presents itself in, that is part of what makes it work."

"How do we always get into these philosophical bullshit conversations?"

"I have all these strange theories bouncing around in my head, and you bring them out of me. What else should we talk about?"

"Let's talk about love."

"No." That is a conversation I definitely don't want to have with him tonight.

"Why not?"

Yeesh. Long list or top ten? I'll go for romantical. "It's a conversation that merits a cold rainy night and lots of excellent cognac. I promise, the next crashing thunderstorm, come over, and I'll get that bottle of dusty VSOP that I found in my great-grandfather's wine cellar, and I'll tell you about love."

"You have too many rules, and I'm starting to worry about your obsession with alcohol." He seems amused with me. "But you win. The next cold rainy night, *Catherine* dear, you and your theories on love are mine. I can't wait to hear them."

"Thank you for your patience, darling Heathcliff," I reply, using our "we're *so* melodramatic" nicknames. "I'll make it worth your wait. And don't worry about the booze, you're just oversensitive to it—occupational hazard. Although, I could be in denial. Perhaps you need to monitor me on a round-the-clock basis. Hmm?" I bat my eyelashes ferociously and lick my lips suggestively. Michael laughs at my antics.

"My, aren't we flirtatious this evening?"

"You bring out the worst in me."

"And you the best in me. That is why we get along so well."

"It's all very lovely, this flirting, but since tomorrow is that dreaded bridal shower brunch you have booked, I ought to go home and get some sleep," I say.

"You're right. Besides, I want to call the little woman before it gets too late."

"Does she know you call her that?"

"No."

"Schmuck."

"Will you let me walk you home?"

"Hon, it's only four blocks." Because of *course* he moved around the damn corner from me—like I need him both nearer *and* further out of reach.

"So? Fine girl like you could get into trouble in two blocks."

"Yeah, but you're staying here!"

"Please, let me walk you, it will make me feel better." Such a gentleman.

"If you insist."

"But first, a hug, for being such a lovely girl and such a good friend."

Michael puts his arms around me and holds me tightly. I could live here, in this apartment, in this embrace. I feel my face go hot, and my eyes start to sting a little, so I pat him on the back and turn away quickly.

"All right," I say. "If we're walking, let's walk."

Outside, it takes several deep breaths of the chilly night air to clear my head. I chalk the emotional rush up to general exhaustion. It takes us only five minutes to get to my place, Michael kisses me on the forehead, and turns around to retrace his steps. I let myself into my apartment. Probably at the moment he is calling Andrea, I'm picking up the newspaper from the kitchen table and turning to the weather page.

jess

In retrospect, it seems very strange. I mean, Harrison and I were relative strangers—the mutual connection to Mark was hardly cause for such complicit trust—but after those first two nights, there just didn't seem to be any point to not sharing the bed. Any sense of propriety was already out the window, the contractor had come back and turned the room into a construction nightmare, and if I'm to be honest here I think it would have felt almost hypocritical to change the arrangement. And he didn't seem to mind when my landlord pushed back my move-in date until right before Mark's wedding. So for the time being we spent our days involved in our separate pursuits, and our nights like some bizarre parody of a fifties television couple, sharing our anecdotes of the day, then chastely kissing one another good-night and retreating to our respective sides of Harrison's king-size bed.

Since U of C starts pretty late in the fall, I had time to slowly readjust to being home, filling my days with prepping my teaching materials, shopping, lunches with the girls and reading. My arrangement with Harrison gave a simplicity of purpose to my evenings.

When he wasn't on call we'd cook dinner together and watch old black-and-white movies on cable. When he was, I'd cook enough for two and leave him a plate. If he wasn't too late getting home we would sit on his tiny back porch-ling (too small to count as a full porch) and enjoy the mild early-summer Chicago night air, or go have coffee at Lula, a really cool café that Anne had turned me on to, or walk over to this local bar he likes, to listen to the Stones on the jukebox. (For a major metropolis, Chicago has a very small-town feel.)

The night after my welcome-home slumber party, he cooked for me for a change, and told me that he had missed me. He made me give him as much dirt as I was allowed, and I promised him that he would get to meet the gang eventually, as long as he promised to behave himself. Mark and Gemma came over one night to watch *Six Feet Under*, and the four of us ended up getting very tipsy on red wine and playing Trivial Pursuit until nearly three in the morning. (Harrison and I kicked their butts.)

Then my new landlord called yet again, informing me that due to the painting schedule, my apartment was not going to be ready for an extra week, so I decided to go to Hama's cabin early. I felt bad imposing for so long on Harrison's hospitality, and Mark's wedding was going to be there anyway, so I figured there would be plenty to help out with. Since I was co–best man with Teddy, I was expected to be at all the attending festivities. A few days of quiet at the cabin sounded like a perfect way to get ready. Not that I wasn't thrilled for Mark, you know, Gemma is great, and

I love my family, but I was in the throes of Peace Corps syndrome, and was not quite ready for the inquisition that accompanies these events when they occur near a big milestone.

One of the hardest things about living for an extended period of time in the third world part of a third world country comes after your return, when everyone around you seems too loud, painfully materialistic and too American. It's called Peace Corps syndrome. If one more coiffed, Lexus-driving suburban babe tells you how she was on safari for ten days and almost died for lack of a decaf skim latte, you might just snap. For those of us who lived the experience, it's very common to have a major superiority complex when we get back. It doesn't last too long, we adjust, and begin to relate to people again, and eventually we find a happy medium. This allows us to enjoy the luxuries of life that money and technology afford us, yet still be true to the part of our heart that will always miss bathing in water brought from the river, and connecting to people who are a thousand times more generous with their last pot of beans than many people here are with a spare million that nets them a write-off.

I had spent these past two weeks slowly allowing myself to interact with the world in small doses, but the deluge of questions I expected from friends and family that weekend was making me light-headed—and it hadn't even happened yet.

Harrison lent me his car for the drive up to Wisconsin, figuring he would grab a ride with Gemma's brother, and then we could go back together. The cabin is way up in the North Woods, a major schlep, but totally worth it. You see, it's not really a *cabin*. Being liberal democrats, "cabin" just sounds so much more down-to-earth than "summer home." But "cabin" makes one think of some backwoods shack, and the truth of the matter is that it's a five-bedroom log house, with air-conditioning and all the comforts of home. It sits on fifty-eight acres of gorgeous property, with a swimming pool, a small lake and three miles of hiking and cross-country skiing trails through the woods.

The house was built from a kit by my grandfather and his two bachelor brothers over the course of a summer male-bonding extravaganza. Papa George and Uncle Tom (don't even think of laughing) have since died, and Uncle Robert is in a senior facility, but Hama is still spry as a june bug and uses the place for two weeks in the spring, two weeks in the fall and all summer long, when she is joined frequently by my mother, Aunt Georgia, my sister Amy, Mark's brother, Teddy (who seduces an endless series of long-legged beauties there) and friends and cousins who stop for a weekend here and there. When things get really hopping, the braver souls are relegated to one of the two one-room cabins that came with the property. These are the real deal, handmade over a hundred years ago by trappers, with bark on pine logs, wide pine flooring and roughed-out doors and windows. They sit side by side a hundred yards from the main house, much the same as they were when they were first built, with the notable exception of the closetlike bathroom Papa George installed in each one. You have to get out of the shower to shave your legs, but get in it to close the door. From your perch on the toilet you can touch everything in the room except the ceiling. I'll be staying in Left for the week, and Teddy will probably end up with Right. The cabins are peaceful and serene and private, perfect for escaping the craziness of my family for an hour here and there.

Hama furnished them identically, queen-size beds, large oak armoires and one overstuffed chair with an ottoman and a reading lamp. They've wonderful old family quilts and afghans, slippers in the armoire (the old flooring gives awful splinters) and fluffy bathrobes in the bathroom. (Of course, to get them you have to get in the shower, close the bathroom door, get the robe off the hook, then get back out of the bathroom to put it on, but it's still a nice touch.)

Hama is on the porch when I arrive, and while I eat cold fried chicken and apple cobbler, we catch up. We've always been close, and it relieves me that she is the same as when I left. One of my greatest reservations about the Peace Corps was the fear that something would happen to her while I was gone. After all, she is 81 years old. It's inexpressibly sweet to find her unchanged. At around 2:00 a.m. Hama decides it's time for bed.

"This is wonderful, sweetheart, but I better get into that bed. These days I get up so damn early I feel like pretty soon I'll be waking up before I go to sleep!"

"Good night, Hama, I love you."

"I love you, too, Jessimillius. Sleep in tomorrow, I've got to go over to Mrs. Olson's in the morning. We'll go into town and play after lunch, okay?"

"Sounds great, sleep well and tell Mrs. Olson I said hey."

"Done."

I grab one of the five big flashlights plugged in next to the door and find my way to the small cabin. I'm dead tired, and the bed is soft and warm. Lying there, listening to the bats eating mosquitoes in the eaves of the cedar roof, I think about Harrison. He wasn't home when I called to tell him I had arrived in one piece. I wondered if he was rediscovering blissful houseguestlessness, and if some beauty was at that moment nestled up against him. This thought bothered me for some reason, but chalking it up to mental exhaustion, I let myself drift off into dreamless sleep.

I awaken closer to eleven than I had hoped, but feeling well rested and happy to be here. I go for a swim to shake the cobwebs from my head, and, after a brief, cramped shower, I get dressed and wander over to the main house. I find a note from Hama reminding me of our lunch date, so I just grab a peach to stem my appetite and look over the refrigerator list. Hama keeps a clipboard on the fridge listing everything that needs to be done around the property. The newest list is devoted to preparations for the wedding—dates and times for people to come set up the tent, tables, chairs, drop off flowers, all the little details that are the reasons sane people elope. It says that Mom, Amy and Aunt Georgia arrive on Wednesday, Teddy, Mark and Gemma and Harrison and Gemma's brother, Charles, on Thursday. There will be a barbecue on Friday night, the rehearsal dinner on Saturday. The wedding is Sunday morning, and everyone will leave Monday, after a large brunch (of course). In between there will be swimming, fishing, hiking and general pandemonium. There is a strange mark on Saturday which says F.?; I'll have to ask Hama what it means.

When Hama returns from Mrs. Olson's, we make our way into town. We stop for lunch at Lou's, where we gorge ourselves on chicken-fried steak and potato salad and fresh blueberry buckle dripping with cream. Hama has an appetite like a lumberjack. After lunch she buys me a new pair of moccasins, just like when I was a little girl. After finishing up her few errands, we stop off for a tiny sliver of fudge before heading home. I can't remember the last time I was so content. When we got back to the house, I help Hama put fresh linens on all the beds, and sweep out Right.

"I don't know who is going to end up in here," Hama says, brushing a cobweb off the lamp. "Teddy already laid claim to one of the rooms in the house—says his current lady friend has allergies."

"Who's in the other rooms?"

"Let's see, your mom and Georgia are sharing the room next to Teddy, Amy is bunking down with me, Mark and Gemma get the attic room for privacy and Gemma's folks get the room off the den. That means that Charles and Harrison will have to flip for the sofa bed, and whoever loses gets Right. Whew, we're a full house this weekend."

"I meant to ask you before, the list says F., question mark, for Saturday, what does that mean?"

"Have you talked to your mom about this weekend?" Hama asks.

"No, why?"

"I really don't know if it's my place to get into this with you."

"Too late! I promise I won't tell, what's up?"

"Your mom may have a gentleman friend coming up on Saturday to stay for the wedding," Hama explains. "He isn't staying here, and that's all she's told me about it."

"Wow. No kidding." That is about all I can think to say.

"Honey, don't think too much, just let life happen. I'm sure it will be fine."

We spend the heat of the day playing gin rummy and sipping iced tea, laughing and trying to predict everyone's potential behavior over the coming weekend. During a light supper we go over the schedule, making individual lists for people. Hama is a big believer in lists. Everyone gets a personalized list of duties, and no one gets to play until they finish their list. Of course, she always throws in things like "take a swim" or "have a cold beer and make funny faces at your sister" or "give your mother a sloppy kiss," so getting through your list is not without its pleasures. When the list making is done, we decide to turn in early in anticipation of the first onslaught the next day.

I return to my little hideaway with a book and a large glass of iced tea, and settle myself on the chair by the window. I'm really starting to look forward to seeing everybody, in spite of my basic apprehensions. I fall asleep in the chair, and wake up sometime in the blackest part of the night with just enough sense to stumble over to the bed.

Wednesday and Thursday are a blur of hugging and laughing and working like dogs. There are tons of strangers running around. I must have signed eight different clipboards for various deliveries and services. (It was on my list.) Harrison lost the coin toss, so Charles gets the sofa bed in the main house. Friday afternoon we all eat like pigs, and fall into comalike naps. Two hours before the barbecue guests are due, I'm asleep in a hammock, Amy and Teddy are head to head on the couch, Teddy's girlfriend, Janice, my mom and Aunt Georgia are all asleep on floats in the pool, Mark and Gemma are on the back porch, Gemma's folks have retired to their room and Charles is snoring away in a chaise lounge. I awaken to the sound of raucous laughter. I open one eye to see Hama and Harrison surveying the scene with much merriment.

"What is so funny?" I grumble in their direction.

"It's a good thing Harrison and I managed to stay awake—otherwise people would show up for a nice party and think they had stumbled into Jonestown!" my grandmother says.

"Well, ring the bell why dontcha, I'm going to grab a shower before things get nuts."

When I'm dressed, I run up to the main house to help finish getting things ready for the party. The guests have begun arriving in droves. I spend the next few hours pouring drinks, clearing plates and fielding endless questions about my plans for the future. Luckily for me, Hama seems always nearby, and is adept at calling for my help before I get cornered by one of our more annoying relatives. Just as Mark and Gemma are waving the last guest down the road, the rest of us collapse in the living room. My sister staggers over to the couch and puts her dark curly head in my lap.

"I'm going to marry rich," Amy blurts out. Quite a statement from someone who traditionally has fallen for musicians and artists.

"Why is that, dearest?" I'm too tired to tease her.

"So we can hire people to do all this crap for us and just sit back and enjoy all our parties."

"For once, we agree," I say.

From the corner of my eye I catch my mother smiling at us and shaking her head. Some things never change. Amy and I are very dissimilar, yet very close. In fact, if we weren't related, I'd probably tell people, "She's like a sister to me." One of the things that bonded me to Beth and Anne was that they have the same kind of energy as Amy and I do. I hate that Amy is living so far away, working for an advertising agency in Seattle, but she swears she keeps an ear to the ground for opportunities in Chicago, so I'm hopeful that she may be nearby in the foreseeable future.

Mark and Gemma return to the house and flop onto the floor where Gemma takes off her shoes, and Mark begins to rub her feet.

"Tell me again why we didn't elope when we were in Las Vegas for that convention?" Gemma says, wincing.

Mark smiles at her. "Because you wanted to snub your nose at all your relatives who thought you were an old maid, and your mother wanted payback for endless bridal shower and wedding gifts."

Mark's soon-to-be mother-in-law throws a pillow at his head, while Gemma tickles him mercilessly until he cries uncle. They all look very happy and connected, and I'm amazingly thrilled for all of them. But I have to admit I feel slightly outside the circle. I've missed all of the events that have led to this real sense of family, I don't know any of the inside jokes…. I'm also feeling the weight of my own absences. It's as if I've lost these two years, Rip Van Winkle style, and when I woke up the world had spun away from me. I pat Amy on the head, and when she refuses to move I lick my finger and stick it in her ear. She jumps up, and I laugh heartily.

"Wet Willie strikes again."

"Bitch."

"I'm over it. I have to get some sleep. Good night, everyone."

"Wait up, Jess, we can brave the woods together," Harrison calls after me.

"So be honest with me," he says as we step off the porch. "Did that or did that not feel like when you're a kid and you go to spend the night at someone's house and their best family friends all come over, and you sit around smiling at references to events that have nothing whatsoever to do with you?"

"My God, how did you know? I mean, they're my family."

"You had that same blank look I did. Like you were really thrilled for all their coziness, but couldn't care less about how they got there."

"Very insightful, Doctor. Perhaps you have chosen the wrong specialty. You would make an excellent psychiatrist."

"I don't think so. If I'm going to be honest here, I find that people who have real problems tend not to discuss them, and the rest mostly whine about unimportant crap."

"Kind of a harsh view, don't you think?"

"My mother was in every twelve-step program ever invented. She dragged me to more than my share of meetings, so maybe I'm negatively biased."

"Was she an alcoholic?"

"No, but she married one. When he left her, she started having a gin and tonic every night before dinner. After ten nights she decided she had 'a problem,' and went to AA. She was an 'alcoholic' for ten days, and has been going to meetings three times a week for seventeen years. She sponsors at least ten people at a time, and they all think she's some sort of guru." His sarcasm is biting.

"No comment," I say.

"Hey, look up."

The night sky is alive with stars, and just over the tops of the trees the northern lights are visible.

"Now close your eyes," Harrison instructs me.

Crickets and frogs and owls are performing a symphony, with the loons singing arias from the lake.

"None of it matters here," he says.

I open my eyes and take Harrison's hand, and squeeze hard. He squeezes back and smiles broadly in the dark.

"I have an idea. Tomorrow, let's get them all back."

"How?" I ask.

"Let's throw all kinds of non sequiturs into the conversation and laugh really hard, as if they're private jokes. You know, like look at me during breakfast and say 'blueberries?' and I'll try to laugh so hard I'll shoot milk out my nose."

"Okay, you got it. Tomorrow, we annoy the shit out of my family."

We arrive at Left, and Harrison bends to kiss my hand.

"Sleep well, fair maiden. Shall I escort you to the morning repast?"

"That would be lovely, say, nineish?"

"I'll knock thrice upon your door."

"Well, let's just hope the bears don't eat you in your bed tonight."

"Bears?"

"Good night, Harrison."

"Did you say bears?"

I close the door to the cabin and listen to him walk the ten yards to his cabin, talking all the way.

"Okay, I'm going to take my unappetizing, skinny, meatless body to bed now. I hope I put enough nasty-tasting mosquito repellent on every inch of my stringy and tough flesh."

What a goofball. Just before I drift off, I briefly wonder why it is I'm so glad he is just next door. If the answer came, I was too asleep to catch it.

beth

It was two years ago today. Moving out, I mean. I didn't even realize it until I picked up a newspaper and even then it took me a minute to remember why the date had any spark of meaning for me. My horoscope said that today was a day to complete unfinished business. So I shouldn't have been in the least surprised that, out of nowhere, and for the first time in over a year, I ran into Sasha.

Literally.

With my car.

I closed up the store, dropped Anne off at her place, stopped by Whole Foods and headed home to walk Petey. But I can never wait to get home to crack open the olives, and they always pack them on the bottom. I was rummaging around in the bag at a stoplight, when the guy behind me suddenly honked loudly at me, and I looked up and there was this man standing right in front of my car peering in at me. Startled, I jumped a little and my foot slid off the brake, and my car leaped forward about two feet, squarely hitting the man before I got my foot back on the brake. He fell onto my hood.

I put the car in Park and jumped out.

"I always thought you might Kill me." The man is brushing off his clothes, and then looks up.

"My God, *Sasha?*" *You have got to be shitting me.*

"Hello, Beth."

People are now honking, so I grab Sasha and push him into my car.

"Are you okay, do I need to take you to a hospital?"

"I'm fine, you Barely Nudged me."

"Thank God. You scared the crap out of me. What the hell were you doing?"

"Crossing the street, minding my own business, when I noticed you. At least I was pretty sure it was you, and I was trying to ascertain the Verity of that when you ran me over."

"I didn't run you over. I barely nudged you. You said so yourself."

"Just teasing. So how are you?"

"A little shaken, but mostly fine."

"Good. And Peter?"

"*Petey.* Sasha, the dog's name is, was and will always be Petey. It isn't like a kid who grows up and stops being called by his childhood nickname."

"How's Petey, then?"

"He's fine. Probably angry with me at the moment, and dying to be walked, but fine."

"Is that where you were headed?"

"Yes, actually. But he'll wait. Where can I drop you?"

"I have nowhere in particular to be. I could come with you."

I don't know exactly what to make of this. I'm hesitant to say no, after all, I just hit him with my car, and Lord knows I can't afford to be sued. On the other hand, I don't really want him in my house.

"Or not, if it makes you Uncomfortable." Nicely played, now I'm the shrew who hasn't moved on in two years if I say no.

"Sure, if you want."

We get back to my place and park. He carries my groceries for me, despite my objections. When we get inside the loft, Petey is jumping and barking, but then he sees Sasha, and is so confused that he sits down.

"Hello, boy." Sasha pats his head.

I grab the leash, and the three of us head out for a walk. I've no idea what to say.

"So I hear you opened your own store?" Sasha jumps in.

"Yeah. When my grandmother died, she left Anne and me a little nest egg, which we used to get the place open. It's been doing pretty well—we lucked into the location about two months before the neighborhood started to really get hot."

"Women's clothes?"

"Women's mostly, but just enough men's stuff so women can be inspired to buy a gift, or so their boyfriends have something to look at while they're there. Accessories, small housewares, fun bath products."

"Good for you. How is Anne?" Odd he'd ask; Sasha and Anne never liked each other.

"Good. We work well together, she's got a much better sense of the clothing trends, and does most of the buying. I cover the rest. She's turning thirty next month."

"Wow. She was Such a Kid when I met her."

"Yep, twenty-two and full of beans."

Petey has decided not to be too affected by the sudden reappearance of Sasha, and obliges us with an enormous dump, of which he seems terribly proud. My least favorite part of dog ownership.

Back at the loft, I offer him a glass of wine, which he accepts happily. It's all of a sudden strangely okay to be talking to him.

"So how are things with you?"

"Okay," he says. "They were pretty bad for a while after you left."

"Sorry about that. I know it must have felt abrupt."

"No. I mean, yes, of course it did, but once I got my head back on it made sense. I suppose I should thank Carla for that."

"Carla?"

"Well, the night you left, I went to the Local Option to hang out with John. He got a little slammed at the downstairs bar toward the end of the evening, so I sat in the corner and watched the dance floor. And there She was. Carla. I mean, I didn't know that at the time, but I saw this woman on the dance floor and I literally couldn't look away. She spun and leaped and wiggled across the empty dance floor. Carla obviously loved to dance. I watched her for most of an hour, both intrigued and repulsed."

"Repulsed? She wasn't some hottie?"

"Not at all, my dear. She was Brutally Average. She wasn't overweight, but had one of those unfortunate bodies that is thickly proportioned around the middle, giving the illusion of excess pounds. Broad-shouldered, flat-chested, not ugly per se, but not attractive, either."

"You still talk like you're giving a dissertation." I teased him.

"I know, can't be helped. So John comes over and sees me watching her, and says, 'She's some piece of work, ain't she?' I agreed. 'She's always in here on Saturday nights, start to finish,' John says to me, 'and she never dances with anyone, always alone. Not that she gets too many offers…' I said I could see where he was coming from."

"You guys are so mean. Just because someone isn't perfect—"

"Do you want to hear this?"

"Okay, sorry." I refill our glasses.

"Fine. So I tell John I'm going to hit the road and he says, 'Tell Beth I said hi, and that the Indigos are playing next week. I know how she loves them.' That stopped me dead, because I realized that you had been gone for weeks and I hadn't told anyone. But I found I couldn't tell John the truth, so I simply said I would indeed tell you."

"This is starting to sound familiar to me."

"As well it might. Stay with me. I thought walking home would clear my head. Just as I started off, I hear the door open behind me, and the click of high heels on the pavement. Not thirty seconds later, there she is, walking beside me."

"No way, a stalker!"

"Well, not really, but I was sort of Taken Aback. I looked at her and she smiled up at me and said, 'Hi there. Nice night for a walk, isn't it?' Her voice was much higher-pitched than one would have expected from her solid appearance, and her teeth were at skewed angles, almost perpendicular to each other. An orthodontist's nightmare."

"What did you do?"

"What could I do? I answered her. She asked me if I

hung out at the Option much, I told her not really. She said, 'I go every Saturday night. They play just the right kind of Saturday-night dance music, don't you think?' I said, 'I wouldn't know, really, I don't dance.' She told me that dancing is her one joy. Then she introduced herself and offered her hand, nails bitten to the quick. I took it, said I was pleased to make her acquaintance. When I told her my name, she laughed, an almost maniacal giggle, before saying, '*Sasha,* that's a girl's name! Guess your ma wanted a daughter, huh?' She was shaking her head from side to side, strings of hair sticking to her forehead, still sweaty from the dance floor."

Now I'm laughing at him. "You do have all the fun, don't you?"

"Of course. So I say, 'It's Russian. My parents were immigrants, and in Russia, Sasha is more commonly a man's name.' Why I felt the need to justify my name to this strange creature was a mystery to me, but so are many things."

"You are so self-actualized."

"All right, I know how it sounds. Anyway, she says, 'Oh. You a Communist?' and I tell her I have no political affiliations, and she tells me she's a Democrat through and through. So at this point, I didn't reply, hoping if I ignored her that she would go away. But she walked along beside me in silence, even though she was practically running to keep up."

"I used to hate that, trying to keep up with you and your gargantuan legs."

"True enough. Thank God after only another minute, we were at my building. So I said, 'This is where I get off, have a pleasant evening.' She says, 'You, too, Sasha. Maybe

I'll see you around. Thanks for the walk.' She was actually sort of sadly sweet. And then she left."

"You didn't ask her up?"

"Of course not."

"I thought you were going to sleep with her, fall in love, tell me that you are now living together."

"You must know me better than that, Elizabeth."

"I suppose. So then what happened?"

"I went upstairs. The apartment was dark and cold, with that eerie purple light from the fish tank. I notice that unless someone had taught Fish VI how to backstroke, I had lost another one—the third since you left—and I use the little net to get him out of the tank."

"Poor little fishies. Have any survived?"

"Afraid not. Number II lasted about six months, but even he eventually went the way of his compatriots."

"I knew I should've taken the tank."

"Probably would have been good. At any rate, I finish the little bathroom funeral, go back to the living room, notice the flashing light on the answering machine, so I go over to listen to the messages. Blah blah blah, Toni, can you take my intro class on Tuesday? Blah blah blah, my mother, reminding me that it's Uncle Ivan's seventy-fifth birthday party, and that I should bring you to the party. This makes me think of you. So I call the number on the notepad next to the phone that you left me. The phone rings, and your machine picks up."

"I knew this was that night."

"Of course. I wait for the beep. Start to tell you about the Indigos, and you pick up the phone. I give you the message. You thank me. It is silent. You thank me again, then tell me you are in a hurry—you're going out. I want to know with who, but instead I say good-night."

"That was such a weird call."

"It felt weird to me, too. So I go into the bedroom, undress and climb into bed, keeping well to the left so as not to touch your side. Your smell is still embedded in the pillows, no amount of washing has been able to rid them of it."

"Oh." I don't know what to say to that.

"No matter. I fall asleep and begin to dream. In my dream, I'm with you, and you are dancing wildly and I grab you and kiss you and when I pull back, you are Carla, and you're laughing at me. And then Carla runs away, and both of you are standing across the room, turning into each other, back and forth, so fast that I can't remember which of you is who, and I woke up crying."

"Oh my God, that is so creepy."

"Tell me about it. I get up, go to the kitchen for a glass of water. When I return to the bedroom I see that, despite the nightmare, the right side of the bed is practically unmarred."

"Well, as I recall, when you had bad dreams with me you never really flailed around too much, just sort of moaned."

"Well, I decided enough was enough. I walked around to your side, got between the sheets, still cool and fresh, and lay in the dark, in this unfamiliar territory of my own bed. I willed myself not to dream, but I did anyway. Only this time it was me who danced. Whirling and spinning and leaping."

"Wow." What the hell do I say to that? This is a really lousy story.

"When I woke up, I felt okay. And I decided that it was

a prod from my unconscious that I needed to move on. So I began to tell people that you had left me, and started to try to live my life without you."

"You seem to be doing okay now."

"I am okay."

Sasha finishes the last of his wine and blissfully announces that he should get going.

"Should I drive you somewhere?"

"No, I'm fine, I'll jump on the El, it's right here."

"Sorry again about hitting you."

"It's fine, I'm sorry I startled you. Anyway, it was good to see you, Beth."

"It was good to see you, too."

Sasha leans forward and awkwardly kisses my forehead, then leaves.

I wonder about him. He ultimately said very little about his life, just that things were much the same for him, still teaching and writing. Other than the weird Carla story, he didn't mention a woman. For the first time since I've known him, he seemed small and out of focus. This makes me feel sad for him, and happy for myself. I've come a very long way in the past two years. And I've made a decision. I'm going to fix up this old loft to suit me. It has been in the same state since I moved in, and since I'm pretty settled in every other way, it's time to make it feel more like a home. I can't afford to be extravagant, but the Home Depot near here has all sorts of do-it-yourself classes. I make a plan to go there after dinner and check out the schedule and see what I can learn. After all, if my horoscope says there is unfinished business to complete, then who am I to argue?

anne

I'm sitting at Mitchell's, engrossed in A. S. Byatt's *Possession*. *Engrossed* being the operative word, because the voice over my head seems to come from out of nowhere.

"Excuse me, miss."

I look up and promptly drop the book into my half-finished bowl of soup.

"I'm so sorry, I didn't mean to startle you." He retrieves the book from its chicken-broth bath, wiping it off with a napkin from the unused place setting across from me.

OH. MY. GOD.

"I'm Chris Schyler. I know we've met, but I can't seem to remember where." He extends his hand.

Vital Statistics:

Chris Schyler

35, construction foreman

Surprisingly literary

Likes blueberry muffins with Kundera novels

Hates people who assume blue collar means illiterate

I let my hand be enveloped by his big callused one. It's electric.

"Anne Gaskell. We didn't really meet."

"I knew I knew you! Where did we not really meet?"

"Lula Café."

"Kundera." I can't believe he remembered.

"That's me." I'm so boring.

"Nice to officially make your acquaintance, Anne Gaskell."

"Likewise, I'm sure."

There is an uncomfortable pause. I can't stand it.

"Would you like to sit down?" I ask, and he sits.

The busboy came and cleared away my soup bowl and soggy napkin, then poured Chris a cup of coffee.

I can't remember what we talked about for the time we sat together. All I knew was that I had sat in Lula's nearly every night for the past six weeks, spending money I couldn't afford, waiting for him to come back. And the day I finally decide to give up and seek my quiet evenings someplace more affordable, he shows up!

We chatted easily—until I caught a glimpse of his wristwatch. I grabbed his forearm and pulled it across the table for a better view.

"A quarter to one. A quarter to one! Oh my goodness, we've been talking for four hours!"

I begin to scramble in my purse for some money, and Chris shakes his head in disbelief.

"Relax, it's on me. Are you going to turn into a pumpkin?"

"Oh, thank you, I couldn't, I mean, I—"

"Really, I'd like to."

"Well, okay, I guess, I mean, thank you."

Chris laughs at my flustered appearance, and I finally join him.

"Oh, I'm such a flake!"

"No arguments. But you've got great eyes." This makes me blush.

"Thanks. So do you." He seems bemused at the compliment, which makes me blush more.

"Thank you." He smiles at me. "I know this is forward, and I'll understand if you say no, but it's a really nice night, and I was thinking that we could go down to the lakefront and continue our conversation."

"I could do that, but I'd have to change my clothes." I gesture at the sassy skirt and blouse I wore to work today, great for being inside, but totally inappropriate for the beach. I must be out of my mind.

"I'd be happy to take you home to change first, I'd even wait in the car."

"My mother would be horrified." So true.

"That may be the best reason to do it." Also true.

"I can't argue with logic like that."

Chris drives to my tiny Bucktown apartment in his cluttered Honda SUV. I run upstairs, throw on a pair of jeans and a thick sweater, pull my hair into a ponytail and put my jacket and some stuff from the fridge into a canvas bag. Like a Girl Scout, always prepared.

We park the car at the lakefront and sit on the rocks, watching the tide and talking. Soon Chris was telling me about his brother Warren, and his sister-in-law and niece. Then he blushed and admitted that he was frequently envious of Warren's life, and was embarrassed by his own sappiness.

"Well, you told me one embarrassing thing, and now I'll tell you one," I offered.

"Absolutely, your turn." Here goes…

"Remember our first nonmeeting at Lula?"

"Of course."

Deep breath. "I've been there almost every day since, waiting for you to come back."

"No!"

"Yes. I spent nearly a month's rent on mocha cappuccinos and blueberry muffins."

"Gave up on banana nut altogether, huh?" He doesn't seem know what else to say.

"You remembered." I blush deeply.

We sit in silence for a minute or so.

"I guess someone really wanted us to meet," Chris finally says.

"I guess so."

He leans over and kisses me softly on the mouth. He is delicious.

"Well, I'm glad we did."

Then he kisses me again.

We sit on the rocks in silence for a long time, my body held close to his, and smile out into the night, giddy. Suddenly his stomach rumbles low and deep. We laugh.

"I thought you might get hungry," I say, opening the bag,

removing a large Tupperware container, a half a loaf of French bread, two forks and a bottle of wine.

"What's all this?"

"Fettuccine with pesto and chicken," I reply, smiling.

I open the wine and realize I've forgotten glasses. Laughing, we share the pasta and drink the cool sweet wine straight from the bottle. Wiping the sauce from the container with hunks of bread, we sit, sated, tipsy from lack of sleep and good wine.

"So tell me, did you always want to have a store?" Chris asks.

"It's really Beth's dream, not mine. She loves the whole thing. But it's much better than waitressing, and I'm so grateful that she wanted to be partners with me—she could've done it on her own."

"And what about your dream? What would you do if you could do anything?"

"Well, I haven't told anyone this, but I want to go back to school and be an occupational therapist." Out loud, it sounds even better than it has in my head.

"You mean, like, working with people after accidents and stuff?"

"Yeah. Or maybe kids with physical disabilities. Want to hear the really dumb part?"

"I'm sure it isn't dumb." He is so *nice!*

"Did you ever see the movie *Regarding Henry?*"

"The one with Harrison Ford and Annette Bening, right?"

I love that he knows the movie. "That's the one. He gets shot in the head and totally loses everything he knew, including the ability to walk and talk. And he works with this occupational therapist who helps him get it all back. I saw that movie and I thought, there are people who can actually DO that, you know—take someone who is broken and help them fix themselves. And I thought, I bet that would be so wonderful to help people like that."

"So what's stopping you?"

"I dunno. I have student loans from college, and there is the store. I don't want to abandon Beth, especially when we're still getting on our feet. But I did pick up the application for a program at Rush, which is supposed to be good. But just to see. I'm not even sure I have the grades to get in. It all just seems like the wrong time."

"Well, you'll know when the right time is. Hey, construction is a dangerous business, I get a lot of guys who have accidents.... I can refer them to you when you are practicing!"

I laugh. "Well, all right, then." I can't believe how comfortable I am with him.

"C'mon, let's walk off our snack."

"Great. Just let me dump this stuff in the car."

We walk along the rock wall until it gives way to sand, take off our shoes and try to walk in the icy September surf. After the first thirty seconds we give up, and walk on the cold firm sand instead. After five minutes or so, we see up ahead that there is a figure lying on the beach, and another running away. Without thinking, we run toward the figure.

About ten yards away we can see it is, in fact, two people, a female, administering mouth-to-mouth to a prostrate male. We reach the pair at the same time as the guy we had seen running returns, and the three of us watch with held breath as the girl's ministrations finally work.

She holds the shivering body, weeping. Not knowing what else to do, we take off our coats and wrap the two wet strangers with them. Chris runs to the car to get a blanket from the trunk.

When he gets back ambulance sirens can be heard approaching, and I've wrapped my sweater around the man's legs. I'm standing in my short-sleeved T-shirt, shivering. Chris lays the blanket around the people, then takes me in his arms. The ambulance arrives, then the police. We give brief statements, and are given back our soggy clothes. The blanket went with the victim to the hospital.

We return to the car in silence, overwhelmed.

"His hands were tied," I say quietly. "He tied his own hands and walked into the water."

Chris had not known. We drive back to my apartment just as the sun is coming up. When we get there, I look at him seriously.

"This has been the best, strangest, worst evening of my life." I don't know what else to say.

"Me, too."

"Somehow I know you will take this the right way.... I don't think I want to go in there alone."

He nods, parks the car and follows me.

My apartment is pretty unremarkable. Small, clean, cozy, with big windows that let the pale light streak across the rooms. I can see him taking it in with benign appraisal. I hang our coats over the radiator to dry off and take him by the hand. I lead him to the tiny bedroom, pull the shade, kick off my shoes and get into the double bed, lifting the quilt for him to join me.

He takes off his boots and climbs in beside me. He holds me tightly, stroking my hair, then he lifts my face and kisses me. I smile at him, this unexpected and wonderful man.

"If this works, it will make a great story."

"It would be worth the story to make it work. Besides, don't forget that your mother will be horrified."

I laugh and snuggle back. Chris rubs his nose in my hair, and we fall asleep.

jess

At nine o'clock sharp there is a knock at my door, and a very chipper Harrison enters my cabin.

"Ready to go, darling?"

"Not nibbled by woodland creatures, after all, eh?"

"They know better. I have a black belt."

"And a brown one, too, I've seen them."

"Well, they have to match my shoes."

We head up to the house where my mom and Aunt Georgia are busy in the kitchen. We help get the food on the table and settle down to enormous cups of steaming coffee. Everyone trickles in, most looking half-asleep, and Hama surveys the group with a critical eye.

"What a bunch of sorry-looking people we have here. Not one of you looks fit to lift a fork. My goodness, I can't wait to see you all on Monday—we might have to call an ambulance to get you to your cars!"

The rental people are in the backyard putting up the tent

and the dance floor. The noise of their hammering and calling orders to each other seems deafening in the clear morning. But once our group manages the first few sips of coffee and the first few bites of food, we liven up a little. And then there's Harrison, liberally peppering the conversation with pointed and nonsensical remarks in my direction. As promised. I laugh meaningfully every time he does this, and we both invoke the "you had to be there" defense. There is much meaningful eye contact around the table. I have to admit it's kind of amusing. After breakfast, my mom calls me into her bedroom, where Amy is sprawled on the bed in her pajamas.

"Girls, we need to talk. There is someone special arriving today. He's not staying here, but he is coming to the wedding, and I want you to be prepared."

"Mom," I begin, since Amy and I had already briefly discussed this, "we're cool with this, we think it's terrific you have been dating. We can't wait to meet him."

Amy nods in agreement, and my mother wrings her hands together.

"You might not feel that way when he gets here."

"Mom, if you like him, we'll like him," Amy says.

"It's your father."

The words hang in the air, making it thick and oppressive.

"Come again?" Amy stammers.

"Your father, I've been seeing your father since winter."

It's like someone's turned off the oxygen in here. My father. *The deserter.* He's coming here today. Amy starts to cry and runs out of the room.

"I thought he lived in Arizona?" I say.

"He's moved back."

"Why?"

"For me. Remember that cruise I took last fall? He was on the boat. A total fluke. We spent a lot of time together—he's changed a lot. He explained things, made them clearer to me. We got to know each other again. Christ, my hands are shaking. He's not the same man, I'm not the same woman, we fit better now than we did then. He's coming to be with me and to see you and Amy, and we both hope you'll come to accept the situation."

"Which is?"

"Which is simply that we're spending time together. We enjoy each other's company. We may be falling in love again. I don't know. We're taking things one day at a time."

"Mom, I want so much to say I'm happy for you, but, good Lord, he left us," I say.

"He wasn't the same—"

"He *left* us, Mom, all of us. He left us with no money, no warning, just a note on the dresser...."

"That's not totally fair. When he got settled, he took financial responsibility for all of us. Did you know that when the divorce was final, he had his lawyer send a letter asking if it was all right to send more alimony and child support than the judge had awarded? *More.* That he insisted on contributing extra to your college trust funds, even though he didn't have to? He remembered birthdays, and holidays, and called every week..."

"And we saw him once every five years, and he never explained why he left. He missed our plays and our first dates and my busted appendix and Amy's broken leg and, I mean, dammit, Mom, you had all the responsibility. He *was* really generous, no question, but did you miss his money? Did you cry into your pillow at night because you needed his money? I sure as hell didn't. Amy didn't. He owed us more than money, and he never came through, so don't act like we should jump up and cheer because he's back. We're not twelve anymore, fantasizing about Mommy and Daddy getting back together. I'm sorry, but we can't just be happy for you, we remember too much."

"We're in counseling."

"We?"

"Your father and I, we've been seeing a therapist together for the past three months."

"No way."

"Yes, way. We don't want to make the same mistakes, we think we can have a meaningful friendship, maybe even a romantic life together. We would like very much if you and Amy would consider joining us for a few sessions."

"Oh my God, what have you done with my mother? I can't begin to process this. Almost twenty years after the divorce, now you're getting counseling. You have lost your frigging minds."

"I had an affair."

Can't I wake up yet?

"Your father was traveling. I was home with you girls, and I was lonely. We were having problems that we couldn't begin to talk about. We didn't have the energy to try to find the vocabulary. I thought he was cheating on the road, so I had an affair. He found out, and I didn't know how to ask for his forgiveness. He thought that meant I didn't want it, so he left."

"Was he?"

"Cheating? No. He wasn't."

Amy has appeared in the doorway. "It was your fault he left? You drove him away?"

"It's not that simple, sweetheart, we were both to blame.

Neither of us knew how to make that relationship work, not then. But we're trying now, and we really would like your support."

"When is he coming?" Amy sniffled.

"At around four."

Amy meets my gaze, and nods almost imperceptibly. I answer for both of us.

"We'll try. We can't promise to approve, not right away, but we'll try."

"That's all we can ask. I love you girls, you know that. So does your father. He wants so much to get to know you again. He knows he can't make up for lost time, but he can try not to lose any more. Please give him that chance. Good or bad, you only get one father in life."

We're hugging and weeping, and I still feel as if the walls are closing in on me. I leave my mom and Amy holding each other on the bed and run down the stairs. I zip out the back door and fling myself into the pool. I swim the length underwater and dive to the bottom, where I stay until my lungs burn and my head starts to pound. When I begin to come up for air, someone grabs me by the arm and pulls me swiftly to the top.

"What the hell are you doing?" I spin around to face Harrison, who's fully dressed and red-faced.

"I thought…I mean…Jesus Christ, you scared the hell out of me, I was walking by and you were just sitting there on the bottom, and… Jesus, don't do that."

He looked really panicked, and I could only imagine the picture I must have made, sitting on the bottom like so much flotsam.

"I'm sorry," I sputtered. "I didn't mean to scare you. Really, are you okay?"

"Are you?"

"I'll get over it. Is that what you're wearing today?"

He glances down at his fully dressed body through the water, and finally gets the joke. Swimming over to the ladder, he starts throwing items out of the water. His leather loafers, his wallet, his money clip, change, sunglasses, leather belt. I start laughing.

"Funny, is it? Well, maybe you like to swim in your clothes, but the rest of us prefer more appropriate attire." He points at me, and I take in my shorts and polo shirt. Luckily I had been barefoot and without valuables. No wonder he thought I was drowned.

I look up and we both laugh. We swim to the stairs and get out of the pool, looking completely ridiculous.

Then we squish off to get changed.

Sitting on the bed in my cabin, towel-drying my hair, there is a soft knock on the door.

"Come in."

It's Harrison, dry and wearing glasses, which I've never seen before.

"I didn't know you wore glasses."

"Extended-wear contacts, one of which is somewhere at the bottom of your pool."

"I'm really sorry, I'll buy you a new one."

"It's okay, just do your swimming at the top of the water from now on."

"Deal."

"You want to talk about it?" He looks at me expectantly.

"Not really, I just got some, well, let's say, surprising, news. I don't yet know what to make of it."

"Your dad?"

"How did you— Oh, Mark."

"He just gave me the basic outline, enough to see how it might be troublesome."

"I just don't think I'm ready to deal with it, you know? I'm just going to get through this weekend and deal with the underlying issues later."

"Well, I just wanted to tell you that if you need saving at any point, give me a wink."

"Like in the pool?"

"Well, I'd prefer to do any further rescues on land if you don't mind, Miss Jess. These are the only dry shoes I've left. Seriously, though, I know when my family gets together like this, some people always get tipsy and start conversations they shouldn't. I can come up with a kitchen emergency at the drop of a hat."

"I'll keep that in mind."

Harrison leans over and kisses my forehead, then gets up and leaves.

My father arrives at four o'clock sharp. He looks very handsome. His hair is grayer than the last time I saw him at Amy's graduation from grad school three years ago. We hug, and he whispers that he is glad we'll be able to spend some time together and catch up. It's the most awkward moment of my life. Luckily, Amy and my mother and Hama show up, so I'm able to escape for the time being.

The rehearsal is quick—it's going to be a casual ceremony—and dinner is full of lively conversation. And, damn him, my father is charming and gracious, and my mother has never looked happier. Helping Hama with the dishes, I ask why she took my mom's side in the whole divorce thing, when, after all, my dad is her son.

"Honey, your mother called me and told me what happened. All of it," she added pointedly. "I told her that whatever was happening between her and Fillmore was their business, but my granddaughters were mine. You girls were the most important thing to me, so whatever was best for you was what I would do. Your father did the rest on his own. He avoided all but the most important family functions, visited me when you and your mom weren't going to be around. It was his way of dealing with it. I'll say only this for my son, he seems to be more of a man now than he was before, and he seems to be making your mother very happy." Then she smiled. "At least we know they're not together for the sake of the children!"

"I love you, Hama. Thank you for being."

"Being what?"

"Just being."

"Silly goose, go take a head count for coffee and tea."

Everyone turns in early, as there is a tight schedule for showers and bathroom time in the morning. Amy will be coming to my cabin to get ready, and I want to beat her to the hot water. There have to be some perks for being the oldest.

I sleep almost as fitfully as if it were my wedding I'm waking up to, with scattered and surreal dreams. I can't wait to get off this damn medication. Mefloquine is the latest antimalarial on the market for extended in-country usage, and I've been on it for over two years. You start a couple weeks before you leave, once a week for the first six weeks, then once every other week until a month after you return. It can take another month for the drug to get out of your system. It may prevent most strains of malaria, but, and let me be frank here, it can seriously fuck with your dreams. I mean, bizarre, violent, brightly colored, almost cartoonlike dreams. Go-into-therapy dreams. Harrison is lucky I didn't kill him in his sleep.

The dreams plague me all night, and when I wake up, that sneak Amy has beat me to the shower. She is kind enough to leave some hot water, and since neither of us is particularly vain when it comes to hair and makeup, we're ready pretty quickly. It's actually kind of nice, getting ready together, the way we used to do if we both were going out. We talk a little bit about Mom and Dad, and decide to just take it like they do, one day at a time.

I can't think about that, because the wedding is absolutely upon us.

And of course, it is beautiful. The early afternoon ceremony is heartwarming and full of love and laughter, good food and good music, and we dance till we drop, and the last guest doesn't leave until almost eleven o'clock. The family gathers in the living room to watch the happy couple open their gifts, which are mostly lovely, and eat leftover cake, which is mostly frosting, and drink champagne, which is mostly bubbles. Harrison, Charles and Teddy and his girlfriend are noticeably absent from the group.

I kiss everyone good-night at around twelve-thirty and wander in the general direction of my cabin. Outside Right, I hear a strange noise, like moaning. I wonder if Harrison drank too much. Then I hear low giggling, and my heart stops. There is a woman in there. He's got a woman in there. I did see him talking to that college friend of Gemma's, the one with the perfect body and the long red hair, and suddenly my heart is in my throat, or perhaps it's cake, but I just know I'm going to be sick.

I rush into my cabin and head for the bathroom. I lean over the toilet, and the feeling passes, which is really good because I would rather have serious pain than throw up. I slowly undress and crawl into bed, feeling miserable and not knowing why. Then there's a knock on the door, and a loud whispering voice.

"Jess, you up? Jess. I need to come in. Jess?"

I stumble out of bed and pull on an old pajama top that I stole from a college boyfriend.

"Jess, let me in." The voice belongs to Harrison.

"What do you want?" He probably wants directions to a nearby drugstore.

"Can I come in, please?"

"Fine. Why not."

"What's wrong?"

"Nothing, I'm tired, what do you want?"

"Can I sleep here tonight?"

"Pardon me?" My head is clearing quickly.

"Charles is in my cabin."

"Charles?" *Charles?* Charles is in Harrison's cabin!

"Yeah, he, um, hit it off with a friend of Gemma's and they're, um, communing in my cabin."

"The redhead?"

"I didn't ask."

"What about the sofa bed in the main house?" Why did I ask that?

"Your aunt is in it."

"But she's supposed to share with my mom...oh. Of course, *mi casa*...."

He comes in, strips down to boxers, then climbs into the bed. I get in beside him.

"Are you mad at me?"

"Not anymore." Shit, wrong answer.

"Anymore? What did I do?"

"Nothing, I just heard them, you know, in your cabin, and I thought, well, you know what I thought."

"And that pissed you off."

"Let me ask you something, that first night, if I had kept up the original charade, would you have made love to me?"

"Before or after I thought I was going to have to marry you?"

"Before, when I was just some chick you brought home from a bar." He thinks for a moment before answering.

"Yeah, I probably would have. Why?"

"I don't know, I was just curious."

"What does this have to do with being mad at me?"

"Not mad, really, just disappointed. I mean, that first night was obviously not the first time you woke up with scotch on your breath and a woman you don't remember bringing home in your bed. That kind of behavior is really scary to me. The drinking is your business, especially with your family history, well, you're the doctor, I don't need to lecture you, but, I mean, I've already lost three friends to AIDS, and I saw hundreds more dying of it in Kenya, and I worry for you. If you had been with that woman, well, I was just sad about it, okay?"

"Thank you." His voice is soft.

"For what?"

"For worrying about me. Wanna know a secret?"

"What?"

"I'm not such a bad boy as everyone thinks."

"Go on."

"I won't say I've never woken up with a stranger, but it hasn't happened since college. The reason I was like that that first night was because I was dreaming about a woman

I met in the bar that night, and in my dream she came home with me. I haven't even had sex in over a year."

"What about the CICU nurse?"

"Nope, rumor, never happened."

"Look, Mark said…"

"Listen to me. I was a little wild in college. I had a rep, guys like Mark expected the worst of me, and I don't kiss and tell. I know women like me, think I'm good looking, whatever, sometimes a nurse or someone walks by and maybe she'll smile, or say hello, and everyone automatically assumes I have carnal knowledge. So maybe I shrug off the questioning glances, it doesn't matter, even if I deny it out-right, they just think I'm avoiding workplace gossip. And to tell the truth, my rep as a lady-killer saves me from a lot of hassles."

"How so?"

"Think about it, most of my friends are paired off, wives, live-ins, and everybody has great single women friends, or sisters or cousins…."

"Like me?"

"No, not like that, just, you know, all those women seek-ing men, and if I'm a rogue and a cad, I can avoid blind dates and setups."

"You allow even your best friend to think you are a slut to avoid unwanted and unsolicited dating help?"

"Basically."

"And you haven't had sex in almost a year."

"Right. Forgiven?"

"There was never any forgiving necessary—like I said, it just worried me."

"I've been tested. I'm a surgeon, we test every three months, okay? You don't have to worry about me."

"How about the other?"

"The drinking? I allow myself up to two drinks a night if I'm out, one if I'm home and to excess only on St. Patrick's Day."

"I didn't know you were Irish."

"I'm not, I just really like St. Patrick's Day. Do I pass muster now?"

"Aw, shut up and go to sleep."

"Jess…"

"Yeah?"

"I'm really honored that you care."

"Yeah, well, it's the least I can do for my husband." I had confessed to him about the photos and the wedding ring, and he was terribly gallant about it.

"All right then, Mother, shall we attempt some rest? We have a long drive tomorrow."

"All right, Father, sleep well." I turn on my side facing away from him, smiling in the dark.

And for the first time since the very first night, Harrison rolls toward me, spooning me, and holds me close until we're both asleep.

Lilith

Tyler called me from the hospital, and told me it would be a good time to come visit Nico, my adopted surrogate father.

Vital Statistics:

Nico Papalopolis

56, drama teacher

Losing battle with AIDS

Likes Frank Sinatra and dry martinis

Hates hospital sheets

Nico was my drama teacher in high school, and became that perfect mix of uncle, shrink, friend and guardian angel. We got even closer when I was in college; he cast me in his outdoor Shakespeare productions every summer and continued to be a wonderful supporter in the early part of my career. When I decided to take my acting sabbatical, he was the one who got me involved in coaching and assistant directing and dramaturgy, so that I could keep a hand in.

Nico has been living with HIV for nearly thirteen years. There have been several close calls, but so far, he's managed to bounce back every time. The new drug cocktail had been working pretty great until about a month ago, but he's going through a very rough patch, and has been in Northwestern Memorial for the past three weeks.

I find a parking space on the Neil Diamond floor of the parking lot, wondering if Neil gets royalties each time the song is played on an endless loop in the elevator vestibule. Nico is on the eighth floor. Tyler, his partner, is standing outside his room when I arrive. I give Tyler a deep hug.

"How is he?"

Tyler looks resigned. "Lucid, for the moment. It was a long morning, but he's better now."

"Morphine?"

"Practically as much as he wants." That doesn't sound good.

"Practically?" The implication frightens me.

He looks at me with tears beginning to brim in his eyes. "You know."

Nico always talked about "being in control of his own death" in an offhand way, but I can't believe that we're remotely there yet. "Not really."

"Really."

"Oh, Ty, I can't believe it, not now."

Tyler shakes off the tears. "Can you blame him? You can see it in his eyes when he comes back from wherever it is that he goes in those weird moments. He knows he's been gone, and it scares him."

"What are you going to do?" I can't imagine facing this, Tyler's strength again astounds me.

"Take him home, make him comfortable, reserve my place in hell." He smiles wanly.

I smile back as best I can. "Aren't you already going to hell for being a lapsed Catholic?"

"Forgivable if I confess before I die."

"What about the sodomy thing?"

"Not in the big ten. Seven deadly, technically, but not the ten."

"But mercy is unforgivable?" I can't imagine what he is suffering.

"Only for myself."

"And if I forgive you?"

"It's a start. You should go in. He's got maybe twenty more minutes before the pain comes back, and once he gets the shot he'll fall asleep. I'm going for coffee and a smoke, I'll leave you some time."

"Okay, I'll wait for you before I go."

"'Kay, Miss Lil. Love you."

"Love you."

I knock softly on the door, and open it. Nico is lying in the bed, looking like just so many bones, the wasted look of someone who is very, very sick, and has been for a very, very long time. He has an oxygen tube in his nose and two IV bags hanging by the bed. The room has loads of flowers, a special quilt on the bed, a porcelain water pitcher next to a large crystal tumbler. Numerous bottles of pills. It's the room of someone who has been in the hospital for a longer stay, has tried to make it homey. Nico looks up when I enter the room, and smiles.

"Lilith, my baby bear, come here and hug an old man."

"Since when are you old?" I go over to the bed and hug him gently, as if he might break, then I kiss him, and try to plump up his pillows, straighten his quilt.

"All right, quit futzing, you make me nervous."

"Sorry, Papa Bear."

"Where's Mama?"

"Went for coffee, he'll be back in time for your shot."

"Went to smoke, you mean. That boy, what an idiot."

"Be nice, he's a grown-up, he can smoke if he wants."

"Filthy habit."

"You would know. You have a few yourself." We fall immediately back into our old banter.

Nico sighs deeply and luxuriously. "Used to. Used to have the most deliciously filthy habits. Look where it got me."

I never let him get away with that sort of talk. "Is it Poor Me Day? I always forget. You want to keep going or do I get to whine about my stuff too?"

"I give up. Baby Bear always was the real head of the household anyway. Everything always just right for Baby Bear, not too hot or cold, not too hard or soft…everything just right."

"Papa Bear was the biggest and strongest, though."

"Not anymore, Lili. Papa is old and tired."

"And wandering out of the cave during hunting season." It's an awful metaphor, but I can't think of another way to broach it.

Nico looks up at me and nods. "Mama told you."

I can't help it, I'm starting to cry, all I can do is nod, looking down at my hands.

Nico reaches over and covers one of my hands with one of his. "It's time. You know it is. I see this look on Tyler's face sometimes and I know I've been speaking in tongues or rambling on, or drifted off somewhere and I don't remember the last real thing I said. It's killing him like this damn disease is killing me, and I won't lie here and waste away."

I wipe my eyes. "But last time, it was so bad, and you got better, so much better...."

"I'm not getting better. I'm dying. And I would rather have some choice, some control."

"It isn't fair to him, it's too much to ask."

"I know. But he will do it because he loves me, and maybe in some selfish way I want that last proof of true love before I go."

"You don't need any proof. You know he loves you." Tyler and Nico have been together nearly sixteen years. Tyler is still thankfully HIV negative.

"It's the last thing we will share, after everything. We need it, both of us."

"When?"

"He'll call you when I'm gone. We've said goodbye and meant it every time we've parted for the past three years. You and I are almost completed."

"Almost?"

"I have some things to talk to you about." Oy.

"Oh, Nico, not today, I don't think I can...."

"Now, Baby Bear, we may not get another chance. Tell me about this boy."

Oh crap.

"What boy?" Maybe I can bluff him.

"Don't be coy with me, little missy. *The boy*. The new boy. The boy who's your shadow these past months, the one you take to all the shows, the one who meets you for drinks on

Wednesday nights, the one Tyler spotted you with sitting in the park in front of the conservatory…"

"Noah."

"More."

"He's an actor. I met him working on Bill's show three—no, four months ago."

"Show muffin?" Nico asks.

"Thought so."

"And?"

"He's more than that, friend. A real friend. We just connected right off the bat. You would like him—he is smart and funny and sweet and caustic and enigmatic and…"

"Good in bed?"

"I wouldn't know."

"But you want to know."

"Oh, Nico, I—"

"You want to know, say it out loud, no use pretending it doesn't exist by not naming it, Baby Bear. You want to know if he is good in bed, if you are good together in bed."

"*'With all the light and darkness that I have.'*" It's an old quote from somewhere, and Nico and I always use it when we're terribly and dramatically serious about something.

"And does he have this same curiosity?"

"I doubt it."

"Because when you told him, he didn't respond." He always does cut to the chase.

"I haven't told him."

"When you kissed him, he didn't kiss back."

This is flipping torturous.

"I haven't—"

"You disappoint me, Lilith. I taught you better than this, to be braver than this."

"He's married."

"He's married, you've got Martin—no reason to live without each other if you believe. Do you believe?"

"Yes."

"So what stops you?"

"It's selfish, I guess."

"More."

"We met and it was like—like those dreams where you are opening a door in your house that you never saw before, and beyond it are all these rooms that you never knew existed."

"More."

"Like your apartment is perfectly fine, you have enough space for all your stuff, so you never look at that little door in the closet, but then one day you open it and everything you need is in the rooms that lie behind, and then, when you wake up and realize it isn't true, suddenly you crave everything you saw. You feel a loss. My life was like a perfectly acceptable apartment. There was enough room in it that it didn't occur to me that there was more room to be had. Then, open door. Everything got wider, clearer. Oh, Nico. I didn't know there was another door."

"Very poetic, Lilith. So you are wallowing in the spaciousness of this man, spending time together, getting to know each other, and…?"

"I thought it was a crush, that he was a show muffin, like you said. I thought it would mellow into a flirty friendship."

"But it hasn't mellowed."

"Nope."

"And now you love him."

"I'm trying not to love him."

"And are you succeeding?"

"I have good days and bad days."

"You and me both. And the selfish part?"

"You know I'm good at honesty. At showing the people I love how much I treasure them. Even the casual little 'my God, you're cute, aren't you ever going to kiss me?' moments. But I can't this time. Just once in my life I want someone else to kiss first. I want someone else to lie awake and wonder what the right words are, if they'll be rejected, if they're ruining a great friendship. I want him to want me so much that he can't help himself, that he has to risk everything for the chance to be with me. I'm tired of living out on a limb, of always being the brave one, the honest one—fuck that! I can't hear the 'I'm so flattered, but…' speech from one more man—certainly not from him. It's hypocritical, and dumb, and maybe I'm the biggest idiot on the face of the earth, but I'm tired, and I like knowing that he likes to spend time with me, that he doesn't dread my calls. I won't risk this friendship so I can know for sure if he wants me. If he wants me, he is going to have to let me know, I can't ask him."

"Tell him." Sure, no problem.

"No."

"Tell him."

"It's too much, too big. He isn't optional now. This friendship is everything to me, if I lost him I would ache forever."

"Don't play drama queen with me, Baby Bear, he is a man, a man like any man, probably a good man, clearly dear to you, but just a man. You will either be together or not. Love each other or wound each other. Know each other forever, or for a time or not ever really know each other at all. But don't tell me you can't live without him, I don't have enough hours left for bullshit."

Now I'm really crying, and I bury my face in my hands.

Nico puts on his soothing voice. "Give me your paw."

I look up and reach out to take his hand.

"Papa Bear has some wisdom for you. Commit this to memory, stitch it on a sampler, but promise me you will live by it for me, then for yourself, once I'm gone."

I wipe my cheeks with my free hand and force a smile. "I promise to try."

"Do not waste life. Every time you let someone leave you without knowing how they make you feel, you have died a little death for nothing. Do not assume that you have more than the moment you are living in. It's never too soon or too hard to tell someone that you love them, that they move you, that you are better for knowing them. Your job is to celebrate love, and to trust in the universe to bring you the people you need and tell you how to be with them when they arrive. You live a life that will end with regretting only things you did, not things you never did. You promise me, Baby Bear, tell everyone, make them hear you, put aside your petty fears and love loud for me, so I can hear you in heaven."

What can I say? "I'll try. Really, I will."

"Do you think he loves you?"

"Deep down, I don't."

"Then he is a fool."

I smile at him. "No, Papa, he is no fool."

"And are you a fool, my Baby Bear?"

"Always."

"That's my girl. The fools have the fun."

"You are the biggest fool of all."

"Just the oldest." I can see that the pain is beginning to return, Nico's jaw is clenching subtly.

"Should I come over Friday?" Supposedly he is going home Thursday.

"Come Friday. If I'm home, I'll be glad to see you, and if I'm not, Tyler will need you." Oh God.

"Don't…" I can't say anything else.

"Chin up, Baby Bear, I'll be watching you."

I take a deep breath and try to smile. "I'll be counting on it. Happily ever after."

"Happily ever after."

When I get home I call Bill and fill him in, and he promises to go visit later in the day so that Tyler can take a dinner break. Then I call the store and make plans to get together with Anne and Beth after work. We decide to splurge and go to Ajax and surprise Robin. Jess is on her way back from Wisconsin tonight, and doesn't have a phone yet, so I leave a message for her at Harrison's asking her to call me when they get back. I'm hoping she'll be free tomorrow so we can have lunch or something. She can tell me all about the wedding, and I can try to forget that yet another dad is leaving my life for good.

jess

The day after the wedding we all had a huge brunch (the mystery woman had disappeared in the middle of the night), packed and loaded cars, kissed goodbye at least four times and hit the road in some strange caravan. My mom and Amy went back to Kenosha where Amy will hang out for a couple days before returning to Seattle, and my dad followed them with Aunt Georgia. Teddy and his girl-friend headed off to Ann Arbor, Charles and his parents to Highland Park, Mark and Gemma to a B&B in the Upper Peninsula for a short honeymoon and Harrison and I went back to Chicago, but only after Hama elicited a promise that we would return for a weekend in August. Harrison and I talked about our families for most of the trip home, at least, as long as I was awake. We're now at my new digs. We found the key with the building manager, and climbed the three flights to a small one-bedroom apartment.

"Not so bad for a sublet," Harrison remarks.

"Not bad at all, they even have linens for the bed." I joke.

"Low blow. Want to grab a bite to eat before I head back north?"

"I'm too grungy to go out, but we could order something in if you want."

"Perfect. Chinese?"

"I love you. Nothing too spicy, okay? I have to grab a quick shower, I always feel disgusting after a road trip."

I shower quickly in my new bathroom, throw on some old leggings and a sweatshirt and go back out to the living room. Harrison is asleep on the couch. I sit on the floor watching him till the bell rings. Sprinting to the buzzer, I let in the deliveryman, and look through my purse for money. The delivery guy does not look thrilled that I have a fourth-floor walk-up, and asks me to sign the credit card receipt.

"You can't buy your first meal in a new apartment, it's a rule," says a gruff voice behind me.

"You don't have to do that."

"I want to."

"Well, thank you."

Harrison had ordered everything on the menu, including paper plates and chopsticks and a six-pack of beer. We hardly spoke as we sat on the floor in the living room stuffing ourselves.

"God, I missed Chinese take-out while I was away. This is like heaven."

"I don't know how you lived without this," Harrison says. "I would die if I couldn't have my Chinese fix every ten days or so."

When the leftovers are in the fridge and the garbage is piled in the sink, Harrison grabs his keys off the counter.

"If there is nothing else you need, I guess I'll head homeward."

"Harrison, thank you so much for everything these past weeks. You have been so much more than kind…." I sort of don't want him to go, frankly.

"Stop, you're making me blush. Look, let's go out this week, catch a movie or something, okay?" He smiles at me.

"Sounds great, I'll call you when I get my phone connected."

"Perfect. You okay here? Anything you need?"

"I'm fine. Go home before you fall asleep. Oh shit, could you do me one favor?"

"Anything."

"Could you call Hama and tell her we got home okay? I promised before I remembered I don't have a phone yet."

"No problem. I'll talk to you in a day or so."

"Okay, thanks again."

He kisses me goodbye, and leaves. I lock up and fall into bed, exhausted. At around 3:00 a.m. I hear the buzzer. Thinking it must be kids or drunks, I ignore it. But then it rings again, very insistently, so I stumble to the intercom and ask who it is.

"It's Harrison."

I buzz him up. It takes forever for his shoulders to appear around the stair bend.

"Hi."

I can't begin to imagine what he is doing here. I step aside. "Come on in, are you okay?"

"I don't know." He looks really worried.

"Did something happen?"

He sits on the couch, which is when I realize he is wearing the pajamas we bought together.

He looks at me. "I just can't get something out of my head."

"What is it?"

"Remember last night—my God, was it just last night? Well, last night when you asked if you had played along with my delusions that first night, if I would have made love to you?"

"Yeah, of course I remember."

"Tonight I got into bed, I was so tired, but I lay down and I couldn't fall asleep, you know, I just kept going over it in my head, why would you ask that? Why? And I figured you wouldn't, not unless that idea had occurred to you for some reason, you know, like an option. Jess, I can't sleep, and I don't really know why I'm here, it's just—shit. I was lying in my bed, and it felt really big and empty, and I thought you might have been angry last night because you thought I would make love to you if I didn't know who you were, but I didn't even try when I did know…"

OhmyGodohmyGodohmyGod.

"I have to kiss you now, please don't be mad, but I've been thinking about it since that first night, and you can throw me out if you want, but I just…"

And then he is kissing me, and I'm kissing him back, and my cheeks are wet and I don't know which one of us is weeping. I take his hand and lead him to the bedroom, where we curl up together in the bed and hold each other, and we fall asleep with our lips pressed together. When we wake up, still twisted together, Harrison brushes the hair off my forehead and smiles at me.

"Good morning, beautiful."

"Good morning."

"I think I have to make love to you now."

And he did. And we were, you know, inevitable.

beth

The night of our first date was the night of the worst rainstorm Chicago had seen in twenty years. The violent waves of Lake Michigan crashed across Lake Shore Drive with such force that four cars and a bus were knocked off the road before they could close down the drive altogether. I was incredibly nervous, and almost hoped that the rain kept him from coming. We had gone to college together and had not been the best of friends.

Actually, we hated each other.

So how do we end up here? Too strange. I had gone to Home Depot and begun looking through the list of classes. There was so much that inspired me to think about the warehouse...everything from basic installation of flooring to really cool painting techniques. I decided on a tiling class, figuring that if I can handle the floor in the bathroom, I might later tackle the kitchen area. When I asked the guy at the information desk about the course, he told me that the person who'll be teaching it was around and suggested I talk to him. He made a call, and a couple minutes later, who showed up but Jeff Phillips.

Vital Statistics:

Jeff Phillips

34, home improvement expert/writer

Genius with porcelain tile

Likes being sober

Hates women who complain about their weight

He actually was very nice, answered all my questions, and then asked me to dinner. I was hesitant, so we compromised on brunch. After all, I was trying to put good karma into the universe, and he seemed much different than the guy I had known peripherally so long ago. Plus, if we ended up friends, he might help me with my home improvement projects. We met at T's, and after getting basic awkwardness out of the way, I found his company, let's say, not unpleasant.

When he asked me again for a dinner date, I thought I said no, but it must have popped out as a yes, because now he's on his way to pick me up. I'm house-sitting for my friend Mara, who is in Japan for a conference, so he's meeting me at her apartment. Since dogs are verboten in these luxury high-rises, Petey is hanging out with Anne and Chris while I'm here, and while I miss him, I don't mind not having to walk him in this downpour.

When Jeff arrives at seven, the news stations are beginning to issue thunderstorm warnings. Mara's apartment on the Near North side is far enough away from the really high-risk areas, but we decide to stay in anyway.

Most restaurants had shut down delivery for the night, so I raided the freezer for the makings of a meal. Way in the back, under the leftover Jenny Craig meals from Mara's last crash diet, I discover a pork tenderloin. I pop this in the microwave to defrost, and start making a salad. I've been eating lots of fish, chicken and fresh vegetables these days in an effort to eat healthier, and have adequately stocked the fridge for my stay, so there are plenty of side-dish options. I decide to steam some broccoli rabe. Once the pork has thawed enough, I rub it with olive oil, garlic, stone-ground mustard, lemon juice, salt, pepper and rosemary, and put it in the oven. Jeff watches me closely, a little crooked smile on his face.

"You cook just like my mom," he muses.

"Is that a good thing or a bad thing?"

"Very good. My mom is great at throwing together impromptu gourmet meals with whatever she finds lying around the freezer."

"Well, maybe she could do something with all those little freezer-burned bags lurking in there."

Jeff opens the freezer and examines the prepackaged diet food. Then he laughs. He holds up a bag. "What do you need with that nonsense, a gorgeous girl like you?" he says, clearly imitating his mom. "You are too thin as it is, let me make you some nice kugel, with sour cream, eh?"

I laugh, and blush, thrilled with the "just off the shtetl" accent, and the reference to my looks.

"A girl in the big city who remembers how to blush. How refreshing."

Jeff's statement only makes me blush more, and I turn away to deal with the food. I put the rabe in the steamer and set a pot to boil for pasta. I turn the pork, which was starting to brown nicely and give off that wonderful Provençal odor of garlic and rosemary.

"I'm covering dinner—you get to pick the music," I say to him, with two distinct motives in mind. The first was to get him out of the kitchen, which suddenly felt too familiar, as if I were entertaining in my boudoir, and the second was to see what his music choice would be. I always test new men in this way. If they chose one of my favorites, they got brownie points, full credit for jazz, half credit for respectable classical and so on. If they put on anything that sounds like make-out music, I "get a headache" before the meal is over. And since Mara and I have almost identical taste in music, I know there is plenty to choose from.

Just as I was putting the pasta in the boiling water, the sounds of Annie Lennox's new album came wafting in from the living room. Full credit for music, Mr. Charm is really doing a number on me. I just hope he doesn't know it….

The rain is really coming down now, beating against the windows loudly, and giving the apartment that cocoonish feeling that comes with bad weather conditions, good food and convivial company.

I pull a bottle of pinot gris out of the fridge, feeling like a yuppie in a wine commercial. Then I drain the pasta and toss it with garlic infused olive oil, chopped fresh basil and grated romano and asiago cheeses. The pork is done, so I pull it out of the oven to let it sit before carving. I toss the salad, put a dab of butter on the rabe and open the wine. Giving myself a mental pat on the back, and sending a telepathic thank-you to Robin for all the cooking lessons, I carry the food to the dining room.

Jeff is standing by the window watching the rain. "I love rain like this," he says, not turning away from the window.

"Me, too. The lightning startles me, the thunder scares me—it's like that great suspense movie fright, terrifying in an exciting, thrilling way."

We stare outside for a full minute, silent.

"Dinner. It's probably getting cold," I finally say.

He takes my hand gently and walks me to the dining room. He pulls out my chair, and then pours me a glass of wine, leaving his own glass conspicuously empty.

"You've come a long way since college," I tease him, remembering some of our exchanges.

"Hey, sweet thing, I bet you're a knockout somewhere under that librarian getup!"

"Hey, asshole, I bet you're a shithead somewhere under that frat-geek getup!"

"Dyke bitch."

"Neanderthal."

"Frigid bitch!"

"Limp dick!"

"Who wouldn't be, around you?"

"Fuck you!"

"Nice smile, too bad about the fangs."

Jeff is obviously remembering, too. "So it wasn't the most illustrious of beginnings," he says, laughing.

"*There's* a major understatement."

He raises his water glass. "To new beginnings."

"To new beginnings."

Dinner is delicious, if I do say so myself, and Jeff keeps up the conversation effortlessly, asking me about the years since college, telling me about his life. He had been a writer, his first book was a reasonable success, the second less so, the third had never materialized. I asked him how he ended up at Home Depot. He said he had become an alcoholic and borderline cocaine addict. The writing stopped being good and his publisher dropped their option.

"So I finally just had this sort of breakdown. I was sleeping twelve hours a day, but having all these horrible nightmares, so I was always exhausted and on edge. Then I started drinking and partying even more. After three months, I freaked. Threw my computer out the window, had a ritual conflagration of my first book in the middle of my living room and almost burned the whole building down. My agent dropped me, my publisher shelved the third project, my fiancée gave me back the ring and moved out, and there I was. Washed up at twenty-eight, looking old before my time, and really feeling alone—country-song material."

"So what did you do?"

"Moved home. Got sober. When my granddad died and left his house to my parents, Dad decided to renovate and restore and told me I could earn my keep by helping him do the work. So I did. Learned from him, took some classes, read a lot. Found I liked working with my hands. Got to know the Home Depot crowd pretty well, used a couple guys there as day labor on bigger jobs. When they had an opening, I thought it would be fun. Enough money to move out of Mom and Dad's and back into my own place. Plus, a lot of the projects got me into a rhythm, and the stories started to come again. I began writing again. Really writing, like I used to. I even called my fiancée, both to apologize, and see if she'd give me another chance."

"Wow. What did she say?"

"She said she didn't think her husband would approve."

"Oh. That must have hurt."

"It really wasn't that bad. She forgave me, and said she

was really happy that I was getting back on track. She even promised to buy the next book I published." He smiles. "If I ever publish another book."

"I'm sure you will. Did you ever see her again?"

"Last year, right around this time. I was walking by Lincoln Park Zoo, and I saw her. She was with this tall, handsome guy—her husband, I imagine—and chasing after this little girl with blond hair and an amazing giggle. What a heartbreaker! Looked just like her mother."

"What'd she say?"

"Nothing. I watched from across the street until they went into the zoo, and then I left. I figured she looked so happy, she didn't need a reunion with me. It was good to see her, though. Really good."

I stared, dumbfounded.

"Yeah, I know, mushy and sentimental. Not what you were expecting from the former beer-funneling champion of Phi Sigma Delta."

"It's a wonderful change."

"Well, you turned out pretty good yourself, for a radical-feminist library monitor."

"For that, you get to wash dishes!"

While Jeff is washing, I dry and put away. Then we retreat to the living room with coffee to listen to the rain. No sooner have we settled in than the power goes out. After ten minutes I realize it isn't going to fix itself too quickly, so I go to fetch candles. On my way back in, I catch my shin on the corner of the coffee table, stumble and land in Jeff's lap.

"That was subtle," he teases.

"Cut that out. I really hurt myself." I'm more angry at myself than him.

"I'm sorry, poor baby, here." He starts to rub my shin gently. It's at least a minute before I remember that I'm still in his lap.

"Thanks," I say, moving to the couch beside him. "It's better now."

I light the candles, and Jeff stands up.

"C'mere." He is walking toward the sliding patio door. He opens the door and a gust of wind blows out the candles.

"Listen," he says as the windblown rain begins to soak the front of his shirt.

"I don't hear anything."

"There's music in this rain." He takes my hand, and before I can protest, leads me out onto the balcony.

We stand there, letting the rain soak us instantly, then he pulls me close to him, and starts to dance. It's lovely and magical and a little frightening, but when he kisses me, I find myself kissing him back, and loving the coolness of the dripping water that lubricates our lips. I don't even realize when I start trembling.

"You're freezing, we should go back in before you catch your death."

I follow him back inside, and we fumble around in the dark until we can get the candles relit. Then we start to laugh.

"How come in the movies when two people play in the rain they get even better looking?" Jeff is looking down at his clothes, which are stuck to him in a most unflattering manner.

"How come all the women in those movies have waterproof makeup on?" I've caught my reflection in the mirror, raccoon eyes and lipstick smeared from nose to chin. "I look like Baby Jane in training."

I find him a towel and a pair of Mara's sweatpants, one of my T-shirts and some socks, and send him to the powder room, while I retreat to the bathroom with my pajamas and try to fix my face and dripping hair.

When I get back to the living room he is sitting on the couch in the candlelight, feet propped on the coffee table. The pants are five inches too short, the heels of the socks hit him midarch, my shirt is the only thing that fits him. His hair is all spiky, like he towel-dried it and left it that way. He looks really good to me.

Before I can tell him this, the lights surge back on, the music starts again and I yelp like a cat from surprise.

Jeff laughs. "Easy, kid, just electricity."

He pulls me to the couch and kisses me again. I shouldn't do this. The last time I did this I ended up with Sasha. One good date doesn't mean…mmm.

"Beth?" He's kissing my neck.

"Yeah?" I'm letting him.

"Can I tell you something?"

"Of course."

"I always had sort of a thing for you in college."

This stops me cold.

"What? We hated each other!"

"You hated me, but I thought you were totally cute, and I wasn't so good at dealing with my feelings. Think back to first grade, didn't the boys who liked you try to beat you up?"

"Well, yes, but they weren't nineteen at the time."

"I'm a late bloomer."

"Well, I'm flattered and a little embarrassed."

"I just wanted you to know."

"Thank you." I lean forward to kiss him, muffin that he turned out to be, but he stops me.

"So I think I should go."

Did anyone else just hear the sound of screeching brakes?

"Oh." I don't really know what to say.

"Look, I want to stay, I really do. More than you can imagine. It has been a great evening. But part of my life these days is about taking things slowly, not jumping in too fast. I really like you, Beth, I think we could be great together, but if we go there, I want to be sure. If I stay, even if we agree it's just to sleep over, things are likely to get out of hand, and I just—"

"Jeff, it's okay. I should be taking things slowly myself. But it's scary as hell out there, and I would be lying if I said I felt good about you leaving. How do you feel about the couch?"

"Does the bedroom door lock?"

"It does indeed."

"Will you promise to lock it so when I wake up at four a.m. and feel a gravitational pull to come snuggle up in bed with you I'm thoroughly thwarted?"

I laugh. "Deal."

"Okay then. And thank you for understanding."

"Thank you for thinking enough of me to want to be careful."

Jeff leans over and kisses me lightly on the lips. I smile at him, get off the couch and dig a blanket and pillow out of Mara's linen closet. Once he's settled on the couch, we have one more brief and delicious good-night kiss, and I retreat to the bedroom, where I lock the door like a good girl. Lying in the dark, I think about the evening, and find myself grinning like a fool. And I wonder what is going to happen next. Not to mention what I'm going to make him for breakfast.

robin

Michael gets up and futzes with the fire in his fireplace, and I pour us both a healthy slug of cognac. He made me dinner for a change, which was lovely. One of the problems with being a chef is that frequently people don't want to cook for you. They think you'll judge them. They obviously don't realize that I often whip up a special batch of Kraft mac 'n cheese for my own supper, especially when I'm out of peanut butter and jelly. It was just a simple salad and pasta with his mom's sauce, but I loved him for not caring and not trying too hard. I also loved him for breathing in and out, and walking upright, and a million other things that are pedestrian and mundane. He walks over and sits beside me on the couch, sips his cognac thoughtfully and smiles at me.

"Okay, kiddo, you're on."

"Meaning?" I know what he means, but I'm hesitant to begin.

"Meaning I've been a good boy. It's pouring cats and dogs out there. I've fed you amply, built you this lovely fire to take off the chill and let you use the Baccarat snifters, despite the fact that you're a major klutz and are likely to break them both by the end of the evening. You promised me your treatise on love, and I do mean to hear it."

Well, crap.

"Okay, okay, I get the picture. Are you sure, considering what you have been through?" Andrea called him over the weekend and told him that she was staying in L.A. His choice, move and be together or be over. He chose over. I'm amazed that love's a topic he is willing to broach. Plus, I've been dreading it, so it's worth trying to stave him off.

"Nope, you and I both know that if Andrea and I were the real deal, I never would have let her leave. Sad but true. It has been over two years we've been friends, and this is probably the only topic we haven't talked about. I wanna hear it."

"That isn't fair—you know all about all my failed romances."

"Not the same thing, and you know it. If you're going to be my personal philosopher, then it's time for the love chapter. I believe I've earned it."

I'm *so* going to be fired. Or will have to quit. But maybe it's time.

"Okay, if you insist. Love is a state of being in which you care about someone else more than you do about yourself. Where someone else's happiness defines your own. It becomes impossible for you to be a truly happy person unless the person you're in love with is happy. If it's you that makes them happy, that's true love, a rare and wonderful beast." I pause for breath, then continue.

"More likely, they will only be happy with someone who is not you. When this happens, you find yourself actively seeking the person who will make the object of your love happy, sometimes even more actively than they themselves may be seeking, because, as I said, if they're not happy, you can't be happy. If you succeed, you are happy because they're happy. Of course, your heart is broken, which makes you miserable, but it's a happy misery, because really being in love with someone means loving them enough to let them love someone else. That is the cycle of love, it's what makes us human, fallible. It's the essence of reality."

He looked up, attempting to make some sense of the theory I had just explained to him.

"So how do you know when you are truly in love?" he asks.

"Just ask yourself if you would be willing to fix her up with your brother."

"What will that prove?"

"Isn't it obvious? You never know when true love will happen for anyone. So if you're willing to fix her up with your brother, despite your attraction to her, that means you are in love. If the idea of her and your brother together makes you angry, jealous, nauseous…then you are just lusting after her, because if you were in love with her, you would seek her happiness at any cost, even the outside chance of becoming her brother-in-law. You might love her as a friend, but you aren't in love with her until there is nothing you wouldn't do to help her get happy."

"I don't have a brother." He grins at me.

"You know what I mean, your best friend, then."

"I see." Outside, the rain beat down, and the rumble of thunder was getting closer and closer.

"I know it's vaguely confusing, but if you let it sink in awhile, it'll begin to make more sense."

"So since I'm back on the market, how will I recognize a woman I could fall in love with? Does she match any set of qualities I have in my head, or will she pop out of nowhere and surprise me?"

"When you find the perfect woman, you'll just know."

"Nobody is perfect." He is so damn sure of himself.

"Exactly."

"You lost me again."

"It's common knowledge that as humans, we have flaws. That's a given. Therefore, in order to be a truly perfect human being, you must have flaws. Our perfection is directly attributed to our flaws."

"So then all people are perfect." Such a logician.

"In their own way, yes."

"Then how do you know when you find the *right* perfect person?"

"Ah, Mikey, that will be the person whose flaws are crossed out by your strengths, and vice versa."

"Don't call me Mikey. I still don't quite understand."

His little smirk is at once irritating and irresistible. I want to smack him. And then kiss him. Or maybe kiss him and then smack him.

"In true love, both people, being perfect, have flaws."

"All right, Robbie, I'm with you so far."

"Don't call me Robbie. Anyway, those flaws don't merge, they get crossed out by the other person's strengths. A true love means a true union. A true union means the melting of two hearts, minds and souls into a single heart, mind and soul, which is redistributed into two bodies. During the rearranging of two into one, flaws and strengths cross each other out. That way, when the one is separated back into two, the union is unmarred." He shakes his head, but I press on.

"As time goes on, new flaws appear, and sometimes it takes a while for a flaw to find a counterbalancing strength, so they stick around and cause trouble. But since new strengths appear as well as new flaws, if the union is strong, eventually even the new flaws get taken out of the picture."

"It certainly is a thought-provoking theory."

"Well, I think there's some truth to it, but then again, it's my theory. I'm less likely to be aware if I'm full of shit than you are."

"No, you've made some very valid points. Maybe slightly unconventional, Robbie, but so was the round-earth theory in its time."

"I graciously accept the compliment that was veiled in there somewhere. And don't call me Robbie."

"How did one of such a tender age become so wise in the subject of love?"

I hate when he does this. "Firstly, I'm not so young. If you didn't know how old I really am, what would be your guess?"

"Honestly?"

"No, please lie to me, you know how I relish it."

"Easy, killer. I don't know, about thirty-eight."

"Fine. It happens to be a fact that girls mature faster than boys, and that the average woman of thirty is as mature as the average male of thirty-six. Since you've told me that I'm not average, but, in fact, appear to be six years older than I really am, that puts me at a forty-four-year-old mentality, making me a year older than you."

"Uncle! I admit it, I'm a mere babe in the woods compared to your overwhelming senior citizenship. That still doesn't answer my question."

"I forgot your damn question."

"How did you get to be so wise in the subject of love?"

"Simple. I've opened myself to it, and as often as possible, embraced it. I've loved long, hard and frequently. Mostly, I've loved people who are unable to return that love to me. But I've loved the true love. Once you have walked that path, you'll go through any heartache in order to achieve that union again." So very true.

"You are lucky. Sometimes, I think I'm incapable of the true love."

"You will love the true love. You can't escape it."

"How are you so sure of me, when I'm not?"

"Faith."

"And you?"

"Someday I'll love the true love again. Till then I'm in search of someone to take me to dinner."

He laughs, clear and honest, and shakes his head from side to side in disbelief.

"Don't laugh at me. I mean it."

"I'm sorry, but that is some ultimatum. Be my true love or buy me dinner. Your choice."

"I didn't give an ultimatum! I can wait for true love…. But I can't stand this enduring loneliness."

"I'm sorry."

He puts a hand on my shoulder and rubs gently. It's soothing. It makes me all tingly. I can feel my face flush, and hope he doesn't notice in the firelight.

So I just keep talking. "It's not your fault. It's the plight of the hopeless, realistic romantic."

"The hopeless, realistic romantic?"

"Yes. It's incurable. Often fatal. A truly horrid condition."

"I've heard of the hopeless romantic, I've even been called one once or twice, but this is a new one for me."

"The principle is basically the same. I've an enduring hope that someday my true love will sweep me off my feet, that he will carry me off into a wonderful new life. But I'm realistic enough to not search for him in every man I meet. What I look for is someone to be my friend. The qualities that attract me to a person as a friend are the same I seek in a love, they're just focused differently. If I gain a friend, that's a wonderful thing. If I become attracted to him in a romantic way, and he happens to lean in a similar direction, that's a bonus. And if, in all this, I stumble upon my true love, that will be a miracle. But I don't look for him—I look for someone to keep me warm at night, to make me laugh. I have infinite patience for the arrival of my true love, but I'm eternally weary of sleeping alone. As you well know."

"I understand." He tweaks my nose.

"Do you? We're perfectly matched friends. You fear ever being able to truly love, but you never lack interesting warm bodies to enjoy life with. I know I'll love again, but I can't find anyone who wants to spend his time with me."

"And just as you have faith that I will love the true love, I believe that someday soon some guy will realize what a catch you are," Michael says.

"Most are fishing for a sleek blue marlin, not a blue whale with a great personality," I reply.

"You promised me you were going to cut that out."

"Sorry, it slipped. Look, I know I'm a wonderful person. When the rest of the male population figures it out, I'll be one psyched chick."

"That's better. So my little philosophess, can you have a one-sided true love?"

God, he is frigging adorable. "Sure. Some of the purest, truest loves have been unrequited. Most of mine have been."

"So you aren't really awaiting the next true love, you are awaiting the one who will love you back."

"Yes. Endless waiting. Romance's equivalent of the DMV. No such thing as the short line."

"Interesting analogy."

"Unfortunately appropriate. Waiting for love is, I believe, the circle of hell that Dante forgot."

"Wasn't there a play by that name?" he asks, joking.

"No, silly, that was *Waiting for Godot,* but it's a common mistake."

"Sure, make fun of me."

"Sorry." We laugh at our own ridiculous banter.

"So are you in love now?" he asks.

Here we go, kids. Fasten your seat belts, keep arms and legs inside the vehicle at all times.

"Hopelessly. Realistically, but hopelessly."

"Really? Anyone I know?"

"I can't tell you that. You know better."

He looks at me in a way I've never seen before, as if seeing me for the first time. This is going to suck out loud.

"Do you love me?"

What can I do but answer him?

"With everything that I am."

He is silent, and alternates between looking into my face and staring out at the fire. Finally he speaks.

"So what do I do?"

"Well, we already had dinner. You can fire me."

"I can't do that, you're the best exec sous I know, and when Gerald moves on, I'm going to need you to take over the kitchen. What do I do about us?"

"I dunno. It isn't a big deal, really, you can just forget it."

"Forget it? *Forget it?!?* How the fuck am I supposed to forget it? How long?"

"Michael, it doesn't matter." I hadn't counted on angry.

"It does too matter, Robin. How fucking long?"

"Stop yelling at me. A year and a half. Give or take."

"You have been in love with me for a year and a half."

"Ever since the picnic." Michael hosts a winter picnic every year at the restaurant. Indoors. Moves all the tables and chairs out, and puts blankets on the floor, and a couple kiddie pools, and does all the cooking himself. At my first one, six months after I got the job, I ended up staying late to help him clean up. We talked and talked and drank a great deal of beer, and he danced with me in the kitchen, and he kissed me a little too long when I finally left around three in the morning. We've never spoken of it since.

"Rob, I never thought, I mean, the age difference..."

"It's eleven years. That isn't so much."

"It isn't so little."

"It doesn't matter anyway." Owie. Why did I ever tell him?

"Of course it matters!"

"It only matters if you want to be with me. Do you want to be with me?"

He looks me right in the eye, which I give him much credit for.

"Yes."

I'm trying so hard not to cry. "It's okay, we can still be friends, I mean, if you want to."

"Robin."

"I think we can just pretend like you don't know, and we won't speak of it again, and…"

"Robin!"

"Stop yelling at me. Jesus! What?"

"I said yes, you little idiot. Yes! I do want to be with you! I'm scared as shit, and deep down I'm wondering if it isn't the hugest mistake in the fucking universe, but you are sitting there, and you are so beautiful, and so crazy, and smart and—*fuck!*" He has lost his words.

"Oh."

"Oh? This is all you have to say?"

"Wow." *Holy shit.*

"Oh and wow. We're fucking doomed."

"Michael."

"What?"

"Do you really think I'm beautiful?"

"Yes, honey, I always have."

"And you really want me? I mean, for real, not because you care about me as a friend, but just for me?"

"Yes, I do."

"Then prove it, would you?"

Michael takes the snifter out of my shaking hands and puts it on the coffee table. He shifts on the couch so he is nearer to me, and puts an arm around my shoulders. With his other hand he strokes my cheek, then he leans over and kisses me. It's like a saving breath.

I get up, take his hand and lead him into his own bedroom. He pulls me close to him, holding me tightly against his lean body, and I can feel his heart racing, which is a real relief, because then I know he really does want me, and is really just as scared as I am.

He buries his hands in my hair and kisses me deeply. I let my hands roam the contours of his body, which I know so well from our platonic nights together, and yet which seem at once new and surprising. We undress each other slowly, and he leads me to the bed, lying me down gently. He is a tender and thoughtful lover, exploring my body slowly, taking me in, caressing and kissing every inch of me until my whole body is alive with sensation. After nearly an hour of these delicious attentions, I can barely contain myself anymore.

"Michael." My voice is throaty and gruff in my need.

"Yes, honey?" Michael is smiling down at me. *My* Michael. His hair is tousled from my fingers, his face is flushed with passion and there is joy in his eyes. Real joy. I'm so happy I think my heart is going to bust right out of my chest.

"I really want you inside me."

"Me, too." Michael leans over and kisses me deeply, then rolls away from me briefly to get a condom out of the nightstand. I reach for him and help him get it on, loving the way his body jumps and twitches at my touch. I lie back down, and Michael kisses me deeply, stroking me with his hand before entering me slowly. I never knew a man could feel so good. I never knew someone could fit me so perfectly, and for the first time in my life I know I'm making love, really making love.

And life is mighty fine.

We spend the night in an endless series of perfect moments. I lose track of how many times I come, and when we've exhausted the nightstand supply, we simply adapt. There is talking and dozing and laughing in the dark, and at four in the morning we end up in the shower with the lights out, soaping each other by feel in the blackness of

Michael's new bathroom, all hot water and steam and slippery limbs. And then soft towels and kisses, and finally, in the pale blue of predawn, there is deep and contented sleep.

The cinnamon wakes me.

My whole body is pleasantly achy, I'm cocooned in Michael's bed and I pry one eye open to see my lover (MY LOVER!) standing next to the bed with a tray. He's wearing boxer briefs and a T-shirt, and has got to be the handsomest man I've ever seen. And he is grinning at me like a crazy person.

"Morning, Catherine."

"Morning, Heathcliff. What's all this?"

"I figured it was my turn to make you breakfast." He puts the tray on the nightstand and leans over to kiss me. There are scrambled eggs with fresh chives, cooked dry the way I like them, and buttery cinnamon toast, and hot tea with milk and sugar. And there is Michael, and his arms around me, and cinnamon kisses, and there is nothing else in the wide world.

anne

The phone rings at 6:45 a.m., just before the alarm clock goes off. It's Mrs. Swerzki, Chris's dad's housekeeper. His father has passed away in his sleep, and she's found him. She is so overwrought that she can barely get the words out, her Polish accent becoming thicker with her misery. Chris thanks her for calling, and tells her to go home and leave a house key in the mailbox for him. He calls Warren's house, and his wife, Donna, wakes him up.

"Dad is dead. We'll be over in an hour."

He hangs up the phone and turns to me, tears swimming in his eyes. I pull him to me, cradling him in my arms, my left hand stroking his hair, my right rubbing his shoulders. When he regains his composure a little, we go to the shower together, and I hold him in the hot spray. He kisses me hungrily and slips his soapy hand between my legs. I reach for him, and we bring each other off quickly, then stand holding each other tightly, as the hot water begins to peter out.

I get dressed while Chris shaves. Calling Beth, I explain that I will be out for the rest of the week, and that I'll call later. She offers her condolences and tells me to take care of Chris. Then I go to my bag to find the number in my PalmPilot of the funeral parlor we had used for my grandmother, in case they need it.

We drive to Warren and Donna's house. Their three-year-old, Alex, opens the door.

"Hey, monkey face, how's my girl?" Chris picks his tiny niece up in a bear hug and carries her inside. I follow mutely.

"Daddy and Mommy are sick," Alex says frankly.

"Why do you think that, sweetheart?"

"Because they don't go to work, and I have to take care of them. Mommy said so. I think they have a tummy ache. I don't go to Mrs. Dagnell when I have a tummy ache."

"Well, let's see if we can make them all better."

"Give them cookies, I'm all better when I get cookies."

We find Warren and Donna in Warren's study, making arrangements. Chris embraces his brother tightly, and I hug Donna. There are tears swimming in Donna's eyes, and, sensing that she was about to cry openly, I pick up Alex and whisper that we should go make Mommy and Daddy some coffee.

I carry the toddler into the kitchen. To be honest, I feel a little awkward being involved in so personal a family tragedy so soon into my relationship with Chris—it has only been three months—but I'm glad that they wanted my help. It's apparent that no one has eaten breakfast, so I decide to make some. It'll keep Alex interested and give Chris, Warren and Donna a chance to be alone. Besides, as any good Jewish girl would, my first instinct in any situation is to feed people. I've inherited just enough of my mother's gifts in the kitchen to be reasonably competent, and ask Alex to help me make breakfast for everyone.

First I put a pot of coffee on to brew, and give Alex a cookie and a wink, telling her not to spoil her breakfast. Then I whip up some veggie omelettes along with some fresh bagels I've found.

Thanking me for my trouble, Donna gets a pitcher of orange juice out of the fridge, and Warren pours coffee.

"You are so wonderful." Chris circles my waist from behind and pulls me to him. "I really love you."

"I love you, too, sweetie, but we had better eat before this gets cold."

The food occupies us for twenty minutes, and thanks to Alex babbling an incoherent story about her babysitter, Mrs. Dagnell, the four adults can eat without trying to make conversation. When we're finished, Donna excuses herself to go take a shower, the two brothers return to the study to finish calling all the necessary people and I ask Alex to help me wash and dry the dishes. When we've finished, I take Alex upstairs to read a story or two. She falls asleep during the second book, worn out from all the excitement, and full of warm food. I tuck her blanket around her and return downstairs, brew a fresh pot of coffee and take it into the study.

"He was so young." Warren is looking at his hands, and Donna is sitting on the arm of the sofa, rubbing his shoulders.

"Sixty-eight isn't exactly a kid, War. And he'd had the high blood pressure thing since Mom left." Chris smiles up at me, taking my hand and pulling me onto the ottoman with him.

"I just wasn't prepared, you know. That phone call is supposed to come later. Jesus, Alex won't even remember him."

"Then you'll have to tell her about him. Think about the good times, the happy memories."

"That won't be too hard, they're so few and far between." Warren sounds surprisingly bitter.

"Give Dad a break, would you?" Chris says. "He had it really rough. He always took the best care of us that he was capable of."

"So we got to go to good schools and he didn't beat us. But he wasn't a father, he was an executor. He provided necessary funds, but not affection."

"Geez, War, the man lost his first wife to cancer, had his teenage son killed before he had a chance at life, then Mom left. He had to support us—raise us—all alone. He might not have been affectionate, but we turned out okay. Speaking of unpleasantness, did you call Mom?"

"Not yet. I figured we ought to wait until all the arrangements are finalized. Do you think she'll come?"

"Don't know, but we ought to give her the chance."

"Chris, I don't get this at all. You are so, I don't know, grounded about this. You were always the irrational angry one, you were always the one that came to me pissed off that Dad didn't notice some good thing you had done, or had been busy when you asked him for help. Why are you defending him now?"

"Because he was our father. And he led a difficult life. And now, not two months into retirement, when the pressure was off, and he could live a little for himself and watch his grandchild grow up, and maybe be a friend to the grown sons who needed him, he died. He never got to enjoy the life he worked so hard to set up for all of us. Never got to see me settle down and raise a family."

Warren and Donna look at me, and then at each other, and then pointedly at Chris. I can't stand it.

"Don't look at me," I said.

The three of them laugh, and Chris hugs me.

"You are very special, I wish you had gotten to meet Dad. I kept putting it off, thinking there was plenty of time." Chris's voice breaks.

"I wish I could've met him, too, sweetie."

Midafternoon arrives quickly, and Chris and Warren leave to go meet the funeral people at the house to get the body, since they're scheduling the funeral for two days from now. I agree to stay with Donna until they get back.

Donna fills me in on some of the details about her father-in-law, since Chris has never been terribly forthcoming about his upbringing. When Warren was six and Chris four, their sixteen-year-old half brother, James, was killed in a freak accident. He played varsity football, and, during one practice, he got tackled by half the team. When they dismantled the pileup they discovered his helmet had somehow come off, and his neck had been broken.

James was the only child from their father's first marriage. His mother had died of lung cancer when he was three, and James was all his father had in the world until he met Warren and Chris's mother, Julia.

Something about James seduced everyone around him, and even though Julia had thought she had no desire for children of her own, after a couple years as James's stepmother, she changed her mind. Or thought she did. But according to Donna, she had never been that maternal. But James had taken to big brotherhood with amazing adeptness, and instead of being resentful of Warren and Chris, he had provided a constant source of support and love. Until James's death, they were a reasonably functional family unit.

But after the accident, James Sr. withdrew, and Julia was ill prepared to deal with two young boys and a grieving husband. It was as if James Jr. had connected all the good parts of their lives. When he was gone, so was that precious connection. It was then that Warren and Chris turned to each other. They fought, as brothers do, but didn't allow petty rivalries to come between them.

It always surprised people that, close as they were, they were nothing alike. Warren had been a shy youth. He dated little through high school and college, and, after he passed his CPA exam, married the first woman he had ever fallen in love with. Donna blushed prettily when she confessed this, and though I had liked her very much the couple times we had met, I warmed to her even more, seeing how much she obviously loved Warren. Chris was a varsity player on every sports team except football, and had been something of a playboy (by his own confession, Donna diplomatically glossed over that part), majored in English literature, and decided after graduation that he preferred to work with his hands. He got a job as a site foreman for a small development company, and continued to lead an exemplary bachelor life. He never had a relationship longer than a couple months.

Until me.

Donna told me how glad she was that he and I had found each other, and assured me that she had never known him to be as happy or as committed as he had been since we got together. I told her that I loved Chris very much, and that I was glad she had shared the specifics of his history with me because I hoped it would allow me to help him in his grief.

For the next two days I try to be as helpful as I can to Chris and his family, and they're all so warm and welcoming of me that I'm somewhat overwhelmed. Chris is seemingly insatiable, our lovemaking, which is always passionate, has taken on an urgency that is pretty astounding. He reaches for me first thing in the morning, in the middle of the night, in the shower, when we return home. I read something somewhere about the connection between death and desire, and I have little internal struggles with wanting to feel badly about the impetus for our romps, and yet not wanting to give up the electricity I feel in knowing how badly he wants me physically.

After the small funeral, we go back to Warren and Donna's to receive condolence callers. By eight o'clock, after putting Alex to bed, and stashing the last casserole in the overstocked fridge, Chris and I decide to get going. I ask if he wants to go sit somewhere and have a cup of coffee. We find ourselves back at Lula.

"How are you doing?" I ask him quietly.

"Okay, I guess. Sad, a little conflicted—I mean, we sure weren't close, but he was my dad, you know?"

"I know. Something tells me all you two needed was an excuse to begin to relate to each other as grown-ups."

"I love you."

"I love you, too, sweetie."

We are quiet for a moment. He takes a deep breath.

"So I was thinking…"

"Don't strain yourself," I tease.

"Okay, never mind."

"C'mon!"

"I was going to say that maybe we ought to move in together."

"You're kidding." I'm stunned.

"I'm not kidding. Both our leases are going to be up soon, and I'm sick of carrying my underwear in a bag all weekend long. And I love you."

I lean across the small table, kiss him softly and say, "I can't think of anyone else I would rather live with."

"And Annie?"

"Yes?"

"The living expenses will be a lot cheaper with just one place, which means you'll probably be able to pay off your loans in record time—in case you want to think some more about OT school."

"I love you so much." I don't know what else to say.

We sit smiling at each other for a minute.

"Honey," I say, "I'm just thinking…"

"Yeah?"

"My mother is going to be horrified."

"Then it must be a good idea."

"Exactly."

the ladies who brunch, as told by jess

"Okay, kids, circle up, and I mean right now!" Beth is adamant. We're sitting in the back room at T's indulging in a rare Sunday brunch, complete with abundant mimosas. We've all been so busy of late that there has been little opportunity to get together as a group, and while we see each other in configurations of two or three, and play catch-up via phone, it's getting harder and harder to keep track of who knows what.

"Me first," says Robin, who rarely likes to take the lead. "I've never been happier in my entire life!" Her relationship with Michael went from zero to sixty in about four days, and in spite of all her worries about their friendship and their working relationship, both had become happier now that they were spending their nights together as well.

"Vey is mere." Beth grins at Robin, knowing how rare and special what she is experiencing can be.

"You can Yiddish at me all you like, I don't care," Robin

says. "He is even better than I imagined, I love him ridiculously, and he loves me, too, and Gerald announced that he is moving to Miami in a few months to head up a new restaurant there, so Michael has offered me the executive chef position when he goes."

"And they say sleeping with the boss is bad for the career!" I quip.

Robin sticks out her tongue at me. "Well, is sleeping with a doctor good for the health?"

I blush. "It certainly doesn't hurt."

"When the hell do we get to meet him, is what I want to know!" Anne throws in. "We've all known Michael for ages, and I let you guys meet Chris…."

"Soon, I promise. It's just that his schedule is so crazy right now, one of the guys in his department went off to Doctors Without Borders, and another had his army reserves unit called up, so he has had extra shifts to cover. But I promise, we will make plans for a couples evening very soon so you all can pass judgment."

"Well, if Martin is out of town I guess I could bring Jay," Lilith offers cryptically.

"I thought his name was Noah?" Robin says.

"Oh, here we go…." Anne is rolling her eyes.

"Stop that, evil thing. Not everyone can have the universe drop the perfect man in our laps. Sometimes things get complicated." Lilith has a very wicked gleam in her eyes.

"What the hell are you two talking about?" I ask, confused and amused all at once.

"All right, a couple months ago Hopleaf hired a new bartender named Jay," Lilith explains. "He just got into town, actor, of course, we've gotten to know each other a bit and have become good friends in a really short span of time, you know, the way you used to be able to do in college? Late nights up talking for hours, and four a.m. post-drinking breakfasts at IHOP, and spontaneous movies in the middle of the afternoon? He is very sweet, very smart—"

"Very young…" Anne cuts in.

"He is slightly younger than I am."

Anne snorts.

"Fine, twisted bitch that you are, he is twenty-four. Satisfied?"

"He's your boy toy. But I thought he was twenty-three?" Anne grins widely.

"You are infuriating! He is going to be twenty-four next month! And it isn't like I'm sleeping with him, we're just getting to be good friends, and spending a lot of time together, and since you all have these great new relationships and I'm the one with the pseudo-boyfriend who I never see, and the married unrequited love—I just mean that if we're going to have some nauseating lovey-dovey couple-y sort of evening, that I would at least have a substitute man to bring!" Even Lilith can't help laughing at herself.

"Don't you mean substitute boy?" Beth pokes Lilith in the ribs.

"Argh, I give up."

"C'mon, don't be like that, after all, if Beth can date Jeff Phillips, the great unwashed beast of the North Shore campus, anything is possible." I wink at Beth.

Beth decides to take one for the team. "Absolutely. Who knows, maybe this young man of yours will sweep you off your feet and make both Martin and Noah a distant memory."

"I highly doubt it. I do have a little crushlet on him, I have to admit. He isn't gorgeous, but he is sexy. Brooding, dark, mischievous, and such a mouth on him, like Ryan Phillipe…"

The owner of T's, a dashing Irishman named Cullom, wanders over to see how the party is faring, bringing another round of mimosas and clearing some of the empty plates.

"Well, I'm sure he's a lovely boy, I mean, *man,* and you can bring whomever you like," Beth says. "I'm happy to host, if you all want to potluck it at my place. I can show off all the work Jeff and I have been doing to spiffy the place up. Maybe a week from Monday?"

"I'll have to check with Harrison, but it could be good."

"Chris and I don't have plans as far as I know, count us in."

"Well, you know the restaurant is closed Mondays, so I'll check with Michael, but it should be fine."

"Martin is actually in town, I think, I'll see if he'll let me drag his ass off the couch for the evening," Lilith offers unconvincingly.

"Excellent. It's a tentative plan."

There is much more merriment before we go our separate directions, having settled not only the upcoming dinner party, but eliciting promises to keep every other Sunday morning for girlie time, now that there are so many other lovely distractions to consider.

Lilith

I usher the last of the guests out the front door, and look around my apartment, which is surprisingly not too terribly messy. I belch loudly, as I'm full of food and lots of wine. Such a classy broad I am. Then I hear my toilet flush, and a few seconds later, Jay appears in my living room.

Vital Statistics:

Jay McElroy

24, actor/bartender

Luscious lips

Likes to dance

Hates people who judge him by his age

I hope he did not hear the disgusting noise that just erupted from me. "I thought you left."

"Nope, just walked Jeanne to her car. Figured you might need some help cleaning up."

"That is very sweet of you." Phew. He appears to have missed it.

"I'm a very sweet boy."

"True enough. But I have to sit for a minute, I've been on my feet all night."

Jay pours us each another glass of wine and sits next to me on the couch, telling me about a show he was in last year.

"So I'm downstage doing my big monologue, and I look over, and in the front row this guy has taken off his prosthetic leg, put it on the floor in front of the stage, and is scratching his stump! I went completely up! I swear, I could've reached out and grabbed the thing."

I'm laughing at the image. "Did you get it back?"

"Eventually. But it was tense for a minute there."

"Total nightmare." A yawn escapes me. "Excuse me."

"I'm sorry, it's so late, you must be exhausted."

"I'm fine, really."

"Can I help you clean up?"

"That would actually be great. It's not much, I just want to get everything into the kitchen."

"Cool. It was a great party, Lil."

"It was the least I could do. I can't believe the theater wasn't going to have a closing party for you guys, after all that hard work, and such a long extension. They're so cheap! I appreciate you staying."

"It's the least I can do. You have been so terrific, introducing me to Bill, getting me the audition."

"That's what friends are for. I know how hard it is being new in town, trying to make something happen." I stand up and grab some glasses off the coffee table.

"Well, I don't know which gods sent you to me, but I thank them all."

"You goose, get the trays."

I head off to the kitchen with the glasses. When I come back into the living room, I almost run into Jay, who's carrying a couple of the decimated food trays. With a quick movement he spins away from the potential collision, with the practiced air of someone who's been in the food service industry for a reasonable amount of time.

"Careful!" He smiles at me. That really is such a yummy mouth on him.

"Do-si-do, cowboy."

I go over and start to turn off the stereo, which is cycling through a fun and funky mix of lounge music that Bill made me. Jay comes back in from the kitchen.

"Don't—I love that song." I turn it up a bit, and Jay comes over to me, takes my arm, pulls me to him and begins to dance.

"And he dances, too, be still my heart."

"Shh." Jay pulls me closer, and after a minute, kisses the top of my head. I look up and he kisses me on the mouth, tentatively at first, then deeper. I don't know exactly what to do, I mean I've sort of wanted this to happen, but I'm very confused. Still, he is a very good kisser, so I try to relax into it a little. He's walking me to the couch, now kissing my neck and shoulders, but suddenly I feel really awful and I pull away.

"Lil? What is it?"

"I'm sorry." I'm such a flipping idiot.

"I never knew I was such a bad kisser."

I laugh in spite of myself. "It's not you—you're amazing—it's me. I'm an unholy mess of a girl." Who is randomly quoting from *The Philadelphia Story,* as if I'm suddenly Tracy Lord, which I SO am not.

"Talk to me."

"I'm attracted to you, I'm, I just, I can't—" I can't even explain it to myself.

"I know, the significant other. I thought you guys were seeing other people?"

"I wish it were that simple."

"It's not him?"

"Worse."

"Herpes?"

As if. "No, goofball."

"Okay then, what?"

"I'm in love with someone." I have to stop saying that.

"Not your man."

"Not my man. A friend. See, the thing is, Martin and I have this arrangement about dating other people for a while, and I have this friend, Noah—you've met him. Anyway, I fell in love with him, quite accidentally, but he doesn't feel the same, at least I'm pretty sure that he doesn't, and I convinced myself a couple months ago to just let it go and move on, you know?"

"Yeah?" He is listening very seriously.

"I was just getting to know you, and we got to be such good friends, and I developed this attraction to you, and I was all excited because I thought if I wanted you, then I really had let go of this other thing. And I've been wanting you to kiss me so badly, but when you did I felt guilty. And I realized I wasn't feeling guilty because I was cheating on Martin, but Noah. And then I felt guilty because I was feeling guilty about the wrong thing." I'm so stupid. I even sound stupid.

"Look, Lil, I think you're great, and I'm just as happy being friends as anything, but you have to figure out your connection to this Noah guy, and what you want to do about Martin, and if those things are the same thing or not."

"They feel very separate to me."

"Are you sure that you aren't in love with this other guy as a reaction to what is missing with Martin?"

"Pretty sure."

"Do you still want to work it out with Martin?"

"Maybe. Sometimes. I don't know."

"Then you have to have closure with Noah. You have to tell him how you feel, and give him the chance to step up, or say no. If he wants you, you still have the freedom of your arrangement with Martin to find out what the deal is, and if he says no, then your heart can let go of the possibility, and you can decide what to do about your relationship."

Sure, piece of cake. "And what makes you so smart, whippersnapper."

"I read *Cosmo*."

"I drink cosmos…."

"That is so 2001."

"Ha-ha. What am I going to do with you?"

"Just what we've been doing. Hang out, laugh, watch silly movies, sit up all night listening to music and talking."

He is a totally amazing boy. "Thank you."

"For what?"

"For being my friend, for wanting me."

"That's the easy part."

"Can I ask you for a favor?"

"Anything."

"Will you stay tonight? I know it's a lot, and I know I'm all fucked up, but I would really like to have someone hold on to me. I would really like for you to hold on to me." Because I'm feeling so alone in the world right now.

"I'm at your service."

"Really?"

"Really."

"One more thing." Might as well make sure…

"Yes?"

"Could you kiss me again?"

"What for?"

"I know it's selfish, but I want to be absolutely sure that it wasn't just an initial reaction."

He leans forward and kisses me deeply, then moves back. "So platonic bed or romantic bed?"

Sigh. "Platonic. But thank you for trying."

"Hey, I'm very obliging. Anytime you need a kiss, you let me know."

"Count on it."

Jay and I finish straightening up, then go to bed. He has to leave at about ten to meet a friend for brunch, but we make plans to get together later in the evening. Then I call Bill and tell him to get his sassy self over to my apartment, *pronto.*

He arrives at eleven-thirty, carrying a box of Krispy Kremes and wearing an air of smugness that is going to irritate me within ten minutes. He follows me to the kitchen, still a minor disaster area after last night's festivities, and we grab large mugs of coffee and retreat back to the living room.

Bill looks at me with a wide grin and begins his interrogation.

"So how late did everyone stay last night?"

I'm not going to make this easy for him, even though it's why I called him and told him to come over.

"Everyone?"

"Well, when Tyler and I left it was just after one, and the only people still here were Larry, Susan, Scotty and your paperboy."

"I should've never told you he had that paper route."

"C'mon, you know I like Jay, I loved working with him on this show, and I'm seriously considering casting him in this workshop next week, but a twenty-three-year-old with a paper route is pretty funny."

"He's twenty-four. All right, I know, I gave him such shit when he told me, but it was just for his first month in town, as soon as he started working at Hopleaf he dropped it."

"So how late were you all up?" Bill is very patient when he is torturing me.

"You are so bad, why don't you ask what you want to ask?"

"Did Jay leave last?"

"Yes."

"Did he help clean up?"

"Yes."

"Did he sit and kibitz with you after the cleanup?"

"Yes."

"Did he fuck you three ways till Sunday, necessitating me getting out of bed at an ungodly hour to bring you doughnuts so you can regain your strength?"

"No."

"Bastard. So when did he leave?"

"Five minutes before I called you."

"This morning? Don't tell me you stayed up all night talking? I swear, Lil, what is it with you and this kid? You're, like, twelve."

"He helped me clean up, we had a dance, he made all the right overtures, I stopped it."

"Are you nuts? He is beyond hot. Please don't tell me he is a bad kisser, not with that pretty mouth. I'll cry."

"He is an amazing kisser. The fantasy can live untouched."

"So? Martin out of town, you guys doing the 'seeing other people thing,' sexy young thing kisses you and kisses you well, and…?"

"I choked. Couldn't do it. Probably should've done it, currently regretting not doing it, but couldn't do it. He was very sweet, and he stayed over, and we cuddled and talked, and he held me and rubbed my back, and I'm meeting him at the bar later for cocktails."

"Don't tell me, this is about Noah."

"You got it."

"You know, Lili-face, no one loves you like me. You are yin to my yang, light to my dark, milk to my cookies, Mona to my Mouse, if you were a man or I were straight we would buy a house in the country and raise children or spaniels or organic produce or something."

"I feel a but coming in here somewhere."

"*But,* you are one fucked-up puppy."

"Give me another doughnut."

"Baby, I know you have been through shit. I know that Martin tries but is no real match for you. While he is safe and comfortable, and I know you love him, you know deep down that just because he doesn't actively make you un-happy, that isn't the same as making you happy."

"Point?"

"I also know that your falling in love with Noah was a wrinkle you hadn't expected. And I think I understand why you love him, really, honey, I do. He is a lovely and lov-able man. But darling, it's attempted grand-theft husband, and that's beneath you, and you know it."

"You and I both know that sometimes the person you are married to isn't the person you are supposed to be with." Meet Rationalization Girl!

"This is still a one-sided conversation! Noah has never done or said anything to indicate that he is interested in anything more than friendship. And don't give me your 'we have great energy' speech, and don't tell me that if he were happy he would talk about his wife, or that you would have met her, or that you would even know her name. It's bullshit, honey, because it suits your purposes."

"My purposes being?"

"You want him. You want him to want you. You want the affair, the grand romance...stolen kisses, secret rendezvous, electric eye contact across crowded rooms.... You think if you get him, it means you were destined to be together, so breaking Martin's heart, breaking up his marriage, it's all validated."

"But if we got together and it was clear that we were meant to be together, doesn't that mean that both Martin and the wife aren't with the people they're meant for?" Denial is so blissful.

"Justify your love, baby. You don't rationalize your way out of this. Let's talk about Paul for a brief moment."

"I have to stop telling you everything until you get more senile, so you'll stop bringing up historical life crises for your own evil purposes."

"Paul. Focus for me. *Paul*. The man who changed your life. Made you a woman...isn't that what you said?"

"Yes."

"Let's look at him for a minute. When you were eighteen..."

"Nineteen."

"Don't fucking dramaturge me, Lilith Eden, whatever, when you were *nineteen* you go to the theater and have this life-altering experience watching this actor."

He can be so snarky. "Yes."

"And while you and your shrink have had all sorts of interesting epiphanies about the connection for you between theater and sex and love and fulfillment and defining your identity, you even got her to agree that this was an exceptional turning point for you as a sexual, romantic adult."

"Yes."

"So seven years later, when you actually MEET the man who has given you this gift, what happens?"

"We become friends."

"Uh-huh…"

"We become friends, and I fall totally in love with him."

"Right. I seem to remember that the first four months of our friendship were all about Paul, and questioning destiny."

"This is not going to be pretty."

"You got all worked up, woe was you, your heart was breaking, his reality was even better than your eighteen-year-old fantasies of him…."

"Nineteen."

"Lilith!"

"Sorry."

"God, you are infuriating. His reality was even better than your *nineteen*-year-old fantasies of him."

"Yes."

"And what happened?"

"I loved him from afar."

"You were working on two shows in a row together!" Bill smacks his head.

"I loved him from anear."

"And you got to be friends."

"And we got to be friends."

"And you got to be friends with his girlfriend."

"And I got to be friends with his girlfriend."

"Good friends."

"Very good friends."

"Essentially better friends than you and Paul."

"Essentially."

"And now they're married, and you wept with bittersweet joy at that union."

"Yes, I did."

"Because part of you will always belong to him."

"Yes, it will."

"But you know that you will never be together."

"No, we won't."

"Even if he and Laurie split up."

"Even then."

"Even if he and Laurie split up and he came to you to confess that he saw you in that audience all those years ago and has been dreaming of you for the past decade and is wildly in love and needs to be with you."

"Even then."

"Because you wouldn't do that to Laurie."

"You can't do that, it's too awful. It's inhuman."

"It's inhuman to take your girlfriend's guy."

"Oh God."

"The wife has a name. And based on what we know of Noah, if he loved her enough to marry her, you would probably like her if you met her. Maybe even be her girlfriend."

"Stop, Bill."

"Just because you don't know her doesn't make it okay."

"I know."

"You know I think your first priority should be figuring out the Martin thing, but we've had that discussion, it's your deal, however you play it. But for now, while you are still together, and not married, you have permission to see other people. And you had a smart, funny, exceptionally sexy young man in your bed last night. A guy who is the first person I have ever felt threatens my best-friend status, that is how connected you seem. A guy who completely adores you, treats you like a queen, can't spend enough time with you and clearly is attracted to you. And is, from your accounts, a great kisser. And you sent him packing because of your feelings for a man who is not yours to take, and from all we've seen, most likely doesn't feel for you what you feel for him."

"I'm one fucked-up puppy."

"This is what I'm saying."

"So what do I do?"

"You tell him."

"Tell him? I thought he wasn't mine for the taking?"

"He isn't, honey, that's why you tell him. Look, I think he is an idiot for not wanting you, for not being madly in love with you, but he isn't. You know it. I know it. We all know it. But you can't let go of that dream where you tell him and he confesses that he feels the same and you run off together. And that is why you can't fix you and Martin, and that is why you can't be open to Jay. You aren't a hopeless romantic, you are a hopeful romantic, and you need him to end it once and for all. Tell him, let him break your heart, and I'll put you back together again. Or Jay will. Or maybe even Martin will. But you gotta break it."

"Oh, Billy Boy. It's gonna hurt so bad."

"Worse than this?"

"I want to think not, but it will."

"I know."

"Why do all the men in my life give me the same advice?" Bastards.

"Who else?"

"Nico told me months ago to tell him. Jay told me last night to tell him."

"Both smart boys."

"I'm supposed to see him Thursday at Hopleaf after his rehearsal."

"Tell him."

"Okay. If the opportunity arises. Really, I will. Cross my heart and hope to die. Preferably before Thursday."

"Want me to be there?"

"Desperately, but don't."

"Fair enough. Is Jay working that night?"

"I think so."

"You'll call if you need me."

"Of course. And Bill?"

"Yes?"

"Don't be threatened by Jay. The highest he can ever get is second-best friend. Okay?"

"Okay."

"I wish Nico were here. I really miss him." As predicted, Tyler helped Nico take leave of this world with control and dignity after his release from the hospital a few months ago.

"I know. Me, too. That bitter old queen was like a mother to me."

"Split another doughnut?"

"Fuck that, one for each of us."

Bill opens the box and hands me one, taking a second for himself. He raises it up into the air and smiles at me, winking through the hole.

"To life and lust."

I smile back. "And exquisite heartbreak."

We clink doughnuts as if we've made a toast.

Bill laughs. "Ain't love grand?"

I shake my head and laugh as well.

"Grand indeed."

beth

The phone rings when I'm about halfway through Jeff's first draft of his new book, deeply relieved that I'm liking it.

"Yeah, um, is Beth there?" Oh my goodness. I glance at the box next to the phone to be sure.

"Eric." Keeping calm.

Vital Statistics:

Eric Ruppelt

42, professor

Secretly loves sci-fi

Likes being the patient one

Hates liars

"What? How did you know it was me?" He sounds flustered.

"I kept your voice. Besides, I've been expecting your call."
And I have caller ID, but that is irrelevant.

"It's been nine years."

No shit. "I know."

"You've been expecting my call for nine years?"

"No, just for the past month or so, since I bumped into
Maria."

"Did you ask her to have me call you?" He sounds very
confused.

"Of course not, I just told her to send my love, and I figured if she did, you would call."

"I didn't even know I was going to call until ten minutes ago, how did you know?"

"She put me back in your head, and you have unfinished
business with me." I'm playing this very cool.

"You always did know me better than I know myself,
Beth."

True enough. "It's what scared you most."

"Well then, I suppose you already know why I'm calling...."

"When do you want to see me?" A reasonable guess.

"Unbelievable. How about Thursday? Coffee at Lula's
after work, say six?"

"Make it seven. And Eric?"

"Yeah?"

"It's good to hear your voice. See you Thursday."

My heart is racing, I'm so glad I stayed calm. If I'm going
to get through this, I have to be a rock.

Eric.

After all this time.

So the deal is this, nine years ago, when I was in grad
school, I developed this serious fixation on one of the

teaching assistants in my department. I know it's such a silly cliché, but he was very cute, and I loved his style, and he liked my writing, and we took to having coffee together after class, or drinks after evening lectures. I made a major play for him, pretending to be fast, which I never really was, pretending it would be just sex, which it never really could, pretending I didn't have real feelings for him, which I clearly did. He was ten years older than I, which bothered him more than the fact that I might someday be in one of his classes. We fooled around a few times, but before I could try to settle him into a routine that might lead to actual couplehood, he got entangled with this very strange professor in the comparative lit department, Maria, eight years his senior, scary glam for an English professor, all dyed black hair and troweled-on makeup and long acrylic nails. None of us had ever liked her, and she was forever rambling on about her personal life in classes, much of which sounded like fiction. She was very possessive, and, within weeks of their uniting, my friendship with Eric was over. I mourned him a little, dropped out of grad school anyway and tried to forget him completely.

Then a few weeks ago I bumped into her at Sauce while I was having a lovely quiet dinner with Jess, and tried desperately not to be happy that she had not aged well. Her skin was ravaged with adult acne, making little mountain ranges beneath the still-heavy foundation. She had gained at least seventy-five pounds, and was not wearing it well, choosing the "funky caftan" look, which does nothing but make a big gal look bigger. Her hair was still a dull black, but now gray roots showed. From a distance I'm sure she could still be striking in her way, but up close she looked tired. I asked about Eric, and feigned nonchalance when she said they were, in fact, still living together. I asked her to pass along my greetings, and waited for the phone to ring.

I get to Lula's twenty minutes late, on purpose. He's the same, older, but still handsome. And he seems nervous. As I approach the table, he stands up.

"Beth, you look great." Which I do.

"Thank you."

"What can I get you?"

"Small pot of tea, milk, no lemon." And a shot of tequila if they have it....

"Still addicted to English tea, huh?"

"Yeah, can't escape it." He walks up to the counter and returns with my tea.

"So how are you?" He seems really nervous.

"I'm great, I decided to bail on the PhD and went into retail instead. My sister and I opened a small boutique a while back."

"Wow, that's amazing. And it's probably for the best. I still haven't gotten around to finishing my dissertation yet and I'm very cranky about the student loans. I heard you were living with someone."

"Yep, for almost six years. But we split up about two and a half years ago."

"I'm sorry, that part I hadn't heard."

"It was a mistake," I explain. "Whirlwind courtship, moved in too quick...when the dust settled, we just didn't have enough in common."

"So you never married, huh?"

"Nope. You and Maria any closer to the aisle?"

"No, I don't think so." Not in the least shocking.

"Have you asked her?"

"Of course, but you know how bad her first marriage

was, she won't even discuss it, says she wants to live in sin for the rest of her life." He seems so indistinct to me.

"And you, Eric, what do you want?"

"I want…I want to know if you can ever forgive me?"

"Eric, you were forgiven ages ago, it wasn't that big a deal."

"Yes, it was. I didn't mean for it to get out of hand like that, and I never meant to hurt you, the look on your face that night at the Hunt Club, it haunts me." I had berated him drunkenly one night for using me. Told him he couldn't have hurt me more had he offered to pay me for services rendered. I'm a shitty drunk.

"Eric, I was a big girl, the whole thing was my own doing. Please, don't ever give it another thought."

"You always were generous with me."

"It was no more than you deserved. But we were talking about you and Maria. Do you believe her when she says she won't marry you because of her first marriage?"

"I don't know, I mean, she was so young, and it was so long ago. And if seven years of living together doesn't prove I'm not out to hurt her, I don't know what will. I'm just not totally happy." This is written all over his face.

"Eric, you have to know if she isn't ever going to marry you. And it has nothing to do with her first marriage."

"What are you getting at?"

"Do you trust me? It's been years, but a long time ago we were good friends. You helped me through a lot of shit, and I only ever wanted your happiness, do you believe that?" More important, do I?

"Yes, of course."

In for a penny… "Leave her. Soon."

"What?"

"She's using you, always has, and you should be married with kids. She won't ever do that for you, no matter how long you hang around proving your steadfastness. Leave, and have a life before it's too late."

"You sound like she's going to kill me." Eric laughs nervously.

"Worse, she will make you doubt yourself, and she will suck the light out of your life, and leave you with nothing." Why is this all coming out like a soap opera? Oh well, I was never great at the tough conversations, nothing to do but press on.

"I can't believe all that, she just isn't into marriage, that's all."

"Eric, she lies."

"What? How do you know?"

"I always knew, and so did everyone else. All that crap about her longtime long-distance boyfriend and his sudden tragic death just when people started to expect to meet him in person. We checked for the obituaries, Eric, we checked the phone book, the address listings, it was too fishy. If there ever was a guy named Ian MacVeagh living in Colorado, under any possible spelling variation, he never had a phone, a residence, a driver's license, a death or a funeral. She made him up. And her woman-of-the-world story—finished high school at fifteen, college at nineteen, married at twenty to a raging alcoholic who abused her... Please, have you ever seen any proof, other than just her word? Photos of the husband or absentee boyfriend? Diplomas? Anything?"

"All the stuff from her first marriage and before that was damaged in a flooded basement." Such an innocent.

"Convenient, how about the amazing Ian? Albums of their precious years together?"

"She threw them out. Too painful."

"Yeah. Right. Eric, she doesn't want to marry you because deep down, she thinks some other guy is around the next corner, some better-looking, richer guy, who is the kind of guy she really deserves, and until then you are good company. And the fact that you're younger is good for her ego. Nothing a fifty-year-old single gal likes better than a forty-two-year-old live-in lover."

"And none of this could be motivated by the fact that she got me and you didn't?" Ouch.

"Eric, you and I could never have been anything other than good friends who had a fling. I knew that at the outset. It wasn't losing you to her that pisses me off, it's that you deserve so much better, and I want you to get it. I want you to be happy."

"So why didn't you say something back then?"

"Like you wouldn't have blown it off as retaliation for jilting me. You're trying to go that route now, and it's been nine years! Besides, I thought you'd eventually get tired of her."

"Why now? Why bother with me now? We fooled around a couple times a lifetime ago, and I freaked and ended a great friendship over it, but why do you care so much after all this time?"

It takes me a minute to answer, but I know I have to tell him the truth.

"Remember that night I told you I wanted to sleep with you, the first time?"

"Of course."

"Remember how I said it was fine because we were just friends, and it was just a physical-attraction thing, that we could sleep together casually, no strings, just take our friendship one step further?"

"Yeah?"

"And how it was okay, you weren't using me because I had my eyes open, and I knew what I was doing, and it wasn't like I was in love with you."

"Yeah, so?"

"I lied."

"You lied?"

"I lied."

"About which part?"

"The last part."

"You were in love with me?"

"Yeah. Well, sort of, at least I thought so. Certainly as much as I could be for where I was in my life."

"Oh God, Beth, no wonder you were so devastated, why didn't you tell me?"

"I knew the only chance I had with you was to be totally casual, and pretend like it didn't matter. If you had known, we wouldn't have ever gotten as far as we did, and broken heart and all, I wouldn't trade those few hours for anything." Well, not so bad, only took me nine years to get that out.

"My God. What the hell do I do now?"

"Eric, I've a list as long as my arm of great-looking, bright, fun, single women, any one of whom would be dying to go out with you. Go home, think about what I said and keep my number. If you leave her, call me, I'll introduce you to all of them, and you can take your pick. Or leave her and never call me again, but get out before you lose any more of your life. Just trust me one last time, you owe me that much. Besides, I think you know, deep down, that what I'm saying is true." The music swells...Lil would be proud of my drama-queen moment.

"I have to think about it. But I'll call you regardless, that is, if you think we could try to be friends again."

"Of course."

"Are you seeing anyone now?"

"Sort of. It's kind of new. He knows all about you. He's glad you finally called me. I think he wants to know if I'm still pining for you before he gets too serious about me, but he swears it's just a brotherhood thing." Actually, this is sort of a fib. Jeff was more than a little uncomfortable, but shook it off, trying to be the upstanding guy.

"And are you? Pining, I mean?"

"No, actually. I'm not the same person that I was. Plus, I really like this guy."

"Will he beat me up?" Eric is only half joking.

"Of course not."

"Good to know. I better go. Thank you, I think. I'll call you, I promise." He starts to put his jacket on.

"I'll be around."

"Yeah, somehow, I knew you would be."

And then he leaves. I quietly finish my tea and go home.

Jeff is coming over later to help me begin installing drywall in my new walk-in closet. And I think we're both feeling like we know enough to move forward, and that's about the best thing I can think of right now.

Lilith

I'm already sitting at a corner table at Hopleaf, drinking Skyy Vanilla and soda, working on my fourth cigarette in a row, when Noah arrives. He wanders over and kisses me on the forehead.

"I'm glad to see you smoking." He doesn't smoke, so I usually abstain around him, but I'm so freaked out today that I can't really be bothered.

"You are?"

"Well, not that I like that you smoke, I wish you would quit, but I'm glad to see you smoking in front of me. You shouldn't censor yourself with me after all this time."

"Not possible." Might as well jump in, after all, this is the only conversation I've been rehearsing for the past eight months.

"Why not? We've been friends for almost a year, why would you be anything other than who you are?"

Sigh. "Because, Noah dearest, who I am doesn't always conform to your rules."

"What rules?"

"Your rules, you have all sorts of rules."

"I don't recall laying down any rules between us."

"Actions and words, darlin'. I've been observing you for these months, and, believe me, you have rules, and I follow them. Because if I don't..." I don't even want to think about it, let alone say it out loud.

"What then?" He's smirking at me. He must think this is part of our bantering, but he is so very wrong.

"You might go away and not come back. And I would miss you." There, that wasn't so hard.

The smile leaves his face. "After everything we've been through, do you think there is anything you could do or say that would end this friendship?"

"Yes, I do."

"Go on, then, Madam Lilith, tell me my rules."

Deep breath. "All right. You will call me back if I call you, but you won't call me first. I'll get a hug hello and a hug goodbye. I may get a kiss on the forehead one but not both of those times, and never a kiss on the mouth. I can take your arm if we're walking together, but not your hand. We can be alone together in public places, but never in private. We can see each other twice in the same week, but if we hit three times in two weeks it will be three to four weeks before I can see you again. I can tell you everything about myself but not ask you about yourself, and if you volunteer anything about yourself, I have to be careful not to ask follow-up questions. And we can't ever talk about family or home...."

"Enough. These are not my rules."

"Whether you believe that or not, Noah, your behavior bears it out."

"I don't know what to say." He looks sort of sheepish.

"Forget it. I shouldn't have said anything."

"No, it's okay, you're just holding up a mirror, and I don't like what I see."

"I'm sorry, I didn't mean to…"

"It's okay. But see. I'm still here. We're still friends. It doesn't change anything, to be honest."

"Baby, it changes everything. I'm only coming to realize how much."

"What do you mean?"

"You know my friend Jay, the bartender? He and I are brutally honest with each other. About everything. No holds barred, especially the tough stuff. And it's amazing. But it's just how we relate to each other. You and I, we dance. We spin around, we touch on issues and joke them away, we glide through the uncomfortable stuff. We stick to music and art and theater and movies and literature and politics and everything, except what is real to us. Our hopes and dreams and fears. We don't discuss anything remotely connected to our deep-down, honest selves. At least I certainly don't."

"Because you are afraid I won't be your friend if I see who you are."

"Yes." Amazing that he can get it in such a simple way.

"Look, I know I don't talk about all that stuff. But you have to know how much I love you and value you. You have been so terrific to me, no one has ever been such a good friend, taken such care. You support my work, take me to shows, find me perfect opening-night gifts. I love spending time with you, our talks, the fact that we love all the same things. My life is so much richer because of you. There is nothing you could say that would change anything about how much I cherish your friendship."

He is so sure of himself. Well, take this…

"How about the fact that I'm so in love with you I don't know what to do anymore? Every time I see you, every time I speak to you, my heart breaks because I want you so badly, and because I know you don't want me, but until I hear you say it, I can't let go of that tiny possibility. I can't let go of the maybe, and God knows I've tried. I need to grieve for you if I'm going to get on with my life, but how could I tell you when we don't talk about these things?" Oh lordy.

Noah is silent for an uncomfortable amount of time. And one thing that is always true about me, I can't stand silence.

"I'm sorry," I say. "I'm so sorry. I've ruined everything."

"I'm married." No kidding.

"I know that."

More silence. Dreadfully long silence. PAINFULLY long silence. I can feel myself aging. And I know that this was a terrible, awful mistake. I'm going to kill Bill. And Jay. And the next time I visit Nico's grave he will be getting his own earful. But in the meantime there's all this frigging silence to deal with.

"I have to go after this drink," Noah says. "Not because we aren't friends, and not because of what you said, but because it's late."

He's a lousy liar. But I have to pretend that it's true.

"Okay."

More silence. He isn't looking at me. This sucks rocks. Finally he speaks again.

"So what is the next show you are working on?"

Small talk? *Now?* Are you fucking *kidding me?*

"Adaptation of Colette's *Claudine* novels that Kim is directing."

"Sounds cool." He won't look at me.

"I'm looking forward to it."

More silence. Noah finishes his beer. Then he stands up.

"I really should go. Rehearsal in the morning. My schedule is not too tight this week.... I'll call you." Right.

"Okay." I stand up. I'm not sure why.

Noah comes over, hugs me, pulls away, then kisses me deliberately on the mouth. He hugs me again. Then he leaves.

When he's gone, I finally let my head bow to touch the table. I'm too drained to cry, but I wish the tears were in me. I need a baptism. There is a hand on my shoulder.

"Hey there, dollface." Jay.

"Hey, yourself."

He pulls up a chair next to me and sits very close, an arm around my shoulders.

"Done?" he asks.

"Done."

"Still friends?"

"I don't think so." Sigh.

"Wanna talk about it?"

"Doesn't matter."

"Liar."

"Not tonight, another night, but not tonight."

"Whenever you want. Another Skyy?"

"I don't think so. Tequila. Patron if you have it. Double. On the rocks."

"You got it."

Jay brings my drink. And when I finish it, a second. Things get somewhat blurry. Some friends show up, I pretend to be happy—we laugh, order fries. Another drink. Before I know it, it's after two, and Jay is walking with me to my car.

"Keys, milady?"

"What?"

"Keys, princess, give me your car keys so that I can drive you home."

Jay is wonderful. I give him my keys. He opens my door and settles me into my seat. He leans over to buckle my seat belt, and I kiss the side of his neck. He's a little damp and somewhat salty, and his hair smells like smoke.

"What was that for?"

"For being my knight in shining denim."

"Anytime." He kisses the top of my head. Then he closes the car door, walks around and gets in. Sarah McLachlan's playing in my CD player, and I sing along loudly, morosely and very very drunkenly. Not to mention out of tune.

Jay's smiling, but not laughing at me, which makes him currently my favorite person in the whole world.

Once inside my house, Jay brings me an enormous glass of cold water and rummages in my kitchen. And I talk.

"I mean, that fucker, he just…fucking sat there…said nothing. Like, hello? Anybody in there?"

I didn't say I talked coherently.

"I know, sweetheart, but you are doing great."

"Nah, I'm all, you know, just crap."

Jay brings me a bowl of Campbell's chicken noodle soup, a peanut butter and banana sandwich and a stack of saltine crackers. Then he refills my water glass. For some reason, I'm ravenous, and focus only on the perfect alternating sensations of salty and sweet, hot and cold, soft and crunchy. Jay smokes while I eat.

By the time I've finished, my head is beginning to clear

a little. We go to the living room, and Jay puts on Frank Sinatra. I love Frank Sinatra. We sit on the couch, and as I gradually get more sober, I'm able to tell him more about what happened. He holds me on the couch and lets me vent.

"Guess I shouldn't have broken up with Martin, huh?"

Jay starts. "What?"

"Yep. Martin called from wherever the hell he is, and we had a tiff and I told him that we should be over."

"Why didn't you tell me before?"

"Makes me feel so stupid. I mean, at the time, it seemed like the right thing to do. How could I tell another man I was in love with him when I have a boyfriend, even if we're 'seeing other people.' That seemed really shitty. So I let him pick a fight, which he always does when he is about to come home, so that he ensures I'll spend all my time making it up to him while he is here, and instead I broke up with him. I'm an asshole."

"You are a brave, wonderful woman."

"I'm a shithead. I broke up with a good man who loves me so that I could tell someone else's husband that I'm in love with him, knowing full well that he wasn't going to pick me. I must be nuts."

"Martin isn't the guy for you, and if falling in love with Noah helped you figure that out, then it's worth it in the long run."

"My life is dung."

"It's not."

"It is old, stinky, maggoty dung."

"You are cranky, and you need some rest."

"You are a good man, you know that?"

"My mother tells me all the time."

Jay turns off my stereo and tells me to put on my pajamas like a trooper, which I do. When he comes back, he has another glass of water, three Advil and two extra-strength Tums. I take my medicine like a good girl. Jay pulls down my covers and motions for me to get in.

"Don't go?"

"I wouldn't dream of it. I'll be on the couch if you need me."

"I need you."

"That was very fast."

I move over, and Jay gets into bed. I snuggle against him, and he holds me very tightly. He rubs my back in a soothing circular pattern and hums softly. I fall asleep to the subtle vibrations.

When I wake up, it's just before dawn. I untangle myself from Jay and tiptoe to the bathroom where I pee for, like, five minutes. But I'm feeling surprisingly good. Not hungover. Not queasy. No headache, no dry mouth. Well, a little dry mouth.

I brush my teeth and drink some more water out of the tap. Then I go back to the bedroom. Jay is sleeping soundly, mouth a little open, one arm bent under his head. I sort of want to kiss him, which seems like a really bad idea, so instead I climb back into bed and curl up with my back to him. He rolls over and spoons me, slipping an arm around my waist. I can feel his breath on the back of my neck, and one of those early-morning semi-erections deftly planted right at the curve of my ass. I can't help it, I snuggle back against him, hearing his little breathy moan as the half erection becomes a full one. He pulls me tighter against him, nuzzling into my hair.

I shouldn't be doing this.

Jay is a good friend, and I'm all fucked up right now.

But he is kissing the back of my neck, and his hand has found my right breast, and my God it feels good.

I turn in his arms, and he leans in and kisses me softly.

"Jay…"

"Mmm, yes, princess?" He's kissing my eyelids, which is really unfair.

"Jay, I don't think this is a good idea."

"Don't think."

He kisses me again, harder, pressing his body against mine in the most delicious way.

"But we…"

"We're dreaming. We aren't awake."

"It doesn't feel like dreaming."

"Sure it does. A sweet dream. And when we wake up, the dream will be a lovely memory."

"Jay, I really don't think this is a dream." He is a silly boy, but his hands have found their way under my T-shirt, and his touch on my skin is awfully nice.

"If you were sure it was a dream, what would you do?"

"I would abandon myself to it." This is true. I know a lot of women whose sexual dreams don't come to fruition, but mine usually do.

"Then dream with me."

Jay rolls me over so that I'm on my back, and, pushing the T-shirt up around my neck, takes both of my breasts in his hands and suckles my nipples, one after the other.

"Oh God…"

"So sweet, just a sweet dream to keep the blues at bay."

I can't stand it anymore, I grab his head and pull him up to kiss him. His tongue is firm and insistent in my mouth, and I pull off my T-shirt while he unbuttons his shirt, kneeling over me. I run my hands over the smooth contours of his chest and stomach, the outline of his erection distinct in his boxer briefs. I trace it with my hand, feeling it twitch beneath my caress. He reaches one hand behind him and finds the waistband of my pajama bottoms, the warm cleft, the source of the wetness. His touch is sure, and whatever remaining willpower or rationality I possess is instantly gone.

Clothes jump off us at an alarming rate; we're a fierce riot of hands and mouths. It's neither lovemaking nor fucking but that sublime space between, and we're both seemingly insatiable. The sun is well up when we drift back to sleep, entwined in a sticky embrace, like those stuffed monkeys with the Velcro on their hands.

Just a sweet dream to keep the blues at bay.

I dimly remember the kiss when he rose from the bed, but by the time my eyes open with any clarity, Jay is gone. And I'm grateful for his absence, for his willingness to allow me to perpetuate the myth of the dream if I need to. I know he won't mention it, won't reference what has happened, or punish me with it at some future time. He'll let me decide whether I want to bring the dream into reality.

Three weeks later, Jay and I are sitting in the Beat Kitchen, in the back room, waiting for Tyler's band to go on. Tyler has been doing amazing since Nico left us, and I think I may have caught a little spark happening between him and his new bass player.

I can't concentrate on that at this particular moment, however, since Noah and his WIFE are sitting at a table across the room with Bill. I'm deliberately not looking in that direction, and Jay is making fun of me.

"How you doing?" he asks, knowing.

"All right, I suppose." I'm a liar. This is ridiculously uncomfortable.

"He keeps looking over here." I don't want to know that.

"Does he look forlorn?" Please?

"More curious."

"Ow." Prick.

"You're much prettier than she is."

Forgiven. "Well, clearly that makes all the difference."

"He's an idiot."

"No, he isn't, and you know it. Admit it, you liked working with him." Bill had directed them both in a staged reading the previous week.

"Appreciating someone for being a good actor and a reasonably nice guy does not mean I don't think he's an idiot where you're concerned."

I must be somewhat sensitive here. After all, Jay and I are still fairly undefined at the moment. We've neither talked about nor repeated the night we spent together, but we continue to see a lot of each other and it's still pretty clear that he would like to take a step forward. I, frankly, am beginning to lean in that direction myself, especially when I remember how good the sex was, but I'm trying to be certain that if I do go there, it's for the right reasons.

"Thank you, baby." I give him my best smile.

"You're welcome. Look, I thought you were relieved that you and Noah are still friends."

"It stings is all. I am lucky, we're still friends…it's getting less and less awkward when I see him. We had a really good time after his reading."

"*Our* reading, thank you very much. You're doing very

well with him, as far as you are concerned, but he never gave you what you needed."

"I'm doing it again, aren't I?"

"You were honest with him, and he was honest with you. I thought that was the whole point."

"Honest? I told him I was in love with him, and he asked me what my next project was. You boys, you never get your pages."

"Our pages?"

"Yes. We write these little scenarios in our heads, and we write your parts, too, and then we wait for the right time to start the scene. Only you never get your pages, and you never say what you are supposed to say, which fucks up our cues. I remember doing Noah's pages very specifically. He was supposed to tell me why we couldn't be together. He was supposed to be flattered. He was supposed to give me all my cues for the charming and heart-wrenching answers I had been practicing all those months. He was supposed to tell me that we were right for each other but that we met too late. Something. Anything. Instead, he made me sit in the deafening silence and watch him finish his drink and—"

"He's looking over here again."

I lean against Jay's shoulder, a hand playing in his hair, smiling up at him, hoping we make an envy-inducing picture.

"He was supposed to be blown away and devastated," I continue, "and instead he seemed not to care."

Jay touches my cheek gently and tweaks my nose. "I'm sorry he didn't get his pages. It's so hard to be you." You have to like a guy who wants you but will still help you make someone else jealous.

I laugh and gaze adoringly at Jay. "Fuck you."

"Let's go...."

"All right. Enough. I always knew he didn't love me, just because he didn't say it the right way..."

"He said it his way. He *was* honest with you—he reminded you he was married, and tried to go back to the way you were. I think he's handled it pretty well. After all, you are still friends. Maybe not like you were, but on the road to recovery, isn't that what you said?"

"Fine. Be logical." Out of the corner of my eye, I notice she's leaving, but Noah's staying. "Don't look, Jay."

"You are such a child. I can't believe you are older than me. Should I pass a note to him in study hall?"

"Behave yourself."

"Want I should get lost so you can be alone with him?"

"God no."

Jay begins to talk like a third-rate mafioso. "Want I should pull him aside and have a talk with him?"

"I'll kill you."

"How about we all play grown-up, and listen to Tyler's band, and have a good time like the past is the past."

"Sure. Reason. Anyone can do that."

"Anyone but you."

"I'm so much better at frantic passivity and thinly veiled neuroticism."

"No arguments here. He's coming over."

"Our father, who art in heaven..."

"You're Jewish..."

"Baruch atah Adonai, elohoynu melech ha-olum..."

Noah arrives at our table. "Hey, kids."

Jay rises, and they shake hands. "Hey, Noah, how's it going?"

"Good." Noah leans over and kisses the top of my head. "Hey you."

Sigh. "Hey you."

Jay motions to an empty seat at our table. "Join us?"

Noah hesitates. "If it's all right...I don't want to intrude...."

I smile at him. "Of course not, sit."

Jay looks at me. "Another round?"

As if he needs to ask. "Absolutely."

"Noah? What can I get you?"

"I'll go...."

"Nonsense, it's what I do." Jay is such a good guy.

"Okay, but let me buy. Guinness." Noah offers a twenty.

Jay waves it off. "I got it." He heads off to the bar, leaving Noah and me alone.

"He's pretty great." Leave it to Noah to say all sorts of things by saying essentially nothing.

"Yeah, he really is."

"You guys are clearly still very close."

Now he seems to be fishing. "Yep. And so it goes."

"It seems like he is good to you."

"He is." I wonder why I'm not making it clearer that Jay and I aren't a couple.

"Good, someone should be good to you."

"You got that right."

I'm looking at this man, this man I loved so dearly, who broke my heart such a very short time ago, and I'm feeling, well, nothing. I mean, that is not entirely true, I still care about him very deeply, but mostly I'm feeling glad that we're friends, and suddenly sure that I'm really and truly on the path to being over him.

Then I spot Jay waiting patiently at the bar for our drinks, waiting patiently for me to tell him what we're going to be to each other, and I'm realizing that perhaps I do want to see what it would be like to be with him. Noah stirs me from my reverie.

"What time is Tyler supposed to start?" Noah asks.

"Midnight."

"Pumpkin time."

"It was nice of you to come." He is sweet, even if he doesn't love me.

"I loved the CD you gave me. They are so loud." This is very true.

"Passion is everything. I'll be kind of sad when they turn this off, though, you know how I feel about Old Blue Eyes."

"Care for a dance?" He can't be serious.

"No one is dancing."

"Maybe they would if we started."

"How can I refuse? A dance and the beginning of a trend, all in one."

"Come on then." He stands up and offers his hand. I take it and he leads me to the dance floor, where he pulls me close to him and begins to sway lightly. He's not a terribly good dancer, but it feels nice, and I'm not at all aware if anyone is watching.

While we're dancing, I see Jay return with the drinks and sit at the table, watching us. He lights a cigarette. Bill wanders over, drink in hand, and joins him at the table. I can only imagine what they're saying. Jay looks over and tilts his head at me. I smile at him in a way that I hope conveys what I'm thinking, which is that tonight I'm going to ask him home with me. For real.

The song ends and Noah and I go back to the table just as Tyler appears from the back room carrying a Budweiser.

"Sorry about the timing mess up, we're up in five," he says to the table. He looks very rock 'n' roll in his tattered jeans and black mesh shirt.

Bill raises his glass. "We should have a toast first. To the first professional performance of Tyler's little band."

"To having intrepid friends in the house," Tyler says.

I raise my glass. "To Nico, who would have hated it."

Noah picks up his Guinness. "To life."

Jay looks at me. "To love."

Bill reassumes control. "To tomorrow, and tomorrow and tomorrow."

We all clink glasses and sip, and Tyler runs off for last-minute preparations.

Bill puts his glass on the table and motions us all to pay attention. "Well, since you are all here, before Tyler makes talking impossible, I suppose I should give you some news."

He hadn't mentioned anything to me. *"News?"*

"Sort of. A show."

Jay looks up. "What show?"

"New play. Ensemble piece. Sweet, funny, romantic...and brilliantly witty. Stoppard meets Cinderella."

Noah speaks first. "Congrats. Who's producing?"

"The little company that could...our *Tartuffe* friends want us back."

I look over at him. "Us?"

"Who has an opening in November?"

Jay jumps in first, ever the eager unemployed actor. "I'm free."

Noah is right behind him. "Me, too."

Well, I'm sure not going to let them all play without me. "Me three."

Bill looks at us like the proud patriarch he fancies himself. "So here's the deal, Jay, my sweet, for you the slightly dopey, but exceptionally handsome, young suitor…"

Jay laughs. "A stretch…"

Bill pats him on the shoulder. "Clearly. Noah, his wise adviser, who falls for the elder sister of the object of Jay's affection…"

Noah bows his head. "What else. And for Lil?"

I know the answer to this one. "Whipping you all into shape," I say.

Bill stops me. "No, dear, for you, the aforementioned sister. She is the unquestionable star of the piece, and steals every scene."

I don't believe it! "You have got to be kidding."

"I never kid about the work."

"I have no words." Which is a first for me.

Bill reads my mind. "Well, that is a first. Quick, my children, let us commemorate this brief silence."

We all toast, and hug Bill. Suddenly the canned music ends, the band enters and Tyler grabs the center-stage microphone.

"Thanks so much for coming out tonight, we would like to dedicate this first song to our friends in the house." We hoot and holler for him.

They begin to play, a tornado of guitars. Jay comes up behind me, half shouting, half whispering in my ear.

"Are you going to be okay with this?"

"Are you kidding? Acting again? I wish we were starting tomorrow! Of course, I'm scared shitless, but in a good way."

"I meant Noah. You're going to be playing lovers, won't that be hard?"

"Not as hard as watching you fawn all over whatever pretty little picketytwick Bill finds to be the ingenue."

"Why?"

"I'm not so interested in competition."

"You are always first in my heart."

"Back at 'cha, handsome."

"Lil, are you flirting with me?"

"Very badly."

"Still trying to make him jealous?"

"Trying to make you see that I don't care if he is jealous anymore."

"Really?"

"Really."

"So now what?"

"I dunno. We listen to the band. Get tipsy. Go home together."

His eyes twinkle at me. "Looking for happy dreams?"

"Looking for happy reality."

His face goes still, as it sinks in that I'm not playing with him.

"Are you sure?" He looks as if he is afraid to smile. So I smile for us both.

"No, are you?"

"I suppose not."

"But we can find out together, right?"

"Absolutely."

He leans forward, and I lean toward him, and the kiss is even more deafening than the music.

dinner for ten, as told by beth

I'm setting the table when Jeff slides his arm around my waist and begins kissing the back of my neck.

"Cut that out, bubba, we have company arriving momentarily." But even as I say it, I'm turning in his arms and smiling at him.

Jeff kisses me deeply and whispers, "We could be very quick, Beth...."

"Mmm. It is a lovely thought, but I think I'll make you wait until they leave...I love the idea of you aching for me all night, it will make you very attentive."

"Cruel and heartless. But fair enough." He kisses my cheek and returns to the kitchen where he's making his famous black bean soup. I've already assembled the salad, just Boston lettuce, cucumbers, red grapes and toasted pecans with crumbled goat cheese, and a homemade dijon vinaigrette waiting. Robin and Michael are bringing the main course, Jess and Harrison are in charge of appetizers and wine, Anne and Chris are bringing side dishes and Lilith and Jay are picking up dessert, since they're coming straight from costume fittings for their new show and won't have had time to cook. It's likely to be a motley meal, since everyone has promised their specialties, and Lord knows potluck is always a strange sort of compilation, but I'm excited to see everyone, especially to meet Harrison and Jay for the first time.

Petey barks twice, just before the buzzer rings, and Jeff calls out that he will answer the door. It's Jess and Harrison, and once Jeff relieves them of the case of wine and the grocery bag of treats, there are quick introductions all around. Jeff takes Harrison on the tour of the warehouse, showing off all the projects he and I have been doing, while Jess and I work on hors d'oeuvres in the kitchen.

"My God, he is gorgeous." I poke Jess in the ribs, and then get back to arranging toasted pita triangles around the stuffed Edam cheese ball Jess made from her mother's recipe.

"Shut up." Jess is grinning ear to ear. "Jeff is looking pretty good himself these days." She fills a couple small bowls with spiced nuts.

"He really is, isn't he?" We are grinning openly at each other.

"Heard anything else from Eric?" she asks.

"He called yesterday, wanted to have lunch this week, but I put him off. I don't know how ready I am to have him back in my life yet. Plus, I think Jeff is still a little leery, you know?"

"Is it safe to come over there, or are you still talking about us?" Jeff yells good-humoredly across the room.

"As if we don't have better things to discuss than you two monkeys," I yell back. Harrison and Jeff cross the room, and

Harrison asks if I'll preheat my oven to warm up his appe-tizer, while Jess begins laughing.

"What is so funny?" I ask.

"Wait till you see…" replies Jess.

"Taste, before you judge! This was the hit of every New Year's party my mom ever threw." Harrison pulls a foil-wrapped tray out of the bag, and lifts the cover to reveal what looks for all the world like an enormous roasted penis covered in some sort of glaze. I look over at Jess, slightly stricken. Jess dissolves in giggles just as Jeff wanders over and says, "What the hell is that thing?"

"Baked salami," says Harrison, pinching Jess, who is try-ing to get hold of herself.

"I see. What is that goop on it?" Jeff pokes the end of the thing with the tip of one finger, while I smack his hand away.

"Secret sauce." This sends Jess into another round of laughter.

"No secrets in this group, mister, fess up." I'm very curi-ous about the sweet-and-sour smell coming off the thing.

"Half chili sauce, half grape jelly, dash of powdered mus-tard," Harrison says proudly. Jeff's jaw drops open.

"That was my mom's secret sauce for sweet-and-sour meatballs!" Jeff seems genuinely shocked.

"Oh my dear Lord." I can't begin to imagine what it could possibly taste like.

"Look, just promise me you'll try one bite when it's ready, and if you hate it, I promise never to foist one upon you ever again." Harrison smiles confidently at the three of them.

"Well, I'll try anything once!" I say gamely.

"He made me promise to try it before we came, under penalty of sleeping on the couch tonight," Jess confesses.

"I'm in," Jeff says, "but I'm a little afraid of what the combination of baked salami and black bean soup is going to do to my digestion."

"There will be no living with any of us tonight!" I say. "If these relationships survive the evening it will be a true testament to deep love."

"Or intestinal fortitude!" Jess says.

Harrison puts the salami, in all its grotesque glory, into the oven to warm through, taking an opportunity to tell the bemused trio that it's Vienna's finest, and he had to make a special trip to the factory-outlet store on Damen to ensure the approval of the sensitive palates of such a culinary group. Jess and I wonder aloud what Robin and Michael will make of it.

The buzzer rings again, and while Jeff gamely unpacks the wine, Robin and Michael, as if on cue, bustle in, their arms laden with large coolers. They have a glow about them that is unmistakable, these are people who are very much in love. They greet the rest of the group eagerly, and begin to unpack goodies, when the buzzer rings yet again, and Anne and Chris enter with their own treats. Robin and Michael have brought a large stuffed veal breast and a perfectly roasted capon, in case anyone has a moral opposition to veal. Anne and Chris have brought a potato gratin, cumin-and-saffron-scented cauliflower and creamed spinach. By the time all these delights are arranged on the buffet, Lilith and Jay arrive carrying a box from Sweet Mandy B's Bakery that they won't let anyone open, saying that dessert is a surprise. The girls exchange meaningful glances, knowing that Lilith is very nervous about bringing Jay into the group, but young as he is, he slides easily into the conversation, and soon the five men are all in the bathroom admiring Jeff's tiling handiwork and using words like *router* and *miter* like refugees from a *This Old House* convention.

We women take the kitchen in hand, under Robin's immediate and sure command, when the men announce that they're going to take Petey for a walk.

"Oh no," says Lilith.

"What?" I ask, just as they leave with a delighted Petey in tow.

"They're going to get high," Lilith replies.

"Really?" asks Anne. "How do you know?"

"Because Jay's good friend Al stopped by earlier, and Al grows some of the best weed on the North Side, and always brings Jay a couple joints when he gets a new batch he's proud of. I jokingly suggested he bring them along, and told him if things started to feel uncomfortable for him, he'd have a way to mellow out. And he said he would be plenty mellow, but maybe the rest of the guys would need it."

"Do you really think they're smoking?" I'm concerned about Jeff—he has been sober for a few years, but temptation is temptation.

"Probably," Jess surmises. "Harrison and Mark used to smoke a lot, and still share a joint sometimes after dinner. I'm sure if it's available, he wouldn't hesitate."

"Chris and Warren have an annual stoner weekend," Anne says. "Donna says they rent a cabin in the Indiana Dunes and Warren buys a quarter ounce from a friend of his at work and they spend two days getting high and eating Cheetos and Mallomars. She figures better a once-a-year brotherly bacchanal someplace safe than a secret habit, especially with kids."

"Someone in the kitchen is always packing, and when Michael gets stressed, he always seems to know which one,"

Robin says. "Frankly, I've been known to indulge, myself, after a long night."

"Well, what kind of hostess would I be if I didn't offer at least a decent alternative! Ladies, I think shots are in order!"

"Absolutely, Beth!" Jess says.

"I'm in," says Robin.

"Not without us!" Anne throws an arm around Lilith.

I grab my martini shaker and fill it with ice. I pour in a healthy slug of Skyy vodka, a splash of triple sec and a larger splash of a Triple Lime Liqueur which tastes like Rose's lime juice but packs a wallop. I shake the concoction while Anne and Lilith rim five shot glasses with sugar.

"To the best girlfriends in the world!" I raise my glass.

"To the loveliest boys, who worship as they should!" adds Lilith.

"To good food and great sex!" Robin says, blushing prettily.

"To surprises!" Anne offers.

"To surviving the appetizers." Jess gives us a wink, and downs her shot.

By the time the guys return from their walk, pink of cheek and slightly pink of eye, they've settled themselves on the couches and are tucking into the Edam with great relish. Jeff immediately comes over to me, and kisses me deeply and meaningfully on the mouth, then looks me dead in the eye. He tastes of his own lovely self, and his eyes are clear and bright, and I'm grateful for his strength and willpower.

Harrison brings a plate to the table, layered with slices of his masterpiece, and a basket of rye cocktail bread. He makes a small sandwich and hands it to Jess with a flourish. Jess crosses herself and takes a bite.

"Oh my God," she says, still chewing, "this is *really* good!"

"I don't believe it," I say. "Make me one."

Harrison passes sandwich after sandwich to the waiting crowd, and soon everyone is laughing, utterly shocked at how delicious the unlikely recipe is.

"It's settled, you can stay!" Anne says.

Three hours later we're crashed out all over the living room. Jeff and I are curled up in one corner of the couch, with Anne and Chris a mirror image on the other end. Robin and Michael have commandeered the love seat; Michael's long legs are propped on the arm, his head in Robin's lap, where she is aimlessly playing with his hair. Jess and Harrison are sharing the overstuffed armchair and ottoman, and Jay is sitting in the other chair, Lilith on the floor between his legs enjoying a neck rub. Petey is sprawled next to Lil, his head resting on her shin. We've eaten copiously, polished off nine bottles of wine and managed to stuff all the leftovers into my vintage refrigerator.

"Who's ready for dessert?" asks Lilith when Jay finishes his mini-massage.

"There is always room in the dessert compartment!" I say. "I'll put on some coffee."

We head over to the kitchen.

"Jay's great," I whisper to Lilith.

"Thanks. It's really weird, he is so young, but I like him, I really do."

"Age is just a number. He's obviously crazy about you, and you seem really happy."

"It's funny, Beth, there's just no pressure," Lilith says. "I can be who I am, enjoy myself, and I don't worry about making the right impression or projecting enough strength, it's just, I don't know, easy."

"As it should be. Heard anything from Martin?"

"He's in town—I'm supposed to have lunch with him on Sunday. Says he wants to talk some things through face-to-face. What about Eric?"

"He wants to see me, but I'm not going there yet. I can talk to him on the phone for now, but I'm playing possum a little when it comes to getting together in person."

"Worried you might be tempted?"

"No, just out of respect for Jeff. It's still so new, I want it to be a little more solid. Eric waited nine years to get my friendship back, if he wants it, another few months won't kill him."

I put coffee mugs, cream and sugar on a tray and walk back to the living room, where a lively discussion about the pros and cons of living together has erupted, divided squarely along gender lines.

"It's such a better deal for the women," Michael is saying. "Half the financial burden lifted, plus you never have to do anything around the house you don't like...no more taking the garbage out or shoveling the walk."

"Oh yeah, instead we're washing your stinky workout clothes, trying to get your whiskers cleaned out of the sink and attempting to teach you how to actually put the new roll of toilet paper *on* the roll instead of on the counter next to the toilet!" Robin argues. "Beth, help me out here!"

"Leave me out of it. I plead the Fifth."

"Careful, Jeff, old man, if she's keeping mum it's just because you haven't moved into this place yet, and she doesn't want to scare you off." Harrison laughs, and Jess pokes him in the ribs.

"Not to worry, Harrison, old chap, I don't believe in cohabitation outside of marriage," Jeff says.

The silence is nearly deafening.

"You're kidding, right?" I'm clearly taken aback.

"Nope, dead serious," Jeff says. "I think it's a cop-out. Two people live together, but they still have that back-door loophole in case it doesn't work out…so if they hit a rough patch, there isn't too much impetus to work through it, after all, they're just renting! It's bullshit, if you ask me. I think if you love someone, are exclusively devoted to them and the relationship, want to live with them, you should get married, make the real commitment and not pussyfoot about."

"But what if your living styles are totally incompatible? Shouldn't you know that before making everything legal?" Jay wonders.

"What about compromise?" Jeff answers. "What about making adjustments? Look, I'm not advocating arranged marriages here, we all spend plenty of time together, nights and weekends and vacations, unless someone has some really strange private habits that they keep secret, I just think it's too easy to make the relationship disposable."

"But divorce is so easy now, isn't it just semantics?" asks Chris.

"Maybe, I'm not trying to preach conversion here, guys, whoever wants to play house without facing the rabbi or priest or City Hall, you have my blessing and support. It just isn't something I could do, that is all. If I love her enough to live with her, then I love her enough to marry her first."

"Well, you make some interesting points, but I for one am glad that I won't have to schlep my toothbrush in my purse anymore!" Anne snuggles into Chris, knowing that in a few short weeks they will be moving into their new place together.

"I'm looking forward to that whole laundry and toilet paper service!" Chris says, and Anne elbows him in the ribs.

"I'm actually leaning toward Jeff's philosophy," Michael says.

Robin pushes him off her lap. "You are not!"

"Am so."

"So then why did you say the other night that you didn't want me to ever leave your place, and that you were glad my lease was coming up in a few months?"

"Because I don't want you ever to leave my place, and I'm glad your lease is coming up. Plus, I think your grandmother's armoire is going to look great in the living room."

"Then why are you saying you agree with Jeff if you want me to come live with you?" Robin looks confused, and her cheeks are pinkening.

"Oh my GOD!" My jaw drops.

"Wow." Anne's eyes fill with tears.

"Oh, honey…" Jess smiles at Robin.

"What the hell am I missing?" Jay asks Lilith.

"Michael is asking Robin a very important question, aren't you, Michael?" Lilith says.

"So very perceptive, ladies, how is it that my little peach crumb over here doesn't read between the lines nearly as well as the four of you?"

"What? WHAT!?! This is so unfair, you guys, I've had too much wine to try to play games, and I'm no good at riddles, and…oh. Oh my." Robin's mouth continues to move but no sound comes out as Michael slides off the love seat and kneels on one knee before her.

"You are my best friend, my partner, my lover, my reason for breathing. I feel like my whole life has been one long exercise preparing me to love you. Will you do me the honor of being my wife?" Michael reaches into his pocket and pulls out a small velvet box.

"Of course I will. I love you." Robin is crying and kissing Michael, and he pulls the ring out of the box and puts it on her finger, and soon all the women are laughing and shouting, and the men are slapping Michael on the back and offering congratulations.

"It's so beautiful!" Jess says, looking at the perfect two-carat emerald-cut diamond in the simple platinum setting, flanked by diamond baguettes.

"That's the most romantic thing I've ever seen, it's like a movie!" Anne is hugging Robin tightly.

"Blah blah blah, whatever, I want dessert!" jokes Lilith.

Coffee is poured all around, along with ponys of a twenty-year-old tawny port that Michael brought, and at last the bakery box is opened.

Cupcakes. Two dozen chocolate cupcakes with vanilla frosting, decorated with hearts and cupids. The assembly laughs.

"Lil, you're clairvoyant," Anne says.

"Not really," Lilith explains. "I helped him pick out the ring."

"You cow! Why didn't you tell us?" I throw a pillow at her.

"I asked her not to," Michael jumps in to defend her. "I needed a female opinion, but I wasn't prepared for the whole *mashpooka* at once!"

"*Mishpucha,*" Robin corrects him and smiles.

"You're teaching him Yiddish!" Anne is laughing at Michael's dreadful pronunciation.

"I'm trying," Robin says, kissing her fiancé on the cheek.

In spite of the gargantuan meal, they each manage two of the decadent cupcakes, and polish off the port with ease. A little after midnight the party breaks up, and by 1:00 a.m., in five different apartments in Chicago, there is joyous love being made.

anne

I collapse on the couch in a sticky sweaty mess while Chris pays the movers and ushers them out the door. He laughs when he sees me sprawled out, leaning on the enormous plastic garbage bags that hold our coats.

"Beer, *principessa?*"

"Yes, please."

Chris heads to our back porch, where a full cooler awaits the arrival of Beth and Jeff, who are coming over tonight to help unpack and arrange furniture. He returns with two ice-cold Budweisers and parks himself on the floor next to my feet.

"How on earth did two tiny apartments contain so much crap?" I wonder aloud, looking around at the jumble of furniture and boxes that fill every inch of available space in our new living room.

"I don't know, but I'm glad it's all in here. One more trip up those stairs might very well have done me in."

Our new place is a third-floor walk-up in an old brick building in Wicker Park. It's a spacious two-bedroom with tall ceilings and hardwood floors. We painted last week with the blessing of our new landlord, so everything is crisp and smells new, but the unpacking that faces us is daunting to say the least.

The buzzer rings just as we're finishing our beers, and Beth and Jeff enter carrying steaming pizza boxes from Bacino's.

"Oh, let's eat instead of unpacking!" I offer, since it sounds like so much more fun.

"Uh-uh, lazybones, no food for you until we have some semblance of order around here." Chris pulls me off the couch.

"Taskmaster."

"Sorry, kiddo, he's right," Beth says. "I'll dump these in the kitchen, they'll keep just fine." Jeff gets a tour from Chris, and I begin to empty the bags of their coats and hang them in the hall closet. Beth returns carrying a folder and looking stricken. I'm about to be in deep doo-doo.

"What's this, Anne?" she asks. I feign dumb.

"What?" She'll never suspect.

"This folder was sitting on your kitchen table. I moved it to put the pizzas down, and something fell out. It appears to be an application for the occupational therapy program at Rush. With your name on it." Beth is far more dangerous when she is calm and specific.

"It's just something I'm thinking about." For, like, two years.

"This is a completed application for the fall," Beth says. "Seems your thinking is reasonably precise."

"It's just something I think I want to do, something I think I would be good at—"

"What about the store?" If looks could kill, someone would be saying kaddish for me.

"Beth, that was always your dream, not mine. I like hanging out with you, working with you, but it isn't very rewarding personally."

"I'm sorry, didn't realize that you were so put upon, that it was such an insult to your delicate sensibilities to do such meaningless work." Damn, she is really pissed.

"Beth, it isn't like that, you know I have a lot of respect for you and the way you have made a success of the store."

"We! *We* have made a success of the store, *our* store, you aren't some fucking employee, you're my partner. Did it not occur to you that perhaps you could've mentioned to me that you were considering leaving?" Beth's eyes are shiny with the beginnings of angry tears.

"Beth, it isn't a full-time program, and I'm still going to need to support myself. I'm not leaving, I'm just going to change some of my hours around to accommodate classes."

"Sure, for now! Or are you planning on offering occupational therapy in the dressing rooms after you finish school?"

"Beth, please, don't be angry, we will have plenty of time to work out the logistics, maybe by the time I finish you will be doing so well you will want to buy me out…."

"You little cow! I don't want to buy you out, I don't even need you in the damn store. I'm trying to figure out why the hell you didn't fucking tell me!" Now Beth is yelling, and Jeff and Chris appear from the back of the apartment looking concerned. "Back off, boys, sister business." Chris and Jeff retreat immediately. Cowards.

"Beth, I didn't want to hurt your feelings. Besides, I might not even get in. I didn't want to get you all worked up until I knew what was what."

"I never would have kept a secret like that from you. Every day we see each other, sisters, best friends, business partners...I can't believe you would have something this big and not share it with me."

She's right. I've been such an idiot. Now I'm crying.

"No way, kiddo. You can't make me comfort you for fucking up. I have to leave before I say something I regret. You unpack, get your shit together. I'll see you in a couple days and we can deal with this then. Mom and Dad know?"

"No. I wanted to tell you first."

"Right. Jeff?" Beth calls down the hall. Jeff and Chris both appear. "We're going. Sorry, Chris, can't do this right now." Chris hands Beth and Jeff their coats while I stand in my new living room in total disbelief. Then they're gone.

Chris comes over and puts his arms around me. "Shh. It's okay. She'll get over it in a day or so."

"I should've told her," I say. "I just didn't want her to talk me out of it." Beth is so logical, if she had come up with any plausible argument against my applying, I probably would have chickened out.

"Maybe you don't give her enough credit. She likes making stuff happen for you. If you had gone to her and said you really wanted this but didn't want to jeopardize the store, she would have come up with a hundred ways to fix it for you. But you didn't give her the chance to be supportive."

"Whose side are you on anyway?"

"I just think she is within her rights to be pissed. And I think she will get over it. In the meantime, what the hell are we going to do about this apartment?" He wipes my face and kisses me gently.

"I dunno. Looks like it's just you and me, kid."

"I happen to like having you all to myself." Chris starts to tickle me.

"Stop tickling! I want to leave Beth a message before she gets home."

"Okay."

I haven't been this nervous on the phone in years.

Beep. "Beth, it's Anne. I'm so sorry about tonight, I didn't mean to hurt your feelings, and I didn't mean to keep this a secret from you. I'm a total idiot, and I don't blame you for being mad, but please forgive me. Pretty please? I'll call you tomorrow."

Chris walks into our new bedroom and sits next to me on the unmade bed.

"Leave her a message?"

"I did indeed. I just hope she forgives me." I hate fighting with Beth, we almost never do it, so when it happens it's really awful.

"She will, don't worry. In the meantime, let's get our heads around this place for tonight, okay?" Chris takes my hand.

"I'm sorry I ruined our first night in our new place."

Chris leans over and kisses me. "The night isn't over yet, you have room to make it up to me." He grins.

"I'll do what I can." I smile back at him.

jess

Harrison and I race up the stairs to his condo, pained expressions on our faces.

"Me first!" yells my beloved, throwing off his coat as he hurries down the hall, leaving me pacing and sweating in the living room.

"Hurry up, mister, or you're in big trouble!" I yell after him.

We've just returned from dinner with Mark and Gemma at Geja's on Armitage, truly one of the best places in Chicago. A dark quiet boîte with the feel of an old wine cellar, Geja's has been doing proper fondue for ages, and the classical guitarist accompanying the delicious food makes it one of the ultimate romantic meals of all time. Unfortunately for us, we had much wine and water with the meal, and coffee after, and then got stuck in traffic on the way home, so by the time we got here, we both had to pee something fierce.

I hear a flush, and mince down the hall. The door opens, and a very relieved-looking Harrison exits, making way for me.

Ahhhhh. I've never been so happy to urinate in my whole life.

When I return to the living room, Harrison is sprawled on the couch.

"I ate too much." He rubs his belly, belt and top button of his slacks undone.

I collapse beside him. "Me, too."

"Mark and Gemma seem great, don't they?" Harrison muses.

"They do indeed. I wonder when she's due?"

"Due?" Harrison looks puzzled.

"She's pregnant."

"Did Mark tell you that?" Harrison looks shocked, surely Mark would have mentioned it to him, too.

"Nope."

"Did Gemma say something?"

"Nope."

"So what makes you so sure, smarty-pants?"

"She only had one glass of wine, and she didn't even drink half of it. Her face is a little fuller and her boobs are a little bigger. And she ate *everything,* and you know how she usually takes those little portions. I would bet that she is in her first trimester, and they're waiting to be sure everything is okay before telling us."

"You're right. I hadn't put it together. You should be a detective."

"I'm a genius, it's true."

"Can I ask you something?" Harrison puts an arm around my shoulders.

"Yes, darling." I scootch over next to him.

"Why were you looking at her boobs?"

"I'm a girl, we always look at other girl's boobs."

"That really sort of turns me on, have to say." Harrison smiles at me lasciviously.

"Easy, lover, I adore you, ache for you, but I need at least another two hours to digest."

"Fair enough. To be honest, I think the spirit is willing but the body is weak." He kisses my forehead and goes to the bedroom to get into comfier clothes. Down the hall I hear his pager go off. "Fuck" is the muffled response. I hear him on the bedroom phone before he reappears. "Sorry, kiddo, have to go back to the hospital."

"Poor baby. Will you be very late?"

"Dunno. Car wreck, two-year-old in the back wasn't in a car seat, and a five-year-old in the front with no seat belt. They're calling us all in."

"Maybe I should go back to my place tonight."

"Stay if you like, but I know you're teaching in the morning, so if it's easier for you to be near school, that's okay, too. If you want, you can drop me at the hospital and take my car—I can grab a cab home if there's even enough time before my shift tomorrow."

"Okay."

I drive Harrison to Children's, arriving at the same time as two ambulances, and he rushes out of the car and into the E.R. I'm back at home in a jiffy. I notice my machine is blinking.

Beep.

"Jess, it's Amy. You might want to call Mom. She and Dad had a big fight, and I think they've maybe broken up. She said she wasn't going to call you right away because she didn't want you to say you told her so. So don't say you told her so, okay?"

Shit.

Beep.

"Hey, it's Beth. We have to think about throwing Robin a shower. I was thinking we should all get together at my place some night this week to make plans. Give me a call and let me know what your schedule looks like."

Beep.

"Hi, it's Gemma! Mark and I just wanted to say how great it was to see you guys tonight. What a super place! And you and Harrison seem really good. Let's do it again soon!"

Beep.

"Jess, it's Lilith, are you there? Pick up if you are there. Hello? Crap. Okay, look, call me if you get this, okay. Even if it is late."

Goodness.

I call Mom first.

"Hello?" She sounds very tired.

"Mom, it's Jess."

"Hi, sweetie, how are you?" Brave face, my mother.

"I'm fine. More important, how are you?"

"Amy is such a little tattler." Well, pissed off is one way to go.

"Amy just wanted me to call you and see how you were doing, she's worried about you. Wanna talk about it?"

"Not really. Not much to tell. Your father proposed and I turned him down. Said I didn't want to get married again. Which I don't. Told him I love him and enjoy his company, but that 'wife' still has too many negative connotations for me, and I would rather live in sin, and asked if he would move in with me. He yelled at me for not trusting him, for not really believing in him. He said he was no Kurt Russell and I was certainly no Goldie Hawn, and he had no interest in a domestic partnership, that he wanted a wife. I said I didn't want to be a wife. He said he didn't want to be a roommate. So I said maybe we shouldn't be together if we wanted such different things and he said he wished I would have told him that before he wasted six thousand dollars on therapy. I offered to write him a check. He left." Holy crap.

"Oh, Mom, I'm so sorry. At the therapy sessions it all seemed to be going so well." Told you so, told you so, told you…

"I know you didn't approve, sweetheart."

"I just wanted you to be happy. I still want you to be happy. Do you think it's over for good?"

"I do. I think we got caught up in the romance of it all. Unexpected reconnection on the cruise, older, wiser, great sex…"

"Mom!" Ewww.

"Oh, be a grown-up, Jessica. Good Lord."

"Fine. But keep it PG–13, would you, please?"

"Ultimately I think I like my life as it is, and I clearly don't love your father enough to make the kind of sacrifices that you should want to make for someone you want to spend your life with. Better we found out now." She sounds okay. Sad, but resigned, and sort of strong.

"I'm really proud of you, Mom. Do you need anything?"

"No, sweetie, I'm okay. You know what you can do for me?"

"What?"

"Give your dad a break. Just because he and I didn't work out this time, either, I do think he is committed to rebuilding his relationship with you and Amy and he wants to be in your life. Let him. He really is a good man. Okay?"

"Okay, Mom. I'll do the best I can."

"All I ever ask. How is everything with you?"

"Good, Harrison and I had dinner with Mark and Gemma, but he got called in for an emergency, so I came home. Classes are good, all is well."

"I like your young man very much. Think he's a keeper?"

"I like my young man very much, too, and yes, I think he may very well be one to hang on to."

"Good."

"Thank you for calling to check up on me, sweetie, I'm fine. I'll talk to you in a day or so."

"Okay, Mom. Call if you need me."

"I will. Good night."

"'Night."

Wow. Such drama. I change into my pajamas and am halfway through grading a stack of freshman papers when I remember that I have to call Lilith. It's just after midnight, but she said call late....

"Hello?" Good, she sounds awake.

"Lil, it's Jess. Got your message—what's up?"

"I'm in trouble. Big trouble. 'Do not pass Go, do not collect two-hundred-dollars' trouble."

"Boy trouble?"

"You betcha."

"Okay, what happened?" What is in the frigging *air* today?

"Okay, so things have been a little weird with Jay lately, you know, he's just still really young, and as mature as he is, there is still some stuff that is sort of irritating."

"I know this, but you said the good was outweighing the bad."

"It was. But the scale has started to shift. A lot. He wants to go out clubbing and take Ecstasy, and I want to stay home and watch BBCAmerica. He wants to take me to these parties his friends have with eight thousand people crammed into a studio drinking warm keg beer, and all I can think is 'dinner parties or Ravinia would be nice.'

"He doesn't have a car, so I have to drive him everywhere. He has a roommate, so we can't ever sleep at his place, which is good, because it's seriously skanky in a bad-bachelor-pad way. I feel guilty letting him pay for dates, because he has no money, but then I'm resentful of always going dutch. I think if we stay together much longer we're going to kill the friendship."

"Oh, Lil, I'm so sorry. But it has been a pretty good run, you've certainly had some fun. I don't think any of us thought it was going to be forever, did you?"

"No, not deep down, I guess not. Then there is Martin…"

"Hold up, since when is there Martin?"

"I saw him a couple weeks ago. He took me for dinner at Sauce, picked me up, picked up the goddamn tab, it was glorious!"

"But it was Martin." Boring. Oh so boring.

"I know, I know. It was just nice to be treated like a grown-up. To be *with* a grown-up. To order the shrimp appetizer *and* the steak Tommy and not think twice about the price. I can't get back together with him, but he wants to. I shouldn't, tho', right?"

"Lilith."

"Okay, I know. That's what Bill said anyway. But I do have to break up with Jay, right?"

"Sounds like you should before you ruin the friendship. Think he'll understand?"

"I hope so."

"Poor Lil. Do you need anything?"

"Wanna break up with him for me? Let me know how it turns out?"

"I would if I could. But you know you can call me if you need me after, okay?"

"Okay. We on for brunch Sunday?"

"Yeah, I think so."

"Beth and Anne make up yet?"

"They talked yesterday. Beth is still a little mad, but I think they'll be fine in a couple weeks."

"Okay. Well, thanks for the talk, Jess, you are such a good friend."

"It's what I'm here for, you call anytime."

"'Kay, 'night."

"Good night."

Good Lord.

I pick up my phone and call Harrison's.

"Hi, it's me. I just wanted to say that I love you very much. I hope tonight turned out okay, call me when you get a chance."

Nothing like other people's relationship woes to make you appreciate the good thing you have yourself.

I go into the bathroom and find I'm out of cotton balls to take my makeup off with. I dig around under the sink, moving aside the box of tampons I bought a few weeks ago. The *still-unopened* box of tampons. I remember that I should've gotten my period at least two weeks ago. Shit. With all the stuff going on at school, I totally didn't even register that my period was late.

I go out to my bag and find my calendar, counting back to my last period. Seven weeks ago. Seven. Shit shit shit.

That can't be right. But I know it is. I throw my coat on, run downstairs and jump into Harrison's car.

The twenty-four-hour Walgreen's is very bright. I grab three different early-pregnancy tests, try not to notice the sympathetic stare of the checkout girl, and rush back to my apartment.

I read all the directions, pee on all the sticks and sit in my bathroom, stunned, as they turn pink, then blue, then into a very distinct set of two lines.

robin

"Ordering two sea bass, one lamb medium rare, one rabbit special. Fire one salmon, one filet rare, two lamb medium, two ravioli special." The kitchen is slammed tonight, and I'm down a line cook, but luckily a friend from Rushmore is helping on his night off, so we aren't completely in the weeds. I have to say I love being at the pass, and since Gerald left, I've been able to transition to executive chef without too much hassle.

Michael comes into the kitchen and hands me a tall glass.

"What is this?"

"Virgin mojito. Thought you might need a refresher. How goes it back here?"

"Just got the last ticket, so we should be good." I send out the salads and appetizers for the final two tables of the night, and tell the apps cook and the garde manger cook to break down their stations, which they begin gratefully.

"You look like you have everything under control," he says.

I take a sip of my drink, essentially club soda with fresh mint and lime, and look up at Michael. "This is perfect, thank you."

"You're welcome." He squeezes my hand and goes back up front.

"Fire two sea bass, one lamb medium rare, one rabbit special. Pastry, where are those chocolate cakes for nine?"

Mindy, our pastry chef, calls out to me. "Just coming out of the oven, Chef. ETA one minute."

I love it when they call me Chef.

We get the last entrées out, and the line, sauté and grill cooks begin cleaning up their stations. I thank my friend Anton for his help and slip him a couple hundred bucks in cash. He makes me promise to bring Michael to Rushmore one of these nights, to celebrate our engagement. I tell Mindy to take off, that I can cover desserts for the last couple tables, but she says she would rather stay, she's working on some prep for tomorrow anyway, so it's not a big deal. For a small staff, we've managed to put together some really talented and committed people, and they're usually a joy to work with.

The boys head off to drink heavily somewhere cheap, as cooks are wont to do, and after Mindy and I get the last desserts out, I go into the little office Michael and I share, change out of my whites and into my civilian clothes and head down to the bar. I'm surprised to see Jay there, talking with Michael.

"This is a lovely surprise." I greet Jay, who looks stricken.

"Hi, Rob, how are you?" He barely looks up at me.

"Okay. What brings you by?"

"I needed to talk to a guy. Michael seemed like a good option."

"Well, I always think so...shall I let you boys chat?"

"Maybe just for a minute—is that really rude?" He looks very upset, poor kid.

"Not at all. You hungry? I could rustle something up for you."

"Good idea, honey, is there any of the ravioli left?" Michael knows this is the easiest thing to throw together, but waiting for the water to boil and doing the sauce will take me at least fifteen minutes.

"Absolutely, I'll do enough for you to share. Back in a bit."

I head back to the kitchen, wondering what's going on. I throw a pot of water on the hottest burner, and grab a sauté pan. Since the pasta was on special tonight, all the fixings are still in the sauté station cooler. The ravioli are large rounds, stuffed with a mixture of ricotta and mascarpone, and spinach and smoked chicken, and walnuts with a hint of sherry. The sauce is about done, a basic marinara, already made, so I add some fresh basil, and a splash of cream. When it's all done, I turn the whole pan out into one large bowl, put some parmesan curls and chopped parsley on top and grab a couple forks out of the silverware station. I stick them in the bowl, take the last half baguette and head back to the bar.

Michael is refilling Jay's wineglass. I hand him the bowl and bread, and go back to the kitchen to tidy up. By the time I return to the bar, ten minutes later, the bowl is empty, the bread is gone and Jay is smiling at Michael and shaking his hand.

"Your guy is the best, Rob, don't ever forget it!"

"I've always thought so." I look at Michael a little perplexed, and he shakes his head. Jay jumps up, downs the last of his wine and kisses me on the cheek.

"I'll see you guys soon, Michael, thanks again, man, you're the greatest."

"No problem, Jay, just call me Thursday."

"Will do. Pasta was perfect. Later, guys." He throws his leather jacket on and strides out of the bar. There is a couple at the other end of the bar, Joe, who lives next door, at his usual spot midbar, and one four top lingering over after-dinner drinks and coffee in the dining room. Other than that, we're empty. Wendy, the last waitress here, wanders over and takes the pasta bowl back to the kitchen.

"What was all that about?"

"Lilith broke up with Jay."

"I knew that was coming. I talked to her the other night, she sounded pretty bummed about it. Whatever you said to him must have helped, though."

"Well, it sounds like most of her reasoning has to do with lifestyle, and he wanted to know if I had any ideas about how he could make more money."

"Well, I'm sure it's more complicated than that, after all, he is pretty young, and he and Lil are in very different places in their lives. What did you tell him?"

"I told him I would hire him as bar manager."

"You didn't." Stay calm.

"I did. We've been talking about hiring someone to cover the bar business so I can focus on the restaurant, and you know that Fitz and I have been thinking about a second location, that will take a lot of time and energy if we're going to make it happen. And Lord knows, we can

afford it. Besides, I trust Jay, and he certainly has the energy."
My lovely man looks so proud of himself. Crap.

"What about the acting? It is one thing to bartend and
keep flexible schedules when he gets a show, but he can't
manage the bar here and be gone for a month at a time."

"He said he'd take a break for six months to get things
organized here, and build the relationships with the reps and
get the books in order. If he gets a show after that, he'll do
the management stuff during the day and hire a bartender
out of his pocket to cover his shifts."

"And this is all so he can make more money to get Lil
back?"

"I figured you would love this idea. Hey, it's romantic!
I'm trying to help out your friend. If Lilith wants a guy
with a car who can take her out to eat, and I can give him
a job that will afford him that, doesn't that make me a
munch?"

"Mensch. And no, it makes you a meddler. What if it isn't
just the money? I think she is using the lifestyle thing as the
easy surface stuff, but deep down she just doesn't want to
be with him anymore. The age difference is too much, she
wants different things. What happens if he goes back to her
with this grand plan and she says no? Now you have a new
bar manager who's doing it for no reason at all. And how
is Lil going to feel coming here knowing he's around? Oy,
this is a total mess. You have to call him, Mikey. You have
to tell him you made a mistake."

"I wouldn't have offered the job to him if I didn't think
he would be great. And if your friend Lilith doesn't want
to date him anymore, that's her problem. And you might
have thanked me for trying to be the big guy here, instead
of trashing my idea. And don't call me Mikey."

"I'm sorry, sweetie. You did a nice thing. And you are right, it is between them."

Michael smiles at me. "I can't stay mad at anyone who makes ravioli that good." He leans over the bar and kisses me.

"I have to run up to the office for a minute. Come get me when you're ready?"

"Should be about twenty minutes, these folks are all on last call."

"Okay."

I go back upstairs to the office and dial Lilith. She needs a heads up.

"Hello?"

"Lil, it's Robin."

"Are you a part of this little conspiracy?" Crap.

"He called you already?"

"Left a five-minute message. 'All our problems are fixed.' Michael is going to give him a fabulous job and he is going to buy his cousin's car and have money to take me out and we're going to be all better." She sounds more amused than pissed.

"It wasn't my idea." Pass the buck, blame the boy.

"I know, honey—you would have run it by me first."

"Of course I would have. Jay and Michael hatched this plan while I made them ravioli. He meant well. Are you very angry?"

"Um, I'm, let's see, not furious, exactly, but not really pleased, either. I had a nice little breakup going and now if I don't give him another chance, I'm a heartless bitch."

"That is what I told Michael. Then again, what if having this job meant that he could do more for you, wouldn't that be good?" I know better, but for now it is all I can do.

"Maybe. Or maybe I've been convincing myself that it is all that superficial bullshit as an excuse to break up with him."

"That is sort of what I thought."

Lilith sighs. "I didn't think it until tonight. God, I'm such a bitch."

"You are not. You are just human. What are you going to do?"

"I'm going to tell Jay the truth. That some of those things might help, or that it might illuminate other fundamental differences in wants and needs. I'll tell him I need his friendship more than I need his romantic companionship, and that if he accepts Michael's offer, it had better be for himself and not for me. That if we continue to see each other and it doesn't work out in spite of the job and the car, he can't take it out on you guys."

"You are amazing."

"I didn't say I was going to be sober when I said it. Or that I would say it to his face. He left his message on my machine, and I fully intend to do the same in return."

We giggle.

"As long as you don't hate us."

"Couldn't possibly. Thank Michael for the thought, will you? It was very sweet."

"Will do. Talk to you later?"

"I'll let you know how it went."

"'Kay, bye."

"Bye."

The door to the office opens as I hang up and Michael comes around behind me and rubs my shoulders.

"Does Lil want to kill me?"

"No, she said you were very sweet, and not to ever do that again!"

"Fair enough. Home, darling?"

"Yes, please."

Michael and I close up Ajax and head back to our apartment. It's still sort of a mess, we just haven't had time to fully integrate our stuff since I moved in. But it's nearly one in the morning and neither of us cares. I head to the shower since I hate going to bed smelling of food.

"Want me to wash your hair?" Michael smiles at me. He knows that after a long day my shoulders ache, and that it hurts to keep my arms above my head.

"Absolutely. I'll do your back." And your front, if you'll let me....

Michael runs the water steaming hot the way I like it, and strips off his clothes. I may be tired but I'm not dead, and the sight of his lean, beautiful body makes my breath catch.

He gets into the shower while I get undressed and holds the curtain open for me. I step into the steam and am immediately enveloped in Michael's warm, slippery embrace. He leans me into the water, soaking my hair, and then begins to lather it up. Which lathers me up, if you get my meaning, because nothing is as wonderful as strong hands in your hair. He kneads my sore shoulders for a moment, and then helps me rinse the shampoo out. He kisses me lightly on the lips, and I grab the soap and have him turn around. His back muscles are well defined under my hands as I gently massage him, paying careful attention to his lower back, the center of pain after a night on his feet. He groans happily.

I let my hands slide around his waist, pulling his body back against mine. I let my hands move down his flat stomach to find he is hard, and he sighs deeply as I stroke him.

He turns in my arms and presses his body against mine, kissing me deeply.

"I think I should take my fiancée to bed."

"She agrees with you."

We rinse off quickly, get out of the shower and towel ourselves dry. Michael takes my hand and we go to our bedroom, where we love each other right into perfect sleep.

beth

I'm waiting patiently at T's, nursing one of their famous Bloody Marys, trying to be nonchalant. I'm about to have brunch with Eric. I haven't seen him since Lula's, but we've been talking on the phone, and it feels strange but good to have him back in my life. I've been avoiding seeing him in person, but he called to say he had big news, and since Jeff is doing a special workshop at the McHenry Home Depot all afternoon, I figured I could risk it.

I don't know why the Eric thing makes me so nervous where Jeff is concerned; after all, I did tell him the whole story and he seems pretty cool about it. Eric means nothing to me anymore romantically, and Jeff is out in the burbs all day anyway, it just better not to bother him with it. I'm always aware of the addict part of Jeff's past, and as strong as I know he is, I also know that stress in one's personal life can make the temptation to zone out pretty hard to resist. Then I think that I couldn't be more egotistical—that my looking in another man's direction would be enough to send Jeff back to the bottle. He just got a request from a well-respected agent to see his latest manuscript, which is a very good sign.

"Sorry I'm late." Eric rushes in breathlessly, and kisses my cheek.

"No problem. I started without you." I gesture to the almost finished Bloody Mary.

"Well then, I'll have to catch up." Eric calls the waitress over and orders me another, and two for himself.

"Very William Powell circa *Thin Man,*" I quip at him. We always loved those old black-and-white movies from the thirties and forties.

"I do what I can, missus." His very bad William Powell imitation.

The drinks arrive, and Eric manages to put his first one away in record time while we make small talk.

"So what is the big news?"

Eric smiles at me. "I moved out."

"No way." I can't believe he actually left her.

"You were right. I did some digging myself, and all the stuff you said about her past seems to be true. I confronted her with it, said that I felt I had been lied to or misled, but that I didn't want to give up. I asked her if she wanted to come clean, if we should get some therapy together or if she should get some therapy on her own, and she blew up at me. So I left. I've been crashing at my friend Zeke's place, but I found an apartment last night, so I should be able to move in next weekend."

"This is a big step. I'm really happy for you. How are you doing with it all?"

"I'm okay, I guess. Sort of numb actually. But it feels like the right decision. And you were right about me, I do want to be married, I do want kids to be at least a viable discussion, but more important, I want to be with someone who's crazy about me, and who I can be crazy about." He polishes off his second Bloody Mary and motions for another round.

"You'll be great, Eric, I just know it. It is a very exciting time for you, the world is your oyster." I'm feeling a little tipsy. And very vindicated. I do so love being right.

"I don't know. Meeting someone at this stage is a daunting prospect."

"I know how you feel. Getting back into the dating scene after Sasha was no picnic!"

"What did you do? Fix-ups? Bars?"

"I did some of the online stuff for a while. You might want to try that."

"Did it work well?" Eric asks.

"Not for me, but I know a lot of people who have had some success. I was pretty unlucky though, now that I think about it." Remembering some of my fiascoes makes me laugh.

"I'm intrigued, what happened?" Eric is smiling at me.

"Okay, the one that actually made me stop was Typhoid Brad."

"Tell me that wasn't really his name."

"Of course not, that's just what I called him. Jdate.com, you know, the Jewish online-dating service? Anyway, I get a note from this guy Brad. Profile seems normal, so I write him back. We e-mail for a while, things seem good, I give him my number. We talk on the phone a couple times. He is funny, smart, we have good conversations, so when he asks to make a date for dinner, I say yes. Saturday night, a real date-date. I was really looking forward to meeting him, you know, to see if there was any chemistry."

"And?"

"And he calls me Saturday afternoon to say he has been fighting a cold, and wants to be in good form to meet me, can we move it to Tuesday? I say sure. Tuesday he calls me to say that he has just gotten out of the hospital, he was so dehydrated from being sick, can we bump it to Friday? I say of course, he should rest up and drink lots of fluids."

"How old is this guy?"

"Forty-two."

"Can't figure out how to drink enough?" Eric was always good at sarcastic.

"I was trying to give him the benefit of the doubt." I laugh. "Anyway, he calls me Friday…"

"Let me guess, abducted by aliens. Suffering from post-anal probe leakage, wants to push it up again."

This really makes me giggle. "Close. Mono."

"Mono? He has mono? What, is he like the world's oldest college freshman?"

"I know! But he is so apologetic, and sweet…you know the kind, 'think what a great story this is going to make' sort of deal? So I tell him to get better, and call me when he wants to reschedule."

"No wonder you called him Typhoid Brad."

"It seemed to suit. So anyway, he e-mails me and calls during his recovery, a couple weeks go by. Finally, one Monday, I get a message on my machine. He is feeling all better, wants to have drinks Wednesday night. I leave a message in return, Wednesday is good, call me and let me know the details."

"So what happens, he comes down with mad cow disease?"

"Nope, blows me off. Doesn't call, doesn't e-mail, doesn't reconfirm, just drops off the face of the earth. I'm sort of thinking in the back of my head that maybe he died, but I figure he is just a weirdo of some kind, whatever."

"Did you ever find out what happened?"

"Well, I did hear from him again."

"What did he have to say for himself?" Eric is leaning on the table, utterly rapt. This is going to kill him....

"The next Sunday I get an e-mail from him. It says essentially this—'I don't know if you got this, or if I'll be available, but if I go I certainly don't want to go alone, so let me know what you think....' And pasted into the e-mail is information about the Fourth Annual Jewish Dating Marathon in Skokie. Four hundred single people, twenty guaranteed introductions in your age category, live Klezmer music, the whole shebang."

"Let me get this straight, he was inviting you to join him at a dating event?" Eric shakes his head in disbelief.

"Yes, indeedy. Puts me off, puts me off, puts me off, BLOWS me off, and then invites me on a first date to a *dating event*. The guy must be insane. I figure he sent it to the wrong person, right? Hit the wrong e-mail address, because no one could be that stupid. So I reply to the e-mail. Said I assumed he sent it accidentally, but wished him luck at the party."

"That is so funny. He must have felt like a moron."

"It gets better."

"It couldn't, don't tell me he *meant* to send it to you?"

"I get an e-mail back from him saying that sometimes you have to do something shocking to get a reaction from someone, and clearly it worked. And that he figured it might be the only way we would actually meet."

"This guy is a piece of work, no wonder he's single!"

"I know, it defies description. So I write back that clearly I've been out of the dating scene so long that I don't know the current protocols—I thought that agreeing to have drinks with him the previous week was a way of actually meeting. But nothing could be dreamier than a first date to a dating event! Please please, I said, take me to the Fourth Annual Jewish Dating Marathon. Nothing sounds more romantic than milling around Skokie with four hundred single Jews looking for love. I said I'd need someone to hold my purse while I was making the twenty guaranteed introductions I'd been promised. I finished by saying he should inform the florist I would be wearing red so that my corsage wouldn't clash."

"That is hysterical. You really put him in his place."

"Apparently not. He wrote back."

"After all that, he didn't get the sarcasm?"

"Here is what he wrote, word for word. 'There was this man. And there was this road. And if I could only remember these dreams, I'm sure they are trying to tell me something.'"

"You are making this up."

"Too weird to be anything but true. Swear to God."

"So he is nuts."

"Oh yeah. No question."

"What did you do?"

"Wrote him back."

"N-uh-uh."

"Yesiree bob."

"What did you say?"

"And I quote myself...'There was this girl. And the limits of time and patience. And a line which, once crossed, means that potentially quirky in an interesting way has become deeply tedious in an unattractive way. If these dreams you speak of show you in a boat, with some fruit and water and sunscreen and a lap throw and a pair of high-heeled shoes and a monkey, it means this— the boat is your life. You have sustenance to keep you alive. Protection from the elements. Some small measure of comfort. The shoes are mine. I left them behind when I jumped overboard. The monkey flew out of my ass as I was leaving, since such an occurrence would need to be possible before I would ever agree to ride on your boat.'"

Eric applauds, and laughs so hard the tears are rolling down his cheeks. "That is the funniest thing I've ever heard. Please tell me he got the message."

"I assume so, I never heard from him again."

Eric wipes his eyes. "I should hope not. By the way, what is it about that experience that makes you recommend on-line dating to me?"

"That's your competition! Think how great you are going to look next to all the Typhoid Brads of the world. Women are going to eat you up!"

"I suppose that is true." Eric motions for the check, and I excuse myself to the ladies' room. When I get back to the table, Eric has already paid the bill, and I promise to get the next one. I tell him I have to get home to walk Petey, and he offers to keep me company, so we head back to the loft.

Petey is very excited to see me, and Eric and I decide to head over to Wiggly Field Dog Park to really give him a workout. We sit on a bench and chat while Petey runs around with some new friends. After about a half hour, we try to put him back on his leash. But Petey thinks we're playing, so he runs away to the far corner of the park. There he finds a small muddy puddle left from last night's storm, and before we can stop him, has rolled in the cool muck most happily. By the time we get over to him, he gets up, gives a mighty full-body shake and covers me and Eric from head to toe with flecks of mud. We're laughing too hard to even scold him. We get the leash back on, walk him home and give him a bath, which means that in no short order we're also wet and soapy, in addition to dirty.

"I'm so sorry. What a mess!" I feel terrible for Eric, who never had a dog and doesn't know how sloppy it can be.

"It's okay. It isn't his fault, he was just having a good time."

"You are a mess. Jeff has some sweats here, why don't I grab them for you, and I can throw your stuff in the wash. Won't take any time."

"Actually, that would be good. If it's no bother."

"No problem at all, hold on a sec." I go to the bedroom, find a change of clothes for Eric and get out of my own things and into a robe. I offer Eric a towel, and he tosses his clothes out of the bathroom to me, and jumps in the shower. I put all our stuff in the washing machine, and get it running, put some coffee on, and brush the tangles out of Petey's still-damp fur. Eric comes out of my bathroom, pink and shiny, wearing Jeff's clothes, which are about two sizes too big. I pour him a cup of coffee and leave him to the television while I jump in the shower myself. As I'm toweling off in the steamy bathroom I hear voices. I figure it is the television, until I hear a loud crash. I run out of the bathroom in my robe, and see Jeff standing over Eric, who's on the floor holding his head.

"What the hell is going on out here?"

Jeff glares at me. "I should ask you the same question."

"Excuse me?"

"You know, Beth, it hasn't been that long, if you were done with me, a courtesy conversation would have been appreciated."

"What the hell are you talking about? Eric, are you okay?" I kneel on the floor and prise his hands away from his eye, which is blowing up rapidly and turning blue. "Jesus, let me get you some ice for that. Jeff, what is the matter with you?"

"Me? *Me!* I come back early from my workshop figuring I would surprise you, and I find some other guy wearing my clothes and you in the shower."

I get some ice out of the freezer and put it in a Ziploc for Eric, who has propped himself against the coffee table.

"It isn't what you think, buddy." Eric puts the ice pack over his eye.

"Good God, Jeff, why didn't you just ask him what he was doing here? This is my friend Eric. We took Petey to the park and he got us all muddy. I'm just washing Eric's clothes before the stains set. Jesus."

"I swear, man, I just took her to brunch, kept her company with the dog. It certainly isn't what you think."

Jeff looks at us both. Then the buzzer for the washing machine goes off, and the realization settles into his eyes. "I'm sorry, I shouldn't have, I mean, jeez, your eye looks really bad. If you want to take a crack at me, you can…."

Eric smiles. "I'll pass, thanks. Look, I can't blame you. She's worth fighting for."

"I think you should go, Jeff." I'm livid.

"Beth, honey, I just, I mean, you have to know how it looks."

"I can't talk to you about this right now. I need to cool

off. This was totally unacceptable. Go home. I'll call you later."

"Fine. I'm sorry. Eric, man, I'm so sorry."

"It's okay," Eric says. "My students will think I'm very cool. No sweat."

"Beth…" Jeff tries to come over to me, but I think the look in my eyes stops him. "Okay, I'll talk to you later." He pets Petey on the head, looks at his hand, which means he has noticed the still-moist fur, reinforcing our story even further, and leaves.

"My God, Eric, I'm so sorry. I have no idea what came over him. Did he just attack you when he came in?"

"Not exactly."

"What did he say?"

"He kissed me." Eric is blushing.

"What?"

"Look, I put the towel like a turban around my head, so that my hair didn't drip on your furniture. I was sitting on your couch watching TV, and I didn't hear him come in. Suddenly someone was kissing my neck. I jumped. He said, 'Who the hell are you?' I said, 'Eric, I'm a friend of Beth's.' He said, 'Where is she?' I said, 'In the shower, and who are you?' And then he decked me."

I have to laugh. I can't help it.

"This is not funny, Beth, that guy has a helluva right hook!"

I go over to put the clothes in the dryer. "I know, it's just, sometimes I like to lounge around in his sweats on a Sunday afternoon, and if I'm recently out of the shower, I always have a towel on my head. I'm trying to picture him sneaking over to kiss me awake, anticipating a little afternoon nookie, and finding you instead!"

"Well, at least you know he can defend your honor."

"What honor? He assumed I was cheating on him! What kind of trust is that? I don't want a guy who is going to punch you out for me, I want a guy who would know when he walked in that there must be a logical explanation."

"Well, maybe he has been burned before, fidelitywise, you should hear him out." Eric is surprisingly calm for someone with a heck of a shiner.

"Innocent until proven guilty. Unless you catch me in flagrante, if you love me you should know I wouldn't do that."

"I think it is 'en.'"

"What?"

"*En* flagrante, not *in* flagrante."

"Thanks, Professor, I'll make a note of it. Will that be covered in the midterm?"

"Hey, a little sympathy for the injured, if you don't mind." He tries to look pitiful.

"I'm sorry, poor thing." I try to look concerned.

"Kiss to make it feel better?"

"Of course." I lean over and kiss his poor swollen eye. He reaches a hand up and cradles the side of my cheek. He tries to pull me in to kiss me, but I move away.

"Eric, I can't."

"Sorry, Beth. That was out of line."

"Look, I know Jeff acted like a brute, but he is still my boyfriend."

"Do you love him?"

"I'm very fond of him. But we haven't been together that long, and I don't know where we're headed." Interesting that I haven't really been thinking about it that much.

"Please tell me he has never hit you." Eric looks genuinely worried.

"Oh God, of course not! I don't know if I'm going to be able to forgive him for hitting *you,* but if he ever laid a finger on me, that would be the end of him. Look, truth be told, I did the right thing after Sasha, you know? Didn't jump back into the dating scene right away, spent some quality time alone, got my house in order. When Jeff and I reconnected, I was feeling is such a good, stable place, and it was romantic. Bumping into someone from my past, finding him changed, and likable, and—"

Eric interrupts me. "In need of taking care of?"

"I never really thought about it. It was nice to be with someone who liked me, who was attentive. And, at the risk of sharing too much information, it was nice to have a decent sex life again!"

"Nothing wrong with that, but how long have you guys been together now?" Eric asks.

"A few months."

"Do you see a future with him?"

I think about it. "Probably not. First off, he won't live with someone before marriage, and after six years with Sasha, I certainly won't marry someone without living with them first. Second, I don't know that we're really partnership material, not for the long haul."

Eric takes my hand, and starts to speak, but I stop him.

"Eric, don't. Don't say anything. Whether Jeff and I are forever isn't important to me right now. I do care about him, I do have a good time with him, and today's appalling behavior notwithstanding, I don't know if we're going to be over or not. You and I are just getting to know each other again after a decade of absence, so you can't be a factor in that decision. *If* Jeff and I break up, that doesn't mean anything for you."

"I'm sorry, I'm just being selfish," Eric says. "I didn't mean to put you on the spot. Tell you what, I'll go on the assumption that we're rebuilding our friendship—nothing more. If you ever get the urge to kiss me, kiss me. If it feels right to us both, then we'll deal with it. But it's up to you. I'll back off, as long as you promise to kiss first if you want to test those waters."

What a goof. "Deal."

"Okay, now we just pretend that nothing happened and go back to light fluffy conversation."

Which we do. We laugh. We talk some more and make plans for an after-work drink the following week. When his clothes are dry, he gets dressed and heads out to meet his friend Zeke to shoot some pool. Jeff calls three times, but I'm not ready to talk to him yet, so I let the machine pick up.

Talking with Eric has certainly opened up some thoughts for me. I thought everything was going fine, but now I'm not so sure. Jeff jumped off the handle like a madman, which scares me a little bit. But if I'm going to be honest, I purposely didn't tell him I was meeting Eric, and I scheduled that meeting when Jeff was supposed to be an hour and a half away all day. But why? I really don't know what I think about Eric. I surely don't want to start something there out of some need to win, to be right after all these years. Then again, when it comes to thinking long term, Eric does seem like a more logical match for me. It's pretty clear that I can't talk to Jeff until I know what that means. And I sure as hell don't know right now.

Lilith

"What on earth is so important that I had to fake sick for you?" I've arrived at Bill's apartment in Andersonville after faking lunchtime food poisoning at my latest temp assignment.

"Come, sit. Can I pour you a glass of wine?" Bill is all calm and smiling hospitality, which makes me far more nervous.

"Am I going to need it?"

"I believe you are, yes." Bill hands me a glass of pinot noir, and sits across from me on a ridiculous purple velvet armchair we found together at a Salvation Army a couple years ago. I sip my wine.

"All right, you are too sparkly to have bad news, so here we go. New boy?" Bill loves Twenty Questions.

"Nope."

"Find something you didn't need on sale?"

"Nope."

"New job?"

"Yep."

"Terrific! Who's producing?" Thank God. Bill hasn't directed a show since our last project, and as much as he likes working with students, and doing workshops and readings, he is only ever really happy with a full-fledged project on his hands.

"I'm producing. But it isn't a show, peanut. It is a theater. A whole theater. Artistic director."

"Bill, that is fan-freaking-tastic! What company?"

"The Greenwood Tree."

"In Milwaukee?"

"Do you know of another?"

The Greenwood Tree Theater, named for a song in *As You Like It,* is a rising young star in the burgeoning Milwaukee theater scene. Very sweet hundred-seventy-five seat three-quarter-thrust mainstage and an eighty-seat black-box studio space. A four-show season, one Shakespeare, one original-text classic, one newly adapted classic and one family show. Plus some great educational programs. Bill and I had seen a couple of their productions on weekend trips to Milwaukee, and the work was interesting. I had heard that their AD had accepted an offer at the Oregon Shakespeare Festival, but Bill hadn't said he'd applied for the job.

"You sneaky queen, why didn't you tell me you were after that job?"

"Because I wasn't. I didn't apply, *they* called me."

"No way!"

"Way. Two weeks ago. Called me up and said they wanted to see if I was interested in exploring the opportunity. I went to Milwaukee, met with the managing director and the chairman of the board. They called me again to see if I would come meet with some key staff, so I did. The offer came this morning."

"Bill, that is so terrific! Artistic director! At thirty-five! You're the new wunderkind of classics, the reluctant 'it-boy' of the Midwest regional-theater community. When do you start?"

"We."

"Pardon?"

"We start in six weeks." Bill is grinning ear to ear.

"We? What the hell do you mean we?"

"Associate artistic director. It was part of my negotiation. I said I would take the job, but that I would need a right-hand person of my choosing to be able to do the work the right way. My hire, no jumping through hoops, same length of contract. Don't make me do it alone, Lil. You know I need your ear, your eye, your input. It's a small company, the pay isn't insane, but very nice considering the cost of living in Milwaukee. Two-year contract with an option, just like me. What do you say, Lili, our own theater! You and me. Pick the season, cast the season, regular paychecks…please say you'll come."

"Oh, Bill, I don't know what to say. It is so wonderful, but Milwaukee? Moving away?"

"C'mon, when will the timing be as right? You don't have a regular job, you and Jay aren't serious enough to really keep you here and it's only a ninety-minute drive, so you'll still be close to family and friends. If we suck, we suck. If we're great, we could move back to Chicago and upgrade."

"I don't know…it is such an incredible opportunity…I love you so much for wanting me with you."

"Tell you what. Come with me this weekend. Meet these

people. If you hate them, or think it feels awful, then no harm no foul. But if you like them as much as I think you are going to like them, we're off on an adventure together!"

"You know what, okay," I say. "Absofuckinglutely. This weekend. No problem." My stomach is full of butterflies, but as the idea is sinking in I'm starting to get really excited. Associate artistic director. Really having a hand in shaping a theater, in creating a season. Overwhelming and scary as hell, but how flipping COOL!

"We're going to have the best time!" Bill reaches his wineglass over to clink mine.

"God, I hope so." I clink back.

Bill and I make our plans to drive out to Milwaukee Friday afternoon to beat rush hour, I take advantage of the unexpected afternoon off to head home and do a little laundry. I call Jay and leave him a message. I want to talk to him about this whole Milwaukee thing before he actually starts working for Michael next week. If I do decide to take this leap, I need to do it without strings. Clean break. Which means if I'm the only reason he is going to take this job, then he still has time to reconsider. I call Beth at the store.

"Girl Stuff, this is Beth, how may I help you?"

"Beth, it's Lil, you busy?"

"Nope. Slow as molasses in here today. Anne just went home to unpack some more boxes since we're so dead."

"How are you guys doing?" I hate when my friends fight, and with Beth and Anne, it just kills me to have things tense between them.

"We're fine," Beth says. "You know me, all bluster and no substance. I yelled, I bitched, I moaned, she apologized, I caved. We're at the slightly-snarky-remarks phase. I'll dig at her, she'll blush, I'll laugh, she'll shake her head, we get on with life. What can I do, the kid has a dream!" Beth laughs her wonderful deep-throated chuckle, and I know that they are fine, which is a big relief.

"I'm so glad to hear it. You know this is going to be good for an extra-special-guilty birthday gift this year!" Beth's birthday is coming up in about three weeks.

"I know. I've dropped eight thousand hints about needing a relaxing spa day. After Anne's little bombshell and Jeff's Incredible Hulk imitation, I really need some detox. I'll bet you a hundred bucks that an afternoon at Kiva is headed my way!"

"Anne told me he clocked Eric. Actually, I think she said he knocked him a kiss and then knocked him on his ass." I feel bad for Beth, but it was a pretty funny story.

"Laugh all you want, I don't know what to do. I really like Jeff, but that quick-to-snap violence thing creeps me out. And that he jumped to conclusions so quickly."

"Have you guys talked about it?" I like Jeff, but the hitting thing scares me, too.

"A little. He apologized. Sent flowers. Swore he wasn't dangerous. I dunno. I told him I needed to take a break for a few weeks and we'll see where we were after that. What about you? Robin told me about the breakup-go-round with Jay, do you really think things will be better if he is more professionally inclined?"

"I think it is possible we may not get a chance to find out."

"Uh-oh, that doesn't sound good. Wha' happened?"

"I got a job offer. In Milwaukee. And I may take it."

I fill Beth in on the details that Bill has shared with me, and she lets them sink in for a minute.

"Sweetie, you know the selfish cow in me wants you to

stay here forever. But this sounds totally amazing. And I think you are right to want to go with a clean break. Talk to Jay, I bet his friendship instincts will be greater than his boyfriend instincts and he'll tell you to go as well. In the meantime, congratulations! I'm so proud of you guys!" I love that she means it.

"Thanks, I'm still shell-shocked. But excited. We're driving out there this weekend so I can meet the company. OHMYGOD, what am I doing? I'm so freaked out because I'm so NOT freaked out, is that the weirdest?"

"I think it is a good sign. Will you be back in time for brunch Sunday?"

"Yep. We're driving back Sunday morning, so I'll meet you guys at T's. In the meantime, don't mention anything to the rest of the girls, I want to give them the news on Sunday."

"You got it. I can't wait to hear how it turns out, I have a really good feeling about it!"

"Thanks, Beth, I knew you were the one to call! If I don't talk to you before, I'll see you Sunday."

"You got it, have a good trip!"

"Will do. Later, gator."

"Bye!"

I hang up the phone, feeling excited and nervous, and run a hot bath. Soaking in the wonderful water, I start laying out my plan of attack with Jay. Beth thinks he will see it for what it is—a great opportunity. But since his latest endeavor with Robin and Michael, I'm afraid he'll offer to come with me. And that is one piece of baggage that will certainly not fit in the overhead compartment.

jess

Harrison catches me coming out of the bathroom, where I've been throwing up as quietly as possible. I don't think it is morning sickness, I think it is nerves. My doctor confirmed yesterday that I am indeed about eight weeks pregnant. I've made an appointment with her in two weeks for a D&C. I can't bring myself to call it an abortion. This morning Harrison is off, and we're supposed to spend the morning together. And I have to tell him that, despite our careful use of condoms, we've managed to prove us both fertile.

"Hey, are you going to shower?" he asks me. Obviously he has not heard me being sick.

"Not yet."

"You okay? You look a little green." No kidding, Doctor.

"Not really."

"What's going on, are you sick?" He feels my forehead for fever.

"Sort of. I'm pregnant." There, that was easy.

"Very funny."

"Really not laughing, Doctor. Eight weeks. Confirmed by one of your gracious colleagues yesterday."

Harrison steps forward and pulls me into his arms. I begin to cry.

"It's going to be okay, sweetie, hush." He is so soothing, and guides me gently back into the bedroom and sits me on the bed.

"I'm so sorry—" I begin. Harrison interrupts me.

"Hey, you didn't do it on purpose, did you?" I can see that he knows I didn't and is trying to lighten the mood. But I have to say it anyway.

"Of course not, it is the last thing I want." His face sinks.

"Certainly not the last thing."

"Well, I mean, c'mon. I'm waiting to hear about my dissertation proposal. If they accept it, that's another three to four years of school, plus research and writing, plus teaching. Can you imagine all that with a kid? And we aren't even living together, let alone married. It is just the wrong time. It's okay—I have an appointment in two weeks. The nineteenth. Can you get the day off?"

"Wait a minute, just *wait*. You have an appointment? Shouldn't we at least discuss it, I mean, don't I get a vote?" I can't believe he is angry.

"A vote? A goddamn VOTE? This was an accident, Harrison. We were not trying to get pregnant, in fact, we were conscientiously trying *not* to get pregnant. I don't seem to recall any hesitation on your part when the time came to slip on old Mr. Trojan. I'm not ready, *we* are not ready."

"Well, what if the baby is ready, ever think about that?"

He must be delusional. "You marched with me at the pro-choice rally!"

"Right. The right to *choose*. Damn important. For both of us, at least I would have thought. I'm not saying it's perfect, I'm saying it is you and me. I love you. And no, we aren't living together, *yet,* we aren't married, *yet,* but I sure as hell have been assuming we were headed there. And headed toward kids together, white picket fence, the whole fucking shebang. So maybe it's the wrong order, maybe not. I'm not saying you shouldn't have an abortion, I'm saying that we should make that fucking decision together. But you cut me out of it. It can't even be a consideration, because you have an *appointment*. Which means that you are pretty fucking certain."

I can't believe he is yelling at me. The tears stream down my face, burning hot.

"We can talk about it, the appointment can be canceled, I just—"

"That is just my point. If you cancel, I'll never know if I talked you into it. Or for that matter, if I talked myself into it because I wasn't part of the original decision, and now I don't want to err on the other side."

"Do you really want this baby? I mean, really? Your med school loans not yet paid off, and me with my loans and making next to no money. You and me and a kid in this condo? Are you saying that's what you want?"

Harrison looks up at me. "I'll never know for sure if we might have taken that path, because you took the decision away from us and made it without me. Don't you know what a betrayal that is?"

"Harrison, I'm so sorry, I had no idea." I don't know what else to say.

"Clearly. And I don't know what it says about us that you didn't."

"What do you want to do?"

"I'll do whatever you want. I'll take off the nineteenth and come with you to the appointment. You can recuperate here, I'll take care of you. And I guess we'll just see."

"What does that mean? Are you going to break up with me? Because I made an appointment in a trying and difficult and emotional time without consulting you? You know what, Doctor. Fuck you. How do I know this whole tirade isn't just a good excuse to dump me and make it my fault? How about that? If you were having all these fantasies about us and our pretty little life together, how come you haven't mentioned them to me? How come you haven't suggested I move in, or fucking proposed, huh? Mr. Teflon, Mr. Commitment-phobic? How come I'm the bad guy, and you're the one who is ready to walk away from the woman you were assuming you were going to spend your life with over a fucking *appointment?*"

"I don't know."

"You don't know much. So I'll make it easy on you. Never mind. I'll get Beth to take me, and I'll recuperate at her house. And then I can be the selfish bitch who made the *appointment* AND left you, and you can be the victim."

I grab my coat and purse, and shove my feet into my shoes, blinded by tears.

"Don't go. Don't walk out on this."

"I can't be here right now. I can't be with you right now." I shake off his arm, and bolt out the door. He is right behind me on the stairs, but there is a cab outside, and I jump in it and give the driver the address of Girl Stuff. My cell phone is ringing its head off before we're halfway up the block, but I shut it off.

The bells on the door ring when I go in, and there are a couple girls milling around inside. Anne is helping them, sees me and calls for Beth. Her head peeks out of the back room, and in two seconds she is across the store holding me. She guides me to the office, where I sink into the tiny love seat across from her desk. She sits on the arm next to me, holding me tight and stroking my hair. I catch my breath, and tell her what happened. Somewhere in the middle Anne comes back, and sits on the floor at my feet.

"I locked up," she says to Beth. "Put the Out to Lunch sign up."

"Good idea."

"Don't make me say it all again, Beth." I'm so tired.

"Short version, Jess is knocked up," Beth says. "Made an appointment to deal with it. Told Harrison, who felt that his right to have a voice was usurped, and threatened to leave her, so she left him first. Close enough?"

"I guess."

"Oh, Jessie, I'm so sorry. What can we do?"

"I'll take her to my place," Beth says. "It'll be okay. Wanna come?"

"Only if Jess wants me." Anne is so sensitive to people in pain, however much it's going to piss Beth off, she is going to be a great therapist.

"The more the merrier."

Anne and Beth close up the store, and we go back to Beth's loft. I'm totally drained. They feed me chicken soup, let me cry some more and make me green tea. Beth even lets Petey up on the couch to cuddle with me, even though that is usually verboten. I fall asleep with his big warm furry body pressed against me.

When I wake up, Anne, Petey and Beth are nowhere to be found, so I assume he needed a walk. Beth's phone rings. Her machine answers.

"Beth, it's Harrison. Are you there? Is Jess there? Have you heard from her? Look, she isn't answering her cell, but if you talk to her or see her, can you call me and let me know that she is all right? I'm sure you probably hate me by now, and if you don't, you will shortly, but I—I just—I need to know that she is okay, okay? So please call me. And tell her I'm sorry."

And I thought I was out of tears.

Beth and Petey come back. Anne has gone home. Beth makes grilled-cheese sandwiches for dinner, and we watch some home improvement shows on TV. We curl up together in her bed, and she holds me while I cry some more, and finally, in the warm embrace of my friend, I sleep.

sunday brunch, as told by beth

"All right, girls, let me know what you think of these." The waiter at T's puts down a round of martini glasses filled with sparkling pink liquid and floating fresh raspberries.

"What is in it again?" I ask.

"Champagne, Skyy Berry, Campari and pomegranate juice."

Anne takes a tentative sip. "Yum!"

"Very seasonal. Have a name for it yet?" Lilith has already finished half of hers.

"We're calling it the springtini."

"Well, keep 'em coming!" Jess says a little too enthusiastically.

The rest of us exchange glances, but say nothing.

"You girls having food today?" The waiter smiles at us.

"You guys ready?" Robin asks.

They take a minute to look over the menu, and order.

"All right, circle up, kids." Jess starts, brave face.

"I want to go last," Lilith says. I wink at her.

"Then I'll start," Robin says. "My mother arrived yesterday. I give it another three or four hours before I kill her. Or Michael does. She has totally taken over the wedding plans, and nothing I say or do seems to change her mind about the event she is envisioning, and it's totally not what Michael and I want. Lucky for me she's at Elizabeth Arden this morning, so I can try to cool off, but I do not know how I'm going to survive until Wednesday."

"Poor thing, is it really that bad?" Anne asks.

"Worse than bad. First, she is very weirdly flirtatious with Michael, which is clearly making him uncomfortable, not to mention pissing me off. Second, she seems to think I'm going to have some big foofy country-club wedding, which is not at all us. And third, every time she talks about the ceremony, she talks about my dad not being around to walk me down the aisle and then bursts into tears. What am I going to do?" Robin looks weary.

"Tell her to piss off," I suggest. "You know, in a nice way!"

"Very helpful." Robin laughs. "Anyone else with sage advice?"

"Why don't you guys elope?" offers Lilith. "I mean, pick some great place and sneak off and just do it, and then come back and have a big party. Then, if your mom wants to do some country-club thing, she can do a brunch or luncheon or something back East for you, and the party here can be whatever you want."

"That is not a bad idea, Rob," Jess says. "A friend of mine did it in the Bahamas over a long weekend, and then had a big hoedown and barbecue when they got back. Took all the pressure off."

"It sounds good. I'll have to talk to Michael. But then you guys won't be there!" Robin has asked me to be maid of honor and the rest of the girls to be bridesmaids.

"We'll be there in spirit, honey," Jess says. "Besides, think about not having to decide on bridesmaid's dresses! We were going to try to surprise you, but last week we all went to try on some of those dresses you talked about, and nothing worked. If it looked halfway decent on Lil and Beth, it looked mediocre on me and dreadful on Anne. We couldn't find a single dress that looked good on all of us."

"It's true, honey. Beth and I looked like we ate the Supremes." Lilith smiles.

"The Junk in the Trunk Twins!" says Beth.

"The Sisters Rubenzaftig!" offers Lilith.

"So you wouldn't be mad if we just ran off?" Robin is beginning to look relieved.

"Robin, we love you and we love Michael and we want you to be happy. If not having to deal with a whole wedding will make you happy, then you should do it." Jess rubs Robin's hand.

"Well, at least it feels like an option. Thanks, you guys. Who's next?"

"I'll go," says Jess. "They accepted the initial proposal for my dissertation Friday, so another three or four years and you'll all have to call me Doctor. I know you all know about me and Harrison and my little procedure next week. I'm about done with Angry, and am now clearly in the Denial phase, which is sort of blissful. And I don't really want to talk too much about it because I haven't cried in about six hours, and would like to try to make it to midafternoon at least."

"Well, we're all here for you, whatever you need," Anne says.

"Absolutely," Robin concurs.

"You guys are so great, I don't know what I would do without you." Jess's eyes start to fill with tears, and she shakes her head. "Someone else go, for Chrissakes."

"Your turn, Beth, what is the latest with Jeff?" Lilith asks.

"I think over, for now. We had a long talk after the Eric debacle, and I think we realized that while we really care about each other a lot, we aren't really 'in love,'" I explain. "And if we aren't in love by now, then where is the relationship really going to go, you know? We decided to take a break for a while and see how we feel with some separation."

"Oh, sweetie, I'm so sorry." Robin leans over the table to take my hand.

"It's really okay. I'm fine. I feel a lot stronger, actually, this time around."

"Does that have anything to do with Eric?" asks Lilith.

"No. At least, not yet. I dunno." I stare at the table.

"It's okay if you think you want to give it a shot with him, no one will think less of you." Anne puts a hand on my shoulder.

"The thing is, I don't think I do," I reply. "I know he wants to, but I think it may be just because I'm safe and he is lonely. Then I think maybe I'm supposed to give him a chance, with all our history. But then I think I'm just thinking that because I don't like being alone. And then I think maybe I should just become a lesbian!" I end loudly.

"Just let me know, sweetness, anytime!" A tall, blond woman with a husky voice and a barbed-wire tattoo around her upper arm winks at me as she walks by. This makes all of us burst into laughter.

The food arrives, along with another round of springtinis.

"Okay, Annie, your turn," I say around a mouthful of veggie omelette.

"Okay, well, I brought something for show-and-tell." Anne pulls a crumpled envelope out of her pocket. She hands it to me.

I look down and read the return address. "Is this the letter?"

"Yep. Will you do it, I'm too nervous." Anne is looking expectantly at me.

I slide a finger deftly across the envelope and pull out a letter. I read it silently.

"Shit. Fuckers." I look up at Anne with concern.

"Well, crap. I guess I can always apply elsewhere." Anne looks down at her plate.

"They deferred you, the bastards. Your application automatically moves to the next semester, so you won't know for sure for another four months." I'm fuming.

"They didn't say no?" Anne grabs the letter, and smiles broadly. "It's a deferral. Not a rejection. It means there wasn't space to consider me this time, so obviously I'm not in their top tier. But I'm not a definite no, either— they like me enough to keep me in the applicant pool for next time."

"You aren't upset?" I ask Anne.

"Well, it would have been great to start this fall, but it's definitely better than a rejection. So I might start midyear? Big whoop!" Anne laughs, and hugs me. "But four more months of waiting, ugh."

"Phew. I thought I was going to have to kick some asses over at Rush!" I take a deep swig of my drink and turn to Lilith. "That just leaves you, princess."

Lilith looks around the table and grins. "I've been offered a job as associate artistic director for a wonderful small theater, and I think I'm going to take it."

The table erupts in buzzing congratulations.

"What theater?" asks Anne.

"The Greenwood Tree," Lilith replies. "In Milwaukee."

The buzz stops.

"You're moving to Milwaukee?" Robin looks perplexed.

"Yes, Milwaukee, only ninety minutes away from here, and a great opportunity, right?" I say forcefully, reminding them that this is probably hard enough on Lilith without their selfish concerns.

"Of course," Jess says. "It's terrific. And we can all meet for weekends up at Hama's cabin! Good for you, Lil!" Jess raises her glass. "Here's to Lilith's new job, and Anne's school and Robin's elopement!"

"Don't forget my breakup and your dissertation!" I add.

"Absolutely. Cheers!" says Robin.

We clink glasses. Jess excuses herself to the ladies' room.

"How is she doing really?" Lil asks when Jess is safely out of earshot.

"Shitty, as you can imagine," I say. "She is staying at my place. Harrison calls every day, but she won't talk to him. He is really broken up, and even though I'm pissed at him, I still sort of understand his point of view. And I really like him still, you know, I really like them together, but I can't talk to her about it yet."

"Poor thing. I can't even imagine." Anne shakes her head.

"And the worst part is, she hasn't told her family, so Mark

called her to tell her that he and Gemma are having a baby!" Beth adds.

"Oh my God, hasn't Harrison said anything to him?" Robin asks.

"Guess not. Considering what's gone on, I guess he thought if she wanted Mark to know, it maybe wasn't his place." I shrug my shoulders.

"But Mark is his best friend, who is he leaning on?" Lilith asks. "It has to be hard on him, too."

"Michael," says Robin.

"What?" I ask.

"Michael. He and Michael went out the other night. I guess he figured Michael would know everything from me, and would be a good ear."

"That Michael, everyone's port in a storm!" quips Lilith. "Just don't let him offer Harrison a job!"

"Don't think the doc is planning to switch careers anytime soon…. Hey, Jay called to officially accept the offer, you know," Robin says.

"I know," Lilith says. "He and I talked last night, and it's over. Clean break. I have to go to Milwaukee and give it my all. And he is really excited about the job, for himself, so I think it will be okay. He really is a sweet boy."

"Hey, we should check on Jess," Anne says. "She's been gone awhile."

"I'll go," I say.

I walk down the short hall where the bathroom is and knock on the door.

"Jess, are you okay in there?" I say through the door. I hear water running and then Jess's voice, which is very faint.

"I don't know, Beth. I'm having cramps and I'm bleeding—a lot."

"Oh my God. Let me in, honey."

"I can't really leave the toilet right now."

"Okay, I'll be right back. You just sit tight." I race back to the table.

"Anne, have Cullom call an ambulance," I say, hoping to evoke an assured in-charge tone.

"Oh my God, what is happening?" Robin jumps up as Anne runs to the front bar to get the owner.

"Be calm, we don't want a scene," I say. "She's in the bathroom, and she's bleeding and having some cramps. We're just going to calmly take her to the hospital and see what is going on. You guys take my car, I'll meet you at Northwestern. And Robin…"

"Yeah?"

"Call Harrison."

Robin reaches for her cell phone, just as a siren is heard in the distance.

I go back to the bathroom, and the door opens. I help Jess walk out toward the front, where Anne is paying the bill. We meet the ambulance outside.

A little over an hour later, a doctor comes to the waiting room, where Michael and Chris have joined us.

She is a slight Indian woman, and has an air about her that is calm but efficient, and she speaks as if she has given this speech hundreds of times. "Your friend is going to be just fine. She had a miscarriage, very common for a first-time pregnancy. We can't find any specific medical reason for it, sometimes these things just happen. But everything looks good, she'll be able to have kids. We had to do a D&C, just to make sure everything was clean, but she did great. We're going to keep her overnight, so as soon as we know what room she is in, someone will come let you know." Very simple and soothing.

Harrison arrives, still in scrubs himself, having been in the middle of a surgery when Michael's call came in. Michael pulls him aside and fills him in, then grabs him in a hug.

jess

I awaken to the sound of someone in my room. The night nurse smiles at me.

"Hi, sweetie, sorry to wake you, but I need to take your vitals," she says. Nothing like the hospital, impossible to rest for more than a fitful hour or two before someone needs blood, or to take your temperature, or give you your meds, or change your IV bag.

"It's okay," I say. I'm numb and my head is fuzzy from the Vicodin they gave me earlier. I must have been asleep when everyone left. I look over at the window seat, which had been full of supportive women all afternoon. Harrison is sleeping, leaning against the wall, but I don't remember him arriving.

"There you go, sweetie. All done. Try to get some rest." The nurse leaves, the door to the room making a loud click behind her. Harrison starts. He looks over at the bed and sees me awake and watching him.

"Hi, honey, how do you feel?" He gets up and moves to the chair next to my bed. He looks horrible.

I shrug. "Tired. Sore."

"Are you in pain? Should I get you some more meds?"

"No. Not pain, just sore."

"Oh, sweetie, I'm so sorry." Harrison leans his head on the bed. I raise my hand and pat his head.

"Me, too."

He looks up at me. I close my eyes. "I wish none of this had happened," he says. "But you are going to be just fine."

"Harrison, you have to go." I can't look at him.

"What?" He has his mouth open.

"Just go. I'm going to be fine, you said so yourself. I wish none of this had happened, too, but it did, and we can't take it back." I swallow hard. "And this little medical emergency doesn't change any of that. We aren't in some movie where an accident happens that makes everyone forget what went before, and live happily ever after. I know I hurt you, and I have to live with that. But you hurt me, too, more than anyone has ever hurt me, and that doesn't go away. I don't know how to process it, certainly not right now. I need you to leave, Harrison, I need to rest. Please. Go home. Please." I roll away from him, squeeze my eyes shut and silently and slowly count to ten so that I don't break down in front of him.

Harrison gets up from the chair. He places a hand on my shoulder. "Honey…"

"Please. Just go away, *please.*" He removes his hand.

"Fine."

He crosses the room, and leaves. I'm left alone, with the number seven stuck in my head. I'm so very tired right now that I can't even cry. Eventually I drift back into a deep sleep.

robin

Michael knocks on the bathroom door. "How's it going?"

"Awful." I open the door. Michael laughs.

"This isn't funny, Mikey." But of course, it totally is.

"Don't call me Mikey. And it's damn funny."

I turn back to the mirror. My reflection is ghastly. I have bright red stripes of inflamed skin all across my face and neck and parts of my shoulders. They are shiny with ointment, and some of them have small blisters.

"Listen, mister, there is nothing funny about it! Look at me, I'm a mess!"

"You certainly are. But our kids are going to love this story."

"If you don't stop making fun of me, kids may not be an option!" I look pointedly at his crotch. He laughs harder. I can't help it, I laugh, too.

"I think you are perfect. But I do think snorkeling is off the menu from now on!"

We're in the Bahamas, staying in a gorgeous suite at the

Atlantis. We're getting married in three hours. A simple ceremony on the beach, just the two of us. But we both woke up early and antsy, so Michael suggested we go snorkeling, which I had never done before. We rented equipment from the hotel, and Michael, who has been doing it for years, gave me a brief course in how to use the mask and snorkel, and we set off for my first underwater adventure. It was beautiful. The ocean was calm and clear, and the small reef near the hotel full of gorgeous fish and coral gardens. I was having such a good time, I even got brave enough to swim around a little on my own. Playing with Michael in the water, swimming around coral formations and making him chase me. Totally fun. Until I zoomed around one corner of the reef and smacked face-first into the trailing tentacles of a large jellyfish.

No kidding.

Those fuckers burn like fire! Michael saw me flailing around and was at my side in a second. He pulled me along back to the beach, the sticky strands slipping away from my skin as we swam fast. Sitting in the shallow water, breathless, he made sure that there were no more jelly pieces anywhere, and then helped me take off my mask. He said it wasn't too bad, and that I didn't seem to be allergic. He said I was lucky I was wearing the mask, so that my eyes were protected. I complained about the stinging, and he explained what you are supposed to do for a jellyfish sting.

I thought he was kidding.

But he wasn't.

And it was unthinkable.

Except it really hurt a lot, and he promised it would make the pain better until we could get me to a doctor.

Nothing more romantic for a bride than to start her day

with her husband-to-be, lovingly peeing on her face behind a palm tree, let me tell you!

Okay, he didn't really pee directly ON my face, he peed into an empty water bottle we found in a garbage can, and then poured it on the affected areas while I breathed through the snorkel. Then we went back to the hotel, where the hotel doctor confirmed that this was indeed the right thing to have done, gave me some ointment and sent us back to our room. He was gracious enough to hold his laughter until the door to his office closed, which we thought was mighty nice of him.

So now, I'm mere hours away from the most important event in my life, and I look as if I was whipped around the face with a hot poker! And every time I look at Michael, all I can think is, *You peed on my face! On our wedding day! A lot of people think it's bad luck for the groom to SEE the bride before the wedding, never mind PEE the bride.*

Oy. The jellyfish poison has obviously affected my brain.

"Robbie, it isn't so bad, the swelling is already going down a little." Bless him, he is trying.

"Don't call me Robbie. And it's a disaster, and you know it. And you heard the doctor, no makeup for three days. *No makeup.* I can't even use concealer to try to make it better for the ceremony! Fucking jellyfish."

"Rob, it wasn't the jellyfish's fault, you swam into him!"

"Her. Only a bitter old-maid jellyfish with no prospects of her own would sting a bride in the face on her wedding day. That was a jellyBITCH!" Michael looks at me to see if I have, in fact, taken total leave of my senses. Then we both crack up.

"Do you want to cancel?" he asks me when the giggles subside.

"Of course not. Will you still have me, in my deformed condition?"

Michael looks me dead in my eye and says, "You are the most beautiful woman I have ever known, jellybitch or no jellybitch. What do you say? Marry me tonight?"

"Of course I'll marry you, Mikey."

"Don't call me Mikey."

He kisses me gently, doing his best to avoid the greasy spots. We sit on the veranda of our suite and have fresh mango juice with champagne, and some light snacks, since we're going to feast at the hotel's fanciest restaurant after the ceremony, and the executive chef here is a guy I knew at CHIC, so there are likely to be eighty-five courses coming at us.

Finally Michael gets up and says, "I should go get ready. Do you need anything before I go?"

"Are you really going?" We had arranged a cabana for Michael near where we were having the ceremony, so that he wouldn't see me in my dress before the ceremony. But now I feel really alone. And what if I can't get the zipper up on my dress?

"Yep. But I'm having someone come up to help you. I arranged it with the spa earlier." His eyes twinkle at me. "Aren't I a munch?"

"Mensch. And yes, you are."

"Love you. See you in an hour."

"Love you, too. I'll be the one in the wedding dress and the welts."

He takes his hanging bag and leaves. I finish my mango mimosa, and get up to lay out my stuff. Beth found the dress for me—made by a local designer whose stuff she was carrying in the store. It's a simple champagne-colored ivory silk sheath, with a silk chiffon overlay that gives it beautiful movement. Anne gave me her pearl bracelet—something borrowed. Lilith loaned me her blue topaz ring—something blue. Jess brought me the linen handkerchief that Hama had carried in her wedding—something old. And Beth found me the perfect beaded clutch purse—something new. I'm trying not to think about how much I wish they were here.

There is a knock at the door. The spa woman. I go to open it.

"Holy shit, Michael said you really got it bad!" Beth is gaping at my face.

"Jesus, it looks like hamburger!" adds Jess, coming in the door behind her.

"You guys, it isn't that bad," Anne says from over Jess's shoulder.

Lilith pushes her way past the others, and says, "Good God! Are you sure we can't put any makeup on those?"

I can't speak.

"Whoa, girl. Don't even *think* about crying. Your eyes are the only thing NOT red and swollen, and you are getting married in, like, forty-five minutes, so pull it together, missy!" Jess is taking control of the situation.

Michael flew them all in to surprise me, the sneak.

I forget all about my stings, and only think about all my best friends being with me, and how much I love the man I'm about to marry. Beth does my hair, and Lilith puts on my eye makeup and lipstick. When I'm dressed, and as ready as I am going to be, the five of us head downstairs, where three golf carts are waiting to take us to the beach.

Michael is standing next to the justice of the peace, wearing a cream linen suit, with a light green shirt unbuttoned at the neck. There's a perfect Caribbean sunset over the water behind him, and Chris is at his side. There's a row of chairs in front of him, my mom sitting there, next to his folks, and his sister and her husband, all of them smiling broadly at me. I still can't believe he got everyone here without my knowing.

The girls all kiss me carefully, and go to sit next to my mother. Jess stays with me and whispers, "I wouldn't have missed being your maid of honor for anything in the world. And you are beautiful." She hands me a single bird of paradise, and walks down the aisle to stand on the other side of the justice.

A trio of steel drums start playing the Beatles' "In My Life," Michael holds out his arms to me, and I kick off my shoes, and run down the aisle to meet him.

Lilith

Bill falls asleep almost immediately after we get out of Milwaukee. I can't really blame him, it has been a very long few weeks between moving and trying to get things started at the theater. We've taken matching apartments in a converted warehouse building near the theater, me on the third floor and Bill on the fifth, figuring it was smarter than actually living together, but still close enough for support. Not perfect, but spacious and serviceable for the time being, and in nice weather it will only be a fifteen-minute walk to work. We both figure it will take a year to get to know the area well enough to find someplace perfect. In the meantime, we're in the middle of rehearsals on the first show of the season, *Cardenio,* widely thought to be one of Shakespeare's "lost" plays, and an interesting text.

Unfortunately, it's an inherited production from the previous AD, so Bill has to tread very carefully so as not to step on the toes of the director or design team, while still establishing a sense of authority and vision. Additionally, the actress cast as the ingenue is right out of school, and, while gifted, very high maintenance. I've been assigned, off the record, as surrogate mother, and have spent the past few days attending to her needs while she gets settled. This seems to mean mostly stroking her ego, letting her bum all my cigarettes and ensuring that she has access to snacks 24/7. Low blood-sugar problems.

We're on our way back for Robin and Michael's official wedding party. I haven't seen anyone since the Bahamas last month, things have been just too busy to get back for a visit, and I'm missing everybody terribly. In truth, I am very lonely in Milwaukee. Bill has been insane, meeting with board members, key community leaders and big funders, not to mention trying to build relationships with the staff.

People have been very friendly, but cautious with us both, especially me. It's great to come into a situation as a team, but there are a couple people, most notably the resident dramaturge and the casting associate, who are a little resentful, since either one of them might have been both qualified and interested in my job had it been available to them.

I know it will get better—moving to a new city without support systems is always a huge transition—but I haven't really made any friends I can trust yet, so I feel somewhat adrift.

And I miss Jay.

I know, I was feeling like the relationship was not working out, and I didn't think we had any potential long term, but I miss him, I really do. I forgot how easy we were together, how much talking with him had become the most important part of my day, how much clarity he had about any situation I might be in. How great the sex was. Sigh. Robin says he is doing great at Ajax, that Michael already doesn't know what he ever did without him. I'm sort of hoping that maybe this weekend we'll have a chance to revisit our situation. Maybe do a trial run on a long-distance thing. Especially now that he bought his cousin's car, and it really isn't a bad drive.

"Are we there yet?" mumbles Bill.

"Sorry, Sleeping Beauty, only halfway. Coming up on Racine in a few minutes. This perks Bill up enormously.

"Racine! Can we get off the highway?"

"Bill…" Racine is very dangerous for us. Roadside temptations of all kinds.

"Aw, *please,* Mom? I've been so good, and I'm hungry!" Bill puts his head on my shoulder. I can't resist him.

"Fine. But let's be careful, shall we?" This is such a mistake.

"I promise!"

I pull off the highway and onto the service road. First stop Apple Holler, where we buy a gallon of fresh cider, a pound of fudge each (maple walnut for Bill, milk chocolate with pecans for me) and two enormous apple turnovers that we eat in the parking lot, getting crumbs everywhere.

Then straight to the Mars Cheese Castle. We taste everything. Cheddar curds. Fresh string cheese. Three kinds of sausage. Chocolate cheese. I mean it. Chocolate cheese. Not chocolate cream cheese, actual cheese. Texture like American, taste like underdone Tootsie Rolls. Odd, and while not unpalatable, we opt out of a purchase. We do, however, buy a bag of white-cheddar curds, a wiggly pound of skinny string cheese that looks like really thick spaghetti, a Swiss cheese in the shape of the state of Wisconsin, a pound of beef sticks and a small summer sausage. We're going to be so sick.

"Next stop, PORN!" says Bill happily, munching on a beef stick.

"Bill, I'm not taking you to the porn shop." I can only imagine, a store that caters to truckers is not going to know what to do with a straight woman and a gay man.

"I WANT PORN! I WANT PORN!" I swear the man is insane.

"Fine! But if we get beat up, it's your fault." I pull into the parking lot of a long silver building with a big pink sign. We enter the front door. It's surprisingly like a grocery store, very brightly lit and clean. I wander over to look at the movies to see if I can find anything food-related to get for Robin and Michael. The selection is vast. And some of the names are ridiculous. I think *Booty and the Ho-fish* is my favorite.

"Lil!" Bill shouts at me across the store.

I turn to find my idiot friend waving a pink rubber phallus the length of my leg over his head.

"Wouldn't this make the best draft catcher?" I can picture it now, stretched across the bottom of Bill's bedroom door to keep the breeze out. The gentleman behind the counter does not look amused, and the couple other patrons, both in plaid flannel shirts, seem completely perplexed.

"Bill, put that back." I use a tone that might imply that I'm speaking to someone with a mental deficiency. Which, clearly, I am.

I manage to get Bill back to the car without incident,

and without purchase, and we return to the highway. About forty-five minutes later I drop him off at his friend Bruce's place where he will be crashing, and head off to Beth's. There is a note on the door saying that she had to run to Girl Stuff—the alarm went off—but I have a key, so I let myself in, put all the sundry goodies in her fridge, walk Petey and crash out on her couch for a quick nap. The party is tonight, and we have to drive back tomorrow afternoon, so it's just going to be a whirl-wind trip.

"Sleepyhead, time to get up!" Beth whispers in my ear.

I get up to hug her, and she pours me a fresh cup of coffee, and we play catch-up. I confess that I think I've changed my mind about Jay, and her face drops.

"What? You think it's a bad idea?" I ask her.

"Honey, he has a new girlfriend," Beth says, patting my hand.

"I've only been gone, like, six weeks, how can he have a new girlfriend already?" This is unbelievable! "Do I know her?"

"I dunno. Some theater person. Jeanne?"

"Jeanne? That skinny little girl? What is she, like, twelve?"

"Lil, Jay is only twenty-four."

"I know that. Don't look at me like that. Oh, this is just crap-a-licious!" I'm so irritated. It figures that he would fall for the first tiny young thing that crossed his path. "I knew she had a thing for him, I just knew it! I knew it at my party when she asked him to walk her to her car, that little slut."

"Lil, isn't that the night he came back and slept over, and made the first pass at you?" Beth is smirking at me in a very irritating way.

"Yeah. Well, that doesn't mean that's what *she* wanted. Jezebel."

"You broke up with him, remember? Almost two months ago. And then you moved. To another state. I think he's within his rights to start seeing someone."

"Guess I fucked up, huh?"

"Everything happens for a reason, sweetie. Is there a chance you want him back just because you are lonely? And horny?" Beth always cuts to the flipping chase.

"Maybe that is part of it, but I also have just been missing him, you know. The way we talked and how much fun it was to hang out together. Not that it matters. Unless..." An idea is forming.

"Lilith, no." Beth is very firm.

"Why not?"

"You may not try to get him back. You may not confess your feelings. You are going to go to this party, and be nice to little Jeanne, and not overly friendly with Jay, and if you flirt with him even the littlest bit, I'm going to smack you about the head in front of everyone, do you hear me?" Goodness, she is strict.

"Doesn't he have a right to know?"

"No. He has earned the privilege of not having to know. I'll make you a deal. If Robin tells me they've broken up, I'll call you, and, if at that point you still want him back, *then* you can call him and tell him. But as long as he is with her, your trap stays shut out of respect for him, for Jeanne and for your own dignity. For now, that boat has sailed, and you sent it on its merry way of your own volition, so let it be."

"Fine." I'm not, really, but she's right.

"There's a good girl. Now c'mon, let's get dressed and go to the party."

★ ★ ★

Everything is beautiful. They've taken the private room at Rushmore, the food is exquisite, the drinks are generous and it's so great to see everyone. They have gone to Aroma Workshop for the party favors, where a scent was made especially for them and put into mini bottles of lotion and spritz cologne. It has a fun little label on it that says "Michael and Robin," and it smells a little like the ocean, in honor of their beachside nuptials. I'm so happy to be in this room. And sad. Because tomorrow I have to drive back to Milwaukee where I don't even know a tenth of the number of people in this room. And to make matters worse, Jay and Jeanne seem totally infatuated with each other and they keep feeding each other and holding hands. He keeps kissing the side of her neck, and I remember that he used to do that with me, and how good it felt. Dammit all to hell.

"Hey you, hanging in there?" Beth brings me another glass of champagne.

"This sucks." I know I'm being petulant, but that is what girlfriends are for, to let you be a whiny baby when you need to be.

"I know. But take a deep breath, I bet within the next couple months you'll probably meet some fabulous guy in Milwaukee and you'll forget all about Jay."

"I don't believe you." Which I don't.

"That doesn't mean it isn't true." I can't argue with this woman.

"Fine."

Anne and Chris wander over and join us, blissfully changing the topic to how things are going for me up north, and filling me in on the latest gossip. Jess still isn't speaking to Harrison, and it looks as if he's giving up. For a while he kept calling her, and dropping by, and sending e-mails, but she always tells him that she isn't ready to talk to him. He decided not to come tonight out of respect for her.

"I'm really worried about her," Anne says. "She spends all her time in Hyde Park now, teaching and working on her dissertation research. We have to practically drag her to brunch if we want to see her at all, and she doesn't want to talk about Harrison. I want to tell her to find a therapist, but I think she would be insulted."

Chris jumps in. "Michael and I took him out last week, and he's still pretty broken up. I guess he has expressed that he's really sorry, that he wants to give it another try and that he realizes how badly he handled the whole thing. But by the same token, he needs her to acknowledge that she was far from perfect herself. But she won't sit down with him to talk about it. And if she doesn't let him in soon, he is going to let it go."

"Jess just needs to process it in her own way," Beth offers. "And ultimately it's none of our business."

"I think she is being an idiot." I can't help myself. "That is a great man, and they were great together, and anyone who bases anything on how someone behaves at such a crazy time is just being stupid and selfish. Nobody is perfect, including Jess, and Harrison was entitled to have whatever feelings he was having. But it seems really immature to just shut the door on the whole thing."

"Nice to know what you think of me." Jess has, apparently, come up behind me while I was ranting, ensuring that I'm now the biggest bitch and worst friend ever. "But I'll tell you what, how about you, of all people, don't presume to pass judgment on my relationships." Her sarcasm is biting. "You have a boyfriend, but he is boring. You fall in love with a married man, and break up with your boyfriend over it, even though you know he doesn't want you. You get lonely and seduce some kid you can be in control of, and then decide that you can't date someone who doesn't have a CAR, so you dump him, too. Then the poor schmuck gives up his dream of being an actor to settle down and make money to try to make things better for you, and what do you do? Sleep with him for a couple more weeks and then take a job in Milwaukee and dump him again. And then you have the nerve to show up here and give his new girlfriend the evil eye all night, because you are lonely and thought he'd just be waiting right where you left him to take care of your needs for the weekend."

People are starting to notice that something is awry in our corner of the room. But Jess is on a roll. "I'll tell you what, all of you. Butt out. What happened between me and Harrison is between me and Harrison. I don't need Anne's wide-eyed I'm-in-the-perfect-relationship optimism. I don't need Beth's patronizing 'whatever you think, sweetheart' Jewish mothering. And I certainly don't need our resident relationship flake telling me that I'm making a mistake."

We're silent, wounded and ashamed. Especially me, since she is right.

"What's up over here, guys?" Robin has wandered over, looking concerned.

"Nothing, sweetie," says Jess, turning to kiss her cheek. "I was just telling these guys that I feel badly, but I have to bail. I have a pounding headache and it's making me bad company. But it's a lovely party, and I'm so happy for you and Michael. I'll talk to you tomorrow and find out what I missed." Jess hugs Robin, coldly says good-night to the rest of us and leaves.

"Why do I think I've missed something?" asks Robin.

"She just felt bad about leaving early," Chris explains, covering for all of us. "Hey, Robin, would you mind introducing me to that chiropractor friend of Michael's? My lower back has been a bitch lately, and Mike said this guy was awesome and might be able to help."

"I can't believe I did that. I'm so stupid." My face is hot and there is a huge lump in my throat. "I'm the worst friend ever."

Anne puts her arm around my waist. "You were just expressing an opinion, Lilith, and, frankly, it isn't like the rest of us don't agree with you." She looks at Beth. "Am I unbearable about me and Chris?"

"Of course not, honey," Beth replies. "You are in love, and you want everyone to have the happiness you are having." Beth reaches over and squeezes her sister's shoulder. "Of course, you guys are totally perfect, so we do kind of want to kill you, but with love!" This makes both Anne and me laugh. "Now, did you two wear the right coats? It's a chilly night, and Mommy doesn't want you catching a cold!"

Anne shakes her head. "If the worst thing about you is a maternal instinct, you are in pretty good shape. At least you aren't a Pollyanna!"

I have to jump in here. "Hey, I'm the one who is totally fucked up about men, and obviously will never have a normal adult relationship, *and* am the one with the big damn mouth who hurts everyone's feelings."

The three of us find comfort in the joking, but it's clear that later tonight, in our private thoughts, we'll think about what Jess said, and what she meant, and wonder how true it is.

I sneak off to the ladies' room and call Jess on my cell phone. Her machine picks up.

"Jess, it's Lilith. Honey, I'm so sorry about tonight. I was way out of line. I'm the last person who should be having an opinion about other people's relationships. But I never would have hurt you on purpose. I only said what I said because I'm worried about you, and I want you to be happy, and you seemed really happy when you and Harrison were together, and so I hate that you seem to be choosing unhappiness on purpose instead of fighting for happiness the way I want you to. I know I have no right to lecture you, but Nico made me promise not to waste the time I have on bullshit with the people I love, and I'm trying. And I would think that everything you have been through, the stuff you saw in Kenya, losing the baby, I just thought it might make you equally aware of how tenuous things can be in this world. I love you. I'm so glad and lucky to have your friendship. And I'm so sorry that I hurt your feelings. Whatever you decide about Harrison, I'll support your decision. I promise. Mea culpa, sweetie. From the bottom of my heart."

I feel a little better, but not as much as I would have hoped.

The rest of the party feels quieter, and I am now so self-conscious about what Jess said about Jay, that I've spent the bulk of the party completely avoiding both him and Jeanne for fear that everyone will be able to read my thoughts the way Jess did. Jay notices this, and when he comes to say goodbye, asks why I avoided him all night. I assure him that I was just trying to catch up with everyone, as it was my first visit back, and that I wasn't avoiding him at all. He doesn't really appear to believe me, but he doesn't press me on it.

Back at Beth's, I set up the Aerobed for myself while Beth takes Petey for a quick walk. When she gets back, we get undressed and settled.

In the dark, I whisper, "Think she'll be okay?"

"I have to believe we'll all be okay," Beth answers. "Otherwise I couldn't get through my days, you know?"

"Well then, we will just have to all be okay."

"Yep. It's the only solution. Good night, Lil."

"Good night, Beth."

Petey pads over to where I'm lying, sniffs my hair, licks my face gently and plops down on the floor next to me. I let my hand hang over the side and rest on his furry warmth, and let the rhythm of his breathing be the last thing I remember.

jess

I can't sleep. It's approximately three o'clock in the morning and I can't shut my head off. This is more and more common; I haven't been sleeping very well since the miscarriage. I know all my friends think I'm crazy for not trying to work things out with Harrison, and maybe they are right. But I can't help being scared. I mean, it was our first fight. And it was so awful. What if the second fight is even worse? Or the third? Maybe it's just better to let it be over so that I never have to find out.

Our first fight.

It really was just our first fight.

I guess we were getting along pretty well, if we never fought about anything before. I have to stop thinking.

I turn on the light. I go out to my desk and take my journal out of the drawer. But I don't really know what to write, so instead I start flipping back through the pages. It opens on something I wrote before I came back from Kenya.

March 2003
Lukume, Kenya

Today I assisted at a birth at a neighboring shamba. It was her first, a girl of only fifteen, and she was scared out of her wits. No doctors, just the women from her shamba and ours, and a thick stick to bite on during the contractions. The women sang almost constantly. I held her hand and tried to tell her how well she was doing, in spite of my still-limited Swahili. We were there for nearly nine hours, in a sweltering hut, and when the little girl was finally born, all the women in the room wept for joy and shouted. There was a lot of blood, the air was thick with the coppery smell of it, but the baby was perfect. And the young mother was proud and exhausted.

I don't know what to do with my feelings about it. She is a third wife, so she has little status, and will have few resources. She is so young, and now her childhood is officially over for good. This baby may or may not survive to the age of five, many don't. And if the child does live, it will be to eke out the same meager existence as her mother.

I look around this little village and see the women, many of whom are not much older than I, and they have six and eight and sometimes eleven children to watch over and try to keep fed. I look at my Form One students, the equivalent of freshmen in high school, who range in age from fourteen to twenty, because so many of them have had to skip years of schooling due to lack of tuition money, or needing to help at home. Hunger and poverty are a way of life here, not as bad as some of the other African nations, but still, an existence that would be unthinkable to the majority of the people I know at home.

And yet, there is a simple and honest love here in these enormous families. Three or four wives on one small plot of land, the father often away trying to make money in larger cities like Kakamega or even Nairobi. Thirty to forty children ranging from babes in arms to people in their late teens, many of whom are already having children of their own. Little girls of only five or six are already entrusted with the care of younger siblings, and these "little mothers" have an air of quiet maturity that is both beautiful and frightening to me.

I think of what I saw tonight, and how glad I am that I was there to witness this tiny life come into the world, and I'm ashamed of my relief that when my time comes, I'll be in a state-of-the-art hospital. I'll have all of the modern conveniences at my disposal. And hopefully, a kind and loving man at my side who won't abandon me eight months of the year to earn his living, but will be a real partner, lover and friend.

They say that pregnancy is contagious, baby fever they call it here. I can see why. Luckily for me, in just a few short months I'll be back home, where, for women like me, babies come only when we have decided that things are in order, that careers are well under way, that personal identity has been assured. Lucky. Very lucky.

This is as far as I can get before the tears blur my eyes too much, and soon I'm sobbing great coughing sobs. I don't know what to do. I do love Harrison, but he really did hurt me. And I know I hurt him, and I wonder if we can fix it. I wonder if he even still wants to try. But I now know I do.

The cab drops me off, in my pajamas and trench coat, at Harrison's. It's nearly four, and the sky is lightening to periwinkle blue. His street is very still. But his car is here, so I know he is home. I still have a key, but I'm too scared to use it, so I ring the buzzer. A minute passes. I ring again. Another minute passes, and then the intercom voice.

"Hello?" He sounds gruff and tired.

"It's me."

The door clicks. I go upstairs. He is in the doorway,

looking puzzled and unkempt. "Are you all right? What happened?"

I collapse into his arms. I can't get any words out.

"Shh. It's okay. Whatever it is, it'll be okay." Harrison holds me tightly and rubs my back. He gently guides me inside, and sits me on the couch. He goes to the fridge and brings me a Tazo green tea, my favorite. I can't believe he still keeps them around. Then he sits beside me.

"Are you okay?" he asks me.

"No. Not really."

"Did something happen?"

"I couldn't sleep. I couldn't stop thinking about everything that has happened and how screwed up it all is, and how scared I am, and how much I miss you, and how afraid I am to love you now." It's all I can say.

He's holding my hand. "Please don't be afraid to love me, Jess. I know we've been through the worst possible thing, and I know that you have been through the worst of it, but I love you, and loving you is the best and smartest thing I've ever done. If we're going to make a life together, there are going to be awful parts, but that doesn't mean it isn't right. It doesn't mean we can't figure it out."

"I know, but I can't help being scared. I don't want you to wake up a few months from now and question whether we stayed together just to prove something to each other or ourselves or our friends. I don't want to spend my life questioning every decision because I'm afraid of how you will react. And we can't pretend it never happened."

"I don't want us to pretend, I don't want us to ignore it, I want us to learn from it and move forward together. Don't you want that, Jess?"

"I think I do. But what if we don't make it?"

"If we aren't going to make it, I don't want it to be because we were too scared to try. Besides, what if we do make it? Can't we be hopeful?"

"I can't promise, but I can try."

"I want to, Jess, I want to so much. I've been a mess without you." Harrison pulls me to him, holding me tightly and kissing my cheek.

"There's something else." I don't like to admit it to myself, let alone him.

"What is it?" He looks at me with tears in his eyes.

"I'm not ready for sex. The idea of sex is just, it's too… I just can't, not yet, and I know that is something I'm going to have to work through." We were being careful, and I still got pregnant, so the very idea of making love scares me to death.

"Of course, honey, that's very common, and totally understandable. I don't mind waiting. We'll do whatever you need to feel comfortable." He embraces me again. "And if you want to see someone together to help us, I can get some recommendations."

This is huge. Harrison believes in therapy for others, but not for himself, and has often said that he can't imagine couples' therapy. For him to be willing to take that step if I want us to is the most unselfish commitment I can imagine.

"Okay."

He smiles softly. "Okay."

"I'm really tired." Finally I'm tired.

"Do you want me to drive you home, or do you want to stay here?"

"I want to stay here, if that is okay." I really do.

"That's good. Really good."

We get up off the couch and go to his bedroom. He spoons me in the dark, stroking my hair, and, finally, I'm able to sleep.

milwaukee

We're still in our slow season at the store, so Anne and I've taken to switching shifts, since there is no point to both of us minding one baby, as it were. I'm on mornings this week, and I'm taking advantage of the quiet to get some plans worked out for the big end-of-season sale next month. The phone breaks my concentration.

"Girl Stuff. Beth speaking."

"Beth, it's Jeff." Wow. We haven't spoken in many weeks.

"Jeff, how are you?"

"I'm fine, you?"

"Okay." Scintillating conversationalists we're not.

"So I was wondering if I could maybe see you, I mean, we said we would take a break, have some space, let the air clear, but I would like very much to get together and talk, if you were ready for that."

Oy. What can I say? "Of course. When?"

"Well, I have today and Wednesday off from Home Depot."

"I'm done here around two today, did you want to meet later?" Might as well get it over with quickly, no sense in obsessing about it for three days.

"Sure. Should I meet you at the loft? Like, threeish?" He sounds sort of weird. I hope everything is okay.

"That would be fine. Just call my cell if something comes up."

"Okay then, I'll see you this afternoon."

Luckily for me, one of my best customers comes in, playing hooky from work and in need of some retail therapy. I get her in and out of nearly everything in the store, and manage to put together some really great outfits for her. I add in several accessories, and some of the new housewares line I found in Canada—funky bright retro appliances and fun dishes and serving pieces. Two hours and nearly three thousand dollars later, it has been a good day for both of us.

Anne comes in for our lunchtime overlap, bringing a couple sandwiches from Potbelly's, with chips and chocolate malteds. I love that kid. We eat and I tell her that Jeff is coming over.

"Wow," she says around a mouthful of her turkey sub, "do you think you are going to get back together?"

"I don't know. I mean, if you need a trial separation from your boyfriend of only a few months, that doesn't exactly bode well."

"I guess. But I thought things were good there? I mean, you seemed happy together, and, until the Eric incident, you certainly never complained."

"I know, Annie, but that whole thing with Eric sort of

made me think about my life, you know? Everything I want. I can't keep coasting in these relationships that don't go anywhere. Sasha was a dead end, Eric was totally inappropriate, even Jeff, who is a great guy, probably isn't the *one*. Why can't I find a guy like Chris? Or Michael? Why can't I find a guy who I can make a life with?"

"Beth, c'mon! How many boyfriends did I have before Chris?" Anne is shaking her head at me.

"I dunno, four?"

"Two. Beth, *two* real relationships before Chris, one in college, and one just after. And what about Robin? Two years of pining for Michael before he came to his senses. You and I both know you don't have the patience for that. When you are supposed to meet him, he'll arrive. I have to believe that." My little sister is so logical about these things, it's really sort of irritating.

"I guess. But now I don't know what to do about Jeff. I still like him and care about him deeply, and I still want him physically, but I don't think we are made for each other. There's a part of me that knows if we get back together it will just be so that I'm not lonely."

Anne takes a sip of her malted. "Then maybe you should be lonely for a while."

"But I did that after Sasha! Almost two years of loneliness and no sex, and I just figured that it was my alone phase, and now it was over. Starting from scratch is just so fucking daunting."

"You have to do what you have to do. Talk to Jeff. He may not even want you back, ever think of that?" Anne smirks at me.

"You are so cruel. Okay, I'm going home to walk Petey and face the music. I'll call you when he leaves."

"Good luck!" Anne kisses my cheek, and I leave the store and head back to the loft.

At three on the dot the bell rings.

"I'm coming, hold on a sec…" I give a yank, and the heavy steel door swings open.

"Jeff, how nice to see you. Come on in." I sound like a Stepford wife.

Jeff kisses my cheek and comes inside. He reconnects with Petey while I get us each a Coke, and we settle on the couch. I figure I had better let him bring up the tough stuff, so I start with small talk.

"How's the new book coming?" Easy place to begin.

"Still in the outline stages." Jeff looks at me with a sort of resignation in his eyes.

"Blocked?"

"Just out of focus, I'll get it back. It's only been a couple months since I finished the last one, I may just be a little burnt." He does look tired.

"What about getting that one published?" I know he was nervous about trying to get back in the game.

"Well, I met with Reynolds this morning…." His ex-publisher.

"How was it? Did they throw you out on your ear?" I figure I'll go for lighthearted and friendly.

"No, actually, they were pretty cool, considering how we left things. They expressed reasonable concern, I offered what guarantees I could and they promised to give the manuscript a thorough reading and get back to me. They've some new editor they want to look at it. It was all I could hope for, really."

"Well, I think they'd be stupid to pass on this one—I loved it."

"You have to say that, you're my, um—" I interrupt him, not wanting him to finish the statement and assign a label.

"No, I don't, I don't have to do anything. I hated *Union,* and all those crappy short stories you did. Like bad Jay McInerny. All parties and no sympathetic characters. I started wondering if you'd hired a ghost to write the first book." It's true, his first book was beautiful, but the second was total shit.

Jeff laughs. "Thanks a lot!"

"Well, I just want you to know that when I say I like your work, I'm not just someone who knows you, I'm also a reader." *Someone who knows you.* Nice qualifier.

"Point taken."

"I'm glad the meeting went okay, though. Were you nervous?"

"Not until after. Then I wanted to bury myself in a bottle of vodka. I haven't wanted a drink that bad in months." This is the stuff that scares me.

"You didn't, did you?"

"I'm fine, I went directly to AA."

"Well, that is good. I mean, I assume." Jeff never really talked much about his recovery process.

"The meeting was pretty good, considering. AA is never a real party, but at least the Whiner wasn't there. I really hate that guy. I mean, I know it's sort of against the party line, and I know you're supposed to support anyone who has the guts to get up and share their stories, but give me a break. If I hear about how this guy's wife left him one more time, I may just offer to buy him a drink." This makes me laugh. But for the first time, Jeff doesn't stop talking about it.

"To tell you the truth, I never followed all the steps, at least not to the letter. I mean, some of that crap is for the birds. I'm not big into God, and mostly I just wanted a place to go when I felt weak, to have someone to talk to. Those first few meetings, at weird hours, three in the morning, two in the afternoon, they got me focused, you know?

"It wasn't a bunch of old rummies, or washed-out barflies, just people with stories. That's actually what saved me—the stories. Doctors, lawyers, stockbrokers, teachers, nice, normal people with stories. Reasons. Excuses. Tears. Amazing confessions, such courage. Blew my mind. So I kept going, I had plenty of time on my hands. Then after a few months, the itch hit me, like an old friend, out of the blue, and I could write again."

It's what his new book is about, five very different people who are all in the same AA group, and how they cope with their problems, and each other. I read it a couple months ago when he finished, and I wasn't sure what to do with it. It's very raw, and real. And I realize he is opening a door and I can ask what I've wanted to ask him.

"Good for you. Hey, that reminds me, I keep meaning to ask you, how much of *Step by Step* is autobiographical?"

"Very little, actually, just the little truisms of drinking, the wheres and the hows—not so much the whys. Any particular issue you're curious about?" He grins at me, since I know he knows what I'm thinking.

"Yeah, the young trader who sleeps with that woman…."

"Okay, yes, I did sleep with someone I met in my first group. It happens more than you might think, really, even though they tell us we aren't supposed to, and it's a big taboo if they catch you. The meetings are really intense. You're stripped bare, everything's on the table and you just make connections with people. Besides, getting back into dating is hard, everyone wants to go out for a drink, or go to dinner and get a nice bottle of wine, and you don't want to broadcast your addiction until you can honestly say you are a recovering alkie with at least several months of sobriety under your belt. She was very nice, and it didn't last. Satisfied?"

I can't believe we've never really talked about this stuff before, and in many ways I feel like everything we've been doing for the past few months has been erased, and we're starting again.

"Why didn't it last?"

"I stayed on the wagon, and she decided to get off."

Ouch. "Did you try to help her?"

"I needed to take care of myself, she was a responsibility I just couldn't take on then."

"I guess that makes sense, I was just wondering why they didn't stay together in the book, but if that's how it goes in life, it makes more sense."

"Look, Beth, I suppose it's as good a segue as any. What are you thinking about us?" Well, that's one way to begin.

"Jeff, I don't really know, to be honest. That whole thing with Eric really scared me. Violence is just something I can't deal with."

"I know, and I'm so sorry, I acted like a complete idiot. I had just had a really hard day, and I was so excited to come back and surprise you, and when I found him here, I just snapped. I know there is no way to condone my behavior. But I've always felt like I wasn't good enough, and when he came back into your life and you seemed to be making an effort to make room for him, I was worried that I'd been some sort of placeholder for a real guy."

"Why didn't you ever say anything? Why didn't you ever tell me that you were worried about him? I told you that I was over him, that what happened between us was ancient history." What on earth did we talk about all those months? I can't seem to remember.

"I have enough marks against me," Jeff replies. "I didn't want you to think I was a jealous maniac on top of it."

"Well, you handled that like a trooper!" We laugh.

"Well, I suppose in hindsight talking through it and not letting it fester in my imagination would have been a better choice!"

It feels good to laugh with him.

"Jeff, I care about you, and I really loved spending time with you, but I just don't know that I see a future with us together. I mean, this is probably the most honest discussion we've had, and it took a breakup to make it happen."

"So you don't think there's anything to fight for?" Jeff seems oddly calm.

"I think we went as far as we could go without it being work, and with a lot of fun. So if there's a genuine possibility of remaining friends, I think that may be a sign to just let it go."

Jeff laughs. "Thank God!"

"Thank God?"

"I was really upset when you said we should take a break, but over the past few weeks I've come to agree. It was so comfortable and easy to be together that we weren't bothering to think about it, but it was pretty obvious that we were never going to be good for the future. I know it's sadly cliché, but I really do hope we can be friends."

"This may be the most adult breakup ever."

"I know."

Jeff and I sit in silence.

"So just friends," I finally say.

"Looks like."

"Wanna have sex?" I'm only half kidding.

"Do you?" His eyes have that look in them.

"Well, I think if we're going to be so mature about everything, one for the road isn't going to kill us. Besides, I certainly haven't had sex since the last time we slept together, and that was ages ago. A girl needs a little maintenance now and again."

He stands up and offers his hand, which I take, and he pulls me off the couch. Then he looks at me, looks way across the loft toward the bedroom, and back at me.

"Race you, buddy," he says, placing significant emphasis on the "buddy."

What the hell. "You're on."

He won the race, but I got one hell of a second-place prize.

anne

I call Rush to check on the status of my application, and a woman puts me through to the admissions counselor.

"Ms. Gaskell, I'm going to be honest with you. Your grades are lower than we would like, and you have some deficiencies in your transcript that concern us. However, your essay is very moving, and the alumni interview got the highest level of recommendation, so we're certainly keeping your candidacy viable. However, it's our policy not to defer an applicant more than once, so if you don't make it this time, you won't be able to reapply for a year."

"I see, well, I thank you for your candor," I manage to say.

"There is another option."

"Which would be…?"

"Ask us to defer your application yourself. If you move the application to next fall, then it won't be reviewed until then. You could take a couple classes in your deficient areas, and, if you got good grades, it would help solidify your application enormously. There are good classes at Northeastern and some of the city colleges that are not too expensive—I can send you a list." She seems to be sending me a message.

"So if I asked you to hold off on reviewing my application until fall, it wouldn't reduce my chances?"

"I think it might improve your chances, particularly if you are able to strengthen your qualifications."

"Thank you for being so honest. I think I would like to do that."

"I'll take care of it, and will send you the list of relevant courses. If you are able to complete two or three of them with high marks, then you will be in excellent shape for next fall."

"Thanks for the confidence! I'll certainly do everything I can!"

I hang up and call Chris, telling him about my latest delay. But he thinks it's terrific, and reminds me that the whole point was to go back to school, which I'll be doing immediately. I hadn't thought of it that way, and it makes me feel better. I jump in the shower, throw on my sweats and head to the store to meet Beth. We're closed today for inventory and presale prep. All the new things for fall and winter are arriving in two weeks, so we always have an end-of-season sale to make room. That means every single item in the store has to be checked for damage, marked down and reorganized. It's going to be a very long day.

Beth is already there when I arrive, wearing a very old set of tie-dye leggings and a black T-shirt from college, and drinking from of a huge Starbucks cup. She hands me a mocha latte, figuring we will both need the caffeine.

"Where should we start?" I ask her, sipping.

"Well, I think we should do the clothes first, since they're easiest, and it will make us feel productive to get a bunch of stuff done. All we have to do is check for damage, put one of these sale tags on and separate them onto the rolling racks by price."

Beth puts on the soundtrack from *The Commitments,* one of our all-time favorite movies. I start on the skirt rack, while Beth starts with tops, and we settle into a sort of Zen state, sorting clothes and singing along with the music.

We're finished in just under two hours. We head to the nearby Cosi to pick up sandwiches, and I fill her in on the change in plans, schoolwise.

"It sounds like this woman is essentially telling you that if you do this the way she suggests, you will be a shoo-in, right?" Beth asks me, picking a piece of tandoori chicken out of her sandwich.

"That's how it felt to me. She is sending me a whole list of classes I can take to beef up my application."

"That is great, honey! So you'll take a couple classes, starting soon, and then go to Rush in a year?"

"Yep. That is, if my partner can help me finagle the work schedule."

"We've been through this already. We'll do whatever we need to do, you know that."

"Thanks, Beth."

"Well, I figure one of these days I'm going to cash in big! I'm putting so many free babysitting nights on your tab that if I ever do have kids, you'll be booked for months on end!"

We finish up our lunch and head back to the store. It takes the rest of the afternoon and much of the evening, but eventually everything is set. The banners are posted in the window, every item has been labeled and organized and

Beth even liked my idea of taking all the damaged items we found and putting them in a big bin labeled As Is, 75% off, instead of pitching them. It's after eight o'clock when we finally lock up, and I invite Beth home to order in dinner with me and Chris. She declines.

"I love you, sweetie, but I'm totally pooped. I'm going home to walk Petey, order a pizza, take a hot shower and watch the *Alias* DVDs I just bought."

"Okay, well, have fun, and I'll see you tomorrow."

When I get home, there is a note on the door. I open it:
Please remove your shoes upon entering.

Chris is such a goofball, I wonder what he has up his sleeve. I open the door, and see that the apartment has a gentle amber glow. There are candles all over the place, and red glass lanterns. In the foyer, where I dump my bag, is a tissue-wrapped package, and another note. I tear off the gold tissue to find the most gorgeous slippers I've ever seen— black silk with Asian embroidery, little red tassels and black suede soles with lots of cushy padding in the bottom. I put them on, and they're heavenly. I open the note:
Go to the bathroom.

I pad down the hall to the bathroom, where there is a hot bath waiting for me, the scented steam thick in the air. There is another tissue-wrapped package on the vanity, with another envelope. This time I open the note first:
Rest awhile, then get dressed for dinner, and go to the living room.

I open the tissue and there are a pair of lounging pajamas in thick, pale pink satin with a Chinese motif of stylized fish and flowers. I lean my head out of the bathroom door, and call for Chris, but there's no answer. He is either not here, or playing possum, and with all the trouble he has clearly gone to, I'm not going to argue with him. I slip out of my dirty sweats and into the tub. I soak for fifteen minutes or so, towel off and slip into my new pj's and slippers, feeling like a Hollywood starlet from the forties. I leave my clothes in the bathroom and go to the living room.

The coffee table and couch have been moved out of the way, and there are huge pillows on the rug, and an enormous round brass tray. There is a teapot on the tray, with a note taped to it that says *Drink Me.* Very Alice in Wonderland. I pour myself a cup of what turns out to be a light green tea, and lean back on the pillows. I hear footsteps behind me, and turn to see Chris carrying a black lacquered tray and grinning at me.

"Are you comfortable, milady?"

I smile back at him. "Very."

He kneels down beside me, putting down the tray, which is covered with gorgeous sushi and other Japanese delectables, and then leans over to kiss me.

"I thought you would have had a very long day, between the school thing and inventory, so I wanted to make a little getaway for you."

I kiss him and hold him tight. "You are so wonderful, and I love you so much, thank you for doing this for me."

Chris tells me that Robin called a friend who works at Tank, a sushi place not far from us, and arranged for the feast. Beth had apparently given him the pj's and slippers a couple weeks ago. She had seen them on her last buying trip and didn't want them for the store, but thought I would love them, and Chris had asked her to keep an eye out for good presents for me. He said they'd given him the idea, and he'd just been waiting for the right time to spring it on me. I told him his timing was perfect.

We ate beautiful dumplings and sushi and tempura until

we were stuffed to bursting, and then I lay back on the big pillows while Chris rubbed my tired feet, the permanent bane of the retail worker. "Feel better?" he asks.

"Perfect. I couldn't be more perfect."

Chris stops rubbing my feet, and climbs over the pillows until he is lying beside me. He leans over and kisses me.

"Nothing I could do to make you more perfect?" He's nibbling my neck in a very lovely way.

"Well, now that you mention it…" I turn my head and kiss him. He tastes of pickled ginger.

I call Beth from the emergency room. "Hey, we're at Northwestern."

"Oh my God, what happened, are you okay?" I know I've woken her up.

"We're fine, we're just waiting to see the doctor. Chris had a small accident." I'm trying not to laugh, because my man is in such pain.

"Is he okay?" Beth asks.

"We think it's his back. Looks like he may have thrown it out."

"How did he do that?"

"Sex sprain. He made me this lovely Japanese picnic on the floor of the living room to surprise me. Big cushy pillows everywhere. After dinner we got a little frisky. When we decided to move the proceedings to the bedroom, we got up, and he whisked me into his arms."

"But you're light as a feather, I can pick you up like that myself!" Beth sounds confused.

"It wasn't picking me up that did it. He took a step forward, stepped on one of the pillows and started to slide, tried to step back and landed smack on the leftover sushi, did a Charlie Chaplin–style banana-peel slip on one leg, managed to drop me off to the side on the pillows, but then sort of spun around and fell down." It couldn't have been choreographed better.

"Oh the poor guy, should I come down there?"

"No, I just wanted you to know that I might be late tomorrow."

"Whatever you need, call me in the morning and tell me what the verdict is."

"Will do."

After about an hour and a half they finally take us back to see a doctor. The X rays show that there are no broken bones or slipped discs, it's just muscle strain. He'll have to ice the injury and rest for at least a week. No heavy lifting for two weeks. And a nice Vicodin prescription just to keep the pain manageable. We get home after 5:00 a.m., and I set him up on the couch, since lying down on the bed is too painful. I bring him a pill and a glass of water.

"Some perfect plan, huh? Just the thing to relax after a hard day, four hours in the emergency room! I can't believe I ruined everything!"

"Hush," I say. "You did perfect. Right up until that double-twisting half gainer, you were batting a thousand!" We start to laugh, and he winces.

"Oh God, it hurts when I laugh. Stop that. I can't believe I'm such a klutz."

"Try to get some sleep. I'll call and leave a message for you at work letting them know you need a couple days and that you will call them in the afternoon. Can I bring you anything else?"

"No, honey, thank you. You're the best."

"Just yell if you need anything, okay?"

"Okay, you get some sleep, too."

I lean over and kiss him gently, and head back to the bedroom. But I can't sleep. I should be exhausted, I shouldn't be able to keep my eyes open, but the bed feels so big and empty without him, and I can't seem to find a good position. I get up and tiptoe back out to the living room. He's sound asleep, head thrown back, mouth open. I pull some of the big pillows from our little picnic over next to the couch, and grab the throw blanket off the armchair. And, lying on the floor, with the sound of his breathing, I drift off.

milwaukee

Lilith steels herself at the stage door, taking a deep breath before entering the Greenwood lobby. She knows her friends are out there, having taken the mini road trip to support her on the first preview of her first directing effort, a contemporary adaptation of *The Importance of Being Earnest,* set in a 1980s advertising agency. The script is a witty piece of writing, and Lilith had fallen in love with it after it was sent to her by a colleague in London. She'd fought so hard to include it in the season that Bill had given up, saying "Fine, you love it so much, *you* direct it!"

And so she had.

The girls knew that opening night wasn't when Lilith got the jitters, it was always first preview. She could tell, in spite of stumbles or technical problems, if something would be good, or if there were unfixable issues that would invariably linger past opening night and through the run. Tonight she felt giddy. The cast was superb, lashing out their sharp-tongued repartee with clarity and ease. The crew had managed the scene shifts and costume changes nearly flawlessly, and everything had looked terrific. But more important, the storytelling was clear, the language precise, the words honored. She hoped that Oscar Wilde would have been delighted with the piece, both a satire of his work and homage to it. Bill had hugged her tightly, and said it looked as if it must have directed itself, so invisible was her touch. It was his highest compliment.

She pushed the door open, and was immediately enveloped in a circle of shrieking love and laughter.

"You are a *genius!*" said Beth. "A fucking theatrical genius! Get the Tony ready!"

"I can't believe how perfect everyone was for their parts, it was like the playwright had those exact people in mind when he wrote it!" Anne gushed.

"I always knew you secretly wanted to be in charge!" Jess adds. "It was spectacular."

"And hilarious!" adds Robin.

Lilith beams and blushes, accepting the compliments of her girlfriends, and knowing that it won't matter if critics or audiences like it, she has done well in the eyes of the people who mean the most to her.

She gathers them up, and they walk to her loft, where they change into their pajamas, crack open some wine and sit on the floor in the center of the open space.

"All right, circle up. Who's first?" Beth starts.

"Well, I have good news!" Robin says. "We got the new space!" Robin and Michael had found the perfect location for an Oak Park Ajax, and had been waiting to see if their bid was accepted. "We begin the build in three weeks, and are hoping to be open in about four months. Michael thinks we ought to look into maybe buying a new condo in the West Loop, to be more equidistant from the two restaurants, but I sort of want to stay where we are."

"Because it's the place you finally got the guts to tell him you loved him," Jess says with loving sarcasm.

"Fuck you, Jessica, because it's the first place I ever had three multiple orgasms in forty-eight hours!" Robin throws back at her devilishly.

"Well, let's put up a plaque for sure," says Beth dryly.

"I'm next," Anne pipes in. "Chris has been offered a really great new job. Senior project manager. It's a huge raise, and he'll be overseeing most of the major work in Chicago. Which is good, because my classes are going really well, so if I get in to Rush for the fall, I'm going to be able to go full-time."

"Miss Beth, you okay with that?" asks Lilith.

Beth shakes her head emphatically. "I'm cool. It's six months off, so denial is still the word of the day. Anne will stay on as my partner, but will be paying for her replacement out of her share of the profits. So no tantrums from me, thank you very much!"

"Teaching is good," Jess says. "Dissertation research is deadly slow. Harrison and I are doing pretty well. He asked me to move in, but I said that I thought it wasn't a great time, and asked him to ask me again in three months."

"Just not sure of it yet?" Lilith wants to know.

"I guess. I mean, don't get me wrong, he is great, we're doing fine. We saw a therapist a few times, just to help work through the miscarriage stuff, and he is a trooper about the sex."

"Still not easy?" Anne asks.

"Well, we finally figured out that with me on the Pill,

and wearing a diaphragm, *and* him in a condom, I have nothing to worry about. It's like girding up to go into battle. But he takes it all in stride, and it gets a little easier every time. I think he feels if he can wean me away from the diaphragm at least, that we'll be in slightly better shape. Especially since I still haven't really gotten the hang of it yet, so when we get in the mood, it takes me, like, fifteen minutes in the bathroom." Jess has to laugh at herself.

"We're all glad you guys are working things out," Anne says.

"Well, the store is good, but I'm still on a dating sabbatical," Beth offers.

Robin clears her throat loudly. "Okay. I'm not seeing anyone in a romantic way. I'm still sleeping with Jeff, but just in a casual bed-buddy sort of way, and we're finding it very nice."

"I don't get you guys," Jess says. "You break up, but you still have sex like once or twice a week! Why not just be boyfriend and girlfriend?"

"Look, we both know we aren't right for each other. We're better as friends. But the sex is good, and we're comfortable with each other, so we keep it casual, and we're fine with it. We both know that when either one of us gets into a relationship, the hanky-panky will be over. But for now, why not?" Beth is blushing a little, but obviously means what she says.

"I'm all for it. I wish I could find someone here to pal around with like that!" Lilith says. "Did you guys know that the single-man-to-woman ratio in Milwaukee is the worst in the whole *country*? Did you?"

"It can't be that bad. Bill seems to be having a good time," Jess observes.

"I know! That is because most of the single men in Milwaukee are gay! No one has so much as bought me coffee since I got here. I recommend you all buy some stock in Duracell, 'cause I'm keeping those people in business!"

"What about that guy you introduced us to before the show, what was his name, Derek?" asks Anne. "He seemed to make you all sparkly!"

"So he does. My lovely local lighting designer." Lilith sighs.

"And?" Beth asks.

"Married."

"Oh no, not again! I forbid it, Lilith, do you hear me?" Beth starts to hit Lilith with a throw pillow. "Not another pining-for-the-married-guy scenario, I won't have it!"

"But, he—" starts Lilith.

"Gets me!" Shout the other four women in unison.

Lilith starts to laugh. "Okay, so maybe I have a pattern problem. There's a really cute intern, just out of college…"

Beth hits her harder, and the others join in, and pretty soon the five on them are collapsed on the floor, out of breath and holding their sides.

They all get their various sleeping areas organized, and when they're settled in, Lilith turns out the lights.

"Thanks for coming, you guys, I really appreciate it," she whispers in the dark.

"No problem," Jess says. "If you keep doing shows that good, we'll keep coming back."

"Of course we will," says Anne.

"Especially with such yummy field trips on the way home!" Robin chimes in.

"Can't you bitches shut up? Sleep time!" says Beth in mock annoyance.

"Ooh, cranky. Fine. Good night, Beth, Jess, Anne, Robin," says Lilith.

"Good night, Lilith, Robin, Jess, Beth," says Anne.

"Good night, Lilith, Jess, Beth, Anne," says Robin.

"Good night, Anne, Beth, Lilith, Robin," says Jess.

"Good night, Jess, Robin, Lilith, Anne," says Beth.

"Good night, John Boy," says Lilith.

"Good night, Mrs. Calabash…" says Robin.

"Wherever you are!" they all say in unison.

Then they giggle. And soon, sleep.

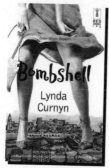